POSTCARDS FROM JAMIE

IAN SKAIR: PRIVATE INVESTIGATOR 2

HILARY PUGH

Housemouse Press

1

It was good to be home. Ian had never felt as at home anywhere as he did here. When he was married to Stephanie, the house had always felt like hers. He was just a rather untidy visitor, even though it was his salary that paid for it. After the divorce and recovering from the gunshot that had ended his career, he moved in with and cared for his grandfather. Living with Grandad the house had never really felt like his, although Grandad, bless him, had always done his best to make Ian feel at home. Ironic, really, that when Grandad died and the house really did become Ian's, the first thing he did was to sell it and move away. That had been the right choice. Here he was now, in his own house and in a place that he had chosen to be. Just himself and his dog, Lottie, in a quiet village with stunning views of the Tay estuary. He had a choice of bridges with either trains or cars to watch, depending on his mood. His catering was taken care of by two pubs and a village shop, and he had a friendly neighbour to chat to over the garden fence. As neighbours went, Lainie Crombie was ideal. She looked after Lottie when he couldn't take her with him. She baked the best Dundee cake he had ever tasted and was promising to knit him what sounded like an entire wardrobe of jumpers, scarves and socks to keep out the cold easterlies that she assured him would roll in from the North Sea during the winter months.

So all in all, his life had taken a turn for the better. What was not to like?

He'd enjoyed his holiday in a rented cottage in a village close to Loch Fyne, where he and Lottie had spent a quiet week sleeping late, going for long walks and eating locally caught fish. Ian had also gone for a digital detox. Private investigating was not the glamorous career most people seemed to think it was. He didn't spend his time snooping around in a deerstalker with a magnifying glass solving crimes that had baffled the local constabulary. Much of his life was spent snooping around the Internet, and sitting outside hotels in his parked car, collecting evidence that people's lives were not as blameless as those they claimed to be leading. He had taken his phone on holiday with him for emergencies, but made a promise to himself not to turn it on unless he absolutely had to. And he'd kept his promise. He had loaded his car with good old fashioned books; a selection of crime novels from the Oxfam shop in Dundee.

The cottage provided a television set and DVD player with a selection of classic films. Ian and Lottie worked their way through Ealing comedies, Casablanca, The Third Man and The Birds. They'd only got halfway through The Birds because while Lottie had remained unmoved by Sam's piano playing and the sewers of Vienna, she became incensed by Hitchcock's birds flapping across the screen and jumped up and down yapping at them until Ian feared for the safety of the TV. He resisted the temptation to turn it on for the news. The world could get on just fine without him needing to know what was happening. He also discovered a box of board games; Snakes and Ladders, Cluedo, Scrabble and Monopoly. Games he remembered from his childhood. He might have enjoyed those, but Lottie's interest didn't reach much beyond wanting to chew up the dice. He wondered if Lainie enjoyed board games. She'd probably be a demon Scrabble player. He might suggest it sometime.

Lottie knew they were home as soon as Ian turned off the main road and drove down into Greyport. She jumped up and sniffed at the window, wagging her tail, until he pulled up in the lane outside his house. As soon as he opened the back of the car, she jumped out and scampered up the path to the front door where she scratched impatiently, waiting for him to follow with his backpack. He put his key in the lock, opened the door and was greeted by the familiar scents of home. He kicked off his shoes and carried his bag into the kitchen, tipping its contents into the washing machine; damp socks, mud-spattered jeans, rain-soaked shirts and Lottie's sodden towel. It had not been a dry, sunny week. Late June and the skies had been leaden with cloud. Most days had been wet and when the rain did occasionally let up, they had been chilled by a brisk wind from the sea. But he hadn't gone on holiday for the weather. He'd gone for a rest, and a rest was what he had enjoyed. He had returned refreshed and ready for... well, he didn't know yet. That was one of the pleasures of being a private investigator. The next case could be dull and routine, or it could be life-changingly exciting. His last case had been exactly that, so he would probably need to settle for the mundane for a while. But that was fine. Work was work and he was his own boss.

He had called in at Tesco on his way home to stock up on food for both of them, so having seen to his laundry, he made himself a cheese toastie and opened a tin of dog food for Lottie. Then he sat down at his computer and logged back into reality once again. He began with his email. There were several about possible new cases. He would deal with those tomorrow. Today he was still officially on holiday. Holiday was holiday and *he* would decide when it was over. He moved all the work emails into a folder, labelled it *Work* and saved them for later. Then he turned to the more personal emails. Several were from friends he had made during his last case; Bridget, the laird's wife telling him that even though the case was finished, he was welcome to visit whenever he wanted to. He definitely did want to. He would drive up there in a day or two with his usual hamper of treats.

Then he opened one from the laird's sister, Ailish Lyton, who had now returned to her flat in London. If he ever needed anywhere to stay in London, she told him, he was welcome to use her flat. If he ever did need to stay in London he would certainly take advantage of the offer. But he rarely went there. London would be crawling with private investigators already. It was highly unlikely that Ian would ever work there. It was a very nice offer though; a luxury flat in the heart of Kensington.

Next he opened an email from Anna, the student he had met during his last case. The young woman who had found him after her own visit to the Kensington flat and who had spent a day playing at being his assistant. A bouncy whirlwind of blond curls and enthusiasm, passionately fond of dogs and currently spending the summer vacation with her family in France. She'd sent him pictures of her stepfather's vineyard and he wondered, not for the first time, how she could bear to leave it and come to Scotland to study.

After that was an email from Caroline; a friend or girlfriend, he was never quite sure which it was. She was on a walking holiday in North Wales with her dog and her sister. Both were schoolteachers and took long holidays. She was not going to be back for another couple of weeks.

There was one more email. A brief thank you from his brother for the e-greeting Ian had sent for his birthday. Ian detected a note of irony in his brother's effusive thanks. He had certainly sent the greeting with more than a touch of irony after a nagging from their mother. Perhaps there were times when he and his brother actually understood each other. Not something that had happened often when they were younger. But family was family. One should try not to hate them for ever.

Just as he was about to close his email, another one pinged in. It was from John Lewis, telling him that the sofa he had bought was ready for delivery and inviting him to log in to their site and pick a suitable date. He had forgotten all about the sofa. He had ordered it weeks ago in Edinburgh. It was the first piece of furniture he had ever bought for himself. Everything else in the house had been inherited from Grandad, or liberated from an unwilling Stephanie after she left him. He had asked Caroline's advice about sofas and she had dragged him off to John Lewis in Edinburgh. No, dragged was the wrong word. Caroline never needed to drag him anywhere. Once they'd established that any kind of long-term commitment was off the cards, he was happy to follow along wherever she wanted to take him. And he had to admit he'd never have managed it on his own. Shopping was a bewildering experience which involved discussions with alarming salespeople and the expectation that he would make choices about things of which he had limited knowledge.

He logged in and selected a day the following week. At the bottom of the form was a box asking him to enter delivery details, in particular any access problems. Why hadn't they asked that when he'd ordered it? He typed in, *steep garden path from road*, hoping they wouldn't take one look and go away again. He then entered, *if van not too big use back entrance*. But how would they know where the back entrance was? It involved a couple of awkward turns from the main road. He had missed it himself the first time he came here. He added his phone number and typed *call for instructions if needed*.

It was good to sleep in his own bed again, and still full of sea air he had slept well. Lottie hadn't forgotten any of her usual daily routine and jumped on him, lead in mouth, on the dot of eight o'clock the next morning. He got dressed and dragged the wet clothes out of the washing machine. He looked out of the window at a sunny, breezy morning which was perfect for drying, so he carried everything outside and pegged it to the washing line. A task not made any easier by Lottie, who was running in circles around him with her lead in her mouth. He'd just pegged out the last shirt when Lottie stopped winding her lead round him and ran to the fence, tail wagging furiously.

'You're back then,' a voice called over the fence. 'Good holiday?'

'Very nice, thanks, Lainie. Everything been okay here?'

'Aye, not so bad. Good to have you both back though. How was the weather?'

'Mostly wet,' said Ian.

'Och, that's a shame. It's been grand here.'

Typical. The west coast of Scotland was known for its mild

weather. Something to do with the Gulf Stream. While here on the east coast they were battered by wind from the North Sea. Another case of him being in the wrong place at the wrong time. Oh well, he'd still had a good break. 'We're just off to the village,' he told Lainie.

'Could you pick up my magazine from the post office?' she asked.

'Of course,' he said. She must have missed him. She rarely asked him to do any shopping for her.

'And drop in for a coffee when you get back?' she asked hopefully.

He nodded. Lainie lived on her own with few visitors. It was the least he could do.

Having walked to the village and back, and shared coffee and pastries with Lainie, it was time to get down to some work. He needed to read his saved emails and decide which cases to take. He skimmed through them briefly. There were a few fairly standard requests that he could work through at his leisure, nothing urgent. He'd just replied to the first one, a background search for an employer in Dundee, when he remembered the call he'd had from Rosalie just before he went on holiday. He'd promised to call her back. It was something to do with a friend who needed him to search for something, or somebody. He looked at his watch. It was late morning, a good time to call. Most of her work, teaching piano to children, happened after school. He picked up his phone and scrolled through his contacts until he found Rosalie Dacres. Lucky he still had the number. He hadn't called her for a long time. They'd kept in touch after she and Piers had got back together, but their calls were infrequent and short.

She answered quickly and sounded pleased to hear his voice. 'You're back,' she said. 'Good holiday?'

'Very nice, thanks.'

'Where did you go?'

'Loch Fyne.'

'Ah, the beautiful west coast.'

'Yeah, beautiful but wet. But I haven't called to talk about the weather. You said you and your friend needed me to do some searching.'

'That's right. Felix is staying with me. He's not been well and it's all rather complicated. It's probably a bit much to ask, but could you possibly come to Edinburgh and talk to him?'

'Of course,' he said. 'You're less than an hour away. I'll come whenever you need me. You know that.' He'd been there for her once before. That was when he thought the two of them might have been more than just friends. It hadn't worked out, but that didn't mean he wasn't there for her if she needed him. He knew Felix was an old friend. Her gay best friend, she had told him. They went back a long way. Studied together in Vienna and then shared a flat in London. Ian didn't know much about musicians, but even he had heard of Felix Lansman, one of the world's best known concert pianists. He was sorry to hear he had been ill and wondered if that was anything to do with whatever searching he wanted. Was Ian about to start tracking down obscure private doctors who dealt with unusual conditions? 'When would you like me to come?' he asked.

'How about lunch on Saturday? Nicola's arriving on Monday and it's going to get a bit hectic. Much nicer if you can talk to Felix when it's quiet.'

'Nicola?'

'Piers' daughter. She's coming for the summer while Toby's in New Zealand.'

'That's right. You did tell me. You and Piers are exchanging offspring.'

'Yes, but Toby's Piers' son. Nicola is nothing to do with me. I've never met her. She sounds like a bit of a handful. Piers is hoping Edinburgh will do her good.'

Ian laughed. 'How old is she?'

'Early twenties.'

'So you won't have much say over what she gets up to.'

'No, and I'm wondering what I've let myself in for.'

'It'll probably be fine. Kids are usually much better behaved away from their families.'

'Toby's not like that.'

'No, but you're a great mum.'

'Not so sure about that. God knows what he'll get up to in New Zealand.'

'It'll be great for him. But it sounds like *you'll* have your hands full.'

'You're not wrong. But it will be the summer break. I'll not have any teaching. Anyway, it'll be lovely to see you on Saturday.'

'It's a date,' he said, then regretted it. *Date* was loaded with implications. 'Have you still got a cat?' he asked.

Rosalie laughed. 'Why do you want to know that?'

'Because I've got a dog and I wouldn't want to start World War Three. I can leave her with a neighbour if—'

'No, bring her. Rainbow died a couple of years ago. We've been catless since then.'

Toby had adored Rainbow. Chosen the name himself with a curiously well-developed sense of irony for a four-year-old, since Rainbow was pure black. That was just before Ian had met them. Rosalie, a single mother, had inherited her grandmother's house and was building a life as a piano teacher and accompanist in Edinburgh. And now Toby was taking a long trip to visit his father in New Zealand before starting university. Amazing how fast time passes.

They ended the call and Ian entered Saturday's trip to Edinburgh in his diary. Then he returned to his email and contacted the other new clients.

2

Rosalie's house in Morningside was very similar to the one Ian and his grandfather had lived in just a few streets away. A sandstone, three-storey house with bay windows, and like many of its neighbours, the front garden had been converted into a paved parking area. Grandad had kept his front garden and grown hydrangeas in it. But he didn't have Rosalie's constant stream of piano pupils driven to lessons in people carriers. Residents' parking was strictly controlled round here. When he lived here, as he had until a few months ago, Ian's parking permit had taken a large slice of his admittedly meagre income. But Grandad had given up his car when he was in his late eighties and he was reluctant to give up part of his garden as well. Thankfully Greyport was different. Kerb-side parking was free and there was plenty of it. Another benefit of moving away from the city.

Rosalie's last pupil of the morning was leaving as Ian arrived, and he pulled into the vacant space. The only other car was Rosalie's, so he assumed that Felix didn't drive and wondered again about how ill he had been, possibly still was. Ian climbed out of the car clutching a bag with a jar of local honey he had bought in Greyport, not wanting to arrive empty-handed. He opened the back of the car and let Lottie

out, attaching her to her lead as she wasn't used to Edinburgh traffic
and even on a quiet road like this he didn't want to risk her taking off
after a cat, or another dog, or even a small child.

He rang the doorbell and Lottie barked. An automatic response,
he supposed, whichever side of the door she was on. She stopped
barking and wagged her tail when Rosalie opened the door.

'Ian,' said Rosalie, kissing him on the cheek. 'It's lovely to see you.
And you look so well.'

The last time they'd met was at Grandad's funeral and he hadn't
been looking his best. 'It's the good Tayside air and plenty of exercise,' he said.

She led him into her drawing room, a room he remembered well.
Years ago he'd been a regular visitor. He had set up a tropical fish
tank here for Toby's birthday. His fourth or fifth. Ian couldn't
remember which. Fish had been Toby's passion. He more or less
learned to read from books about fish. And then Ian had reunited
Rosalie and Piers. They had parted after a series of misunderstand-
ings. Piers hadn't even known that Rosalie was pregnant. But Rosalie
had discovered that Piers was going to be in Edinburgh and Ian did a
little sleuthing, chummed up with Piers and engineered a meeting.
Something that had been right for everyone - except Ian himself.
After that his visits became less frequent. But although he missed
Rosalie and what they might have had together, he had to admit that
life was pretty good right now for all of them.

Rosalie took the honey from him. 'I do miss Eric,' she said. 'He
was the last of that generation. Everything is different now.'

She was right. Rosalie had moved to Edinburgh after inheriting
the house when her own grandmother Adele died. Adele had been
part of a close-knit group of very elderly, very lively neighbours, who
swam and danced together, but who had now all passed on. His
grandfather Eric had been the last of them and had felt this keenly as
Ian drove him to one funeral after another.

'Felix will be down in a moment,' said Rosalie. 'He sleeps late.'

'You said he hadn't been well?'

'He had a breakdown a few months ago. Wandered off after a

concert and was found about to throw himself off a railway bridge near the Carnegie Hall.' She sighed and studied the label on the honeypot before dabbing her eyes with a tissue and smiling up at him. 'Rachmaninov's second piano concerto,' she added.

'Sorry?'

'That's what he'd been playing. It was one of his signature pieces. He's not touched a piano since.'

Sad, Ian thought. Life at the top must be very stressful. Sometimes just bumbling along had its advantages. 'But he's recovering now?' he asked.

'He needed a few months of quiet and rest. He'd driven himself into the ground. Years of world tours, finishing one concert then jetting off to the next, living out of suitcases in hotels, no real home of his own. He drank too much and used cocktails of drugs to keep him awake or send him to sleep. It was a case of being at the top with nowhere to go except down.'

'And you rescued him?'

She shook her head. 'He spent several months in a clinic. A very expensive one near Harrogate where he had therapy. But when he started to recover he had nowhere to go, so I brought him here.'

'He's no family?'

'He has his mother. She visits occasionally but she lives in a tiny flat in Paris and would never have coped.'

'You've been very kind.'

'He's been a friend for a long time. He's temperamental and difficult, but we've always been there for each other. We shared a flat in London until he won the Rebikov Prize in Moscow and after that his career really took off. That was about the same time that I got pregnant, Gran died and I moved up here.'

And five years later Ian had met her and Toby when he'd gone with Grandad to the birthday party of one of their friends, a man who had been Rosalie's grandmother's dancing partner, or was he her synchronised swimming pal? It might even have been both.

The door opened and Felix appeared. Ian had checked the Internet for pictures of him; a well-built Mediterranean type with black hair and gleaming dark eyes. Ian had found a video of him performing with an orchestra and had marvelled at his confidence and charisma. He was a stunning pianist, well known for the energy and passion of his interpretations. Technically brilliant, apparently. Ian was no pianist himself, but he could believe it after watching him for a few moments on YouTube. The man who stood in the doorway was a shock. He must have lost several stone in weight, his hair was thin and greying, he had dark circles under his eyes and fidgeted nervously. Rosalie led him into the room, sat him in a chair and introduced them. Felix nodded at Ian and then sat staring at his hands.

'Shall we have lunch first or would you like to tell Ian why we've brought him here?'

Felix looked up at Ian. 'I want you to find Jamie,' he said. Lottie strolled over to him and he patted her on the head and smiled weakly at her. 'Can you do that?'

'I will certainly try,' said Ian. 'But I'm going to need a little more to go on.'

'Let's have lunch in the garden,' said Rosalie. 'Then you two can sit and chat.'

She carried a tray with plates of quiche and salad out through French windows and they sat round a wooden table under an umbrella and ate.

'Tell me about Jamie,' said Ian as he finished his meal and took out his notebook. 'Is he a friend, a relation?' Even a well-loved family pet, he wondered. But probably not if Felix had spent his life travelling from one concert to the next.

'He worked for my father,' said Felix. 'I was in love with him. He's the only person I've ever loved.'

'You'd better tell Ian about your father,' said Rosalie.

Felix sighed impatiently. 'You've heard of Lansman International? A chain of hotels. Used to be at least one in every European capital.' He sounded tired, cynical even.

Ian nodded. He thought he had heard of them. He remembered some kind of disaster, maybe five or six years ago, when a hotel chain had gone bankrupt. He thought that was Lansman's. He'd not realised there was a family connection.

'My father, Leopold Lansman, owned and ran them until he died and they collapsed.' Again he showed no emotion, just an air of tiredness and impatience.

Ian remembered now. There had been some scandal over the finances. Leopold had been murdered, stabbed in the back at the Park Lane hotel. No one had ever been arrested. Something else nagged at Ian's memory. Leopold's son had been the prime suspect but had disappeared along with any remaining assets he could scrape together. Presumably Leopold Lansman had more than one son. 'You had a brother?' he asked.

Felix nodded. 'Franz. An even bigger criminal than my father. Brutal he was, in business and in his personal life.'

'Where were you living when all this happened?'

Felix looked at him blankly. 'Nowhere really. I was on the move most of the time. Sometimes visited my mother in Paris.'

'You came here a few times,' Rosalie reminded him. 'Toby used to call you Uncle Felix. Do you remember that?'

Felix looked vague.

'It must have been a dreadful shock,' said Ian.

'I suppose it was, but I was focussed on my career.'

'He was incredibly driven,' said Rosalie.

'I'd had to battle with my father over it,' said Felix, becoming livelier, but also angrier. 'He wanted me to join the business with him and Franz, but I only ever wanted to play the piano. It was Franz who persuaded him I would be useless in a hotel. Not because he knew I would be unhappy but because it would divide the business in two and Franz wanted it all for himself. My father sent me to a music professor in Geneva, where we lived at the time, and asked for an opinion. I played to him, and he persuaded my father that I had a career ahead of me.'

'So your father relented and let you study music?'

'Purely out of self-interest. He thought I would be good for publicity. Give the hotels a bit of cachet.'

'And Jamie? How did you meet?'

'We met in London,' said Felix. 'My mother and I spent a month there. I was due to record the Bartók concerto. I hadn't performed it for years, so I booked some sessions with a Bartók expert at the Royal College. Mother wanted to shop. We stayed at Lansman's in Park Lane of course. We had a private flat there. I got chatting to Jamie, who was working as an intern at the hotel. Turns out we went to the same school – not at the same time, Jamie's younger than me.' Felix seemed to drift off into a daydream. He smiled at them. Then remembered something and frowned. 'Franz and I were only at the school for a year or so. Father thought it would give us a bit of English polish which would be useful for hotel work, but realised quite quickly that it wasn't working and we were packed off back to Switzerland. Er, what was I saying?' He seemed to be getting confused and drifting away from his meeting with Jamie.

'You were saying you and Jamie had been to the same school,' Ian prompted.

'We even had the same piano teacher. Jamie played beautifully, but he told me he never had any thought of a career in music. He played because he loved it and it showed.' Now Felix spoke more softly. 'After school he went to university and then worked as an intern for my father.'

'And he was working at the hotel in Park Lane when you met?'

'We fell in love. That was the last truly happy summer I remember. We talked about getting a flat in Vienna. Jamie was going to apply for a job there once his internship had ended, but a few months later my father was murdered and Jamie and Franz both disappeared.'

Ian wrote it all down. 'There must have been witnesses. People who were working in the hotel?'

Felix shook his head. 'I don't know. Mother and I didn't come back to London. I'd just finished a tour of Japan and was staying with her in Paris.'

'Was there a funeral?'

He nodded vaguely as if trying to remember. 'My father's body was sent back to Geneva and Mother and I went to the funeral. But we only stayed a couple of days, I was on tour again after that. I don't remember much about it. It's all a bit of a blur.'

Ian wondered how hard the police in London had tried to solve the case. What usually happened when foreign nationals were murdered? It sounded as if they had just released the body and wiped their hands of it. He'd check newspaper reports when he got home. 'Do you know that Jamie was at the hotel that night?'

'I'm sure of it. That was the last time he was seen. Franz would have worked him hard, and it was very unlikely that Jamie would have been given time off if Franz had anything to do with it.'

'And no one knew where Franz was? Not even your mother?'

'She heard nothing. But she wasn't close to him. He'd disagreed with my father over money he'd transferred to her. My father had been stashing huge amounts of cash away into her account in Switzerland. It meant he didn't have to pay UK taxes. It left my mother a rich woman after his death. Enough to buy the flat she was renting in Paris. She even tried to trace Jamie for me, but the police in London suspected that he and Franz had planned it together and were living off the proceeds somewhere in South America.'

'I'm sorry to ask this,' said Ian. 'But are you sure that isn't what happened?'

Felix looked at him, shocked and horrified by the idea. 'I'm absolutely certain,' he said angrily. 'Jamie was the sweetest, gentlest person in the world. And he loved me. I know that.'

Had Felix really known him that well? Couldn't this just be a case of a rose-tinted memory of love? 'I realise you've been through a tough time recently. Is that why you want to find him now? After six years.' *How hard did his mother try to find Jamie? And why did she give up?*

'Rosalie told you I was found trying to jump off a bridge?'

Ian nodded.

'At the clinic they blamed exhaustion and the stress of my career. *I* know that it was because I couldn't bear another day without Jamie. Do you believe in telepathy?'

'I'm not sure,' Ian said, hesitantly.

'Because a week after I was sent to the clinic, I started receiving postcards. The last one was from somewhere in Scotland.'

'And you think Jamie sent them?'

'I know he did.'

'You can't be sure they were from him,' said Rosalie kindly. 'There was no message.'

'They *were* from him,' said Felix petulantly.

'Do you still have them?' Ian asked.

'Of course I do.'

Yes, of course he would have kept them. He was in love with this guy. 'Perhaps I could take a look at them.'

'They're up in my room,' said Felix. He pulled himself out of his chair. But just as he was about to go inside, the garden gate swung open and a woman appeared. Lottie started barking and Felix sat down again. 'I'll get them later,' he muttered.

3

She was wearing canvas shorts and hiking boots. Strong and healthy, Ian thought, even with the dark circles under her eyes and the general air of one who was not quite sure where they were. She had the look of someone who had just got out of bed after a rough night – or who had just landed after a twenty-four-hour flight.

Ian recognised her immediately. He had only met Piers once, and that was more than ten years ago. But there could be no mistake - this was Piers' daughter and Toby's half-sister, Nicola. They had the same dark curls; Toby kept his cropped short, while Piers, Ian remembered, had shoulder-length hair and Nicola's cascaded down to her waist. Nevertheless, it was the same hair. Also the same brown eyes and breezy confidence.

'Hi,' she said, dumping a rucksack on the ground and massaging her shoulders. 'I'm Nick.'

Rosalie sprang to her feet. 'Nicola,' she said, pulling her into a hug. 'It's great to see you. We didn't expect you until Monday.'

'Got an earlier flight. Tobes said you wouldn't mind.'

'Of course I don't,' said Rosalie. 'Toby's safely settled in then?'

'Yeah, planning a skiing trip with Dad. Then some kind of winter camping survival thing. I was glad to get away from all the boy talk. Too much testosterone flying around. You can't imagine.'

Ian thought he probably could. Toby skied like a pro, having spent his winters from the age of about six in the Cairngorms in whatever rugged conditions they threw at him. It would be paradise for him to ski in the summer as well – or rather getting a go at two winters a year. And winter camping sounded like something he'd enjoy. Having a father on the other side of the world was obviously paying off. Piers was definitely an outdoorsy type. Whenever he wasn't singing he sailed and climbed rocks, probably rode horses bareback as well.

'Come and sit down,' said Rosalie. 'How was your flight?'

'Confusing,' she said. 'We flew to LA and arrived before we'd left. Then on to London which was going forward in time again. And then to Edinburgh. So I've no idea what time it is now, or even what day it is.' She sank breathlessly into the chair.

Rosalie laughed. 'We've just finished lunch.'

Nicola got out her phone and stared at it. 'Says it's one-thirty, Saturday the first. I turned it on once the plane landed. Seems it adjusted quicker than me.'

'Well,' said Rosalie, 'you're probably hungry. I know what airline food's like and there's plenty here so tuck in.'

'Thanks,' said Nicola, grinning and filling a plate with food.

'Let me introduce you,' said Rosalie. 'Felix Lansman over there is staying with me for a while.'

'Felix Lansman?' said Nick, her eyes widening. 'I heard you play Bartók in Auckland a couple of years ago. You should have come to see Dad. He'd have been thrilled. Did you ever meet him?'

Felix looked vague. 'Don't really remember where I've performed. Left it all to my agent.'

'Felix and I were sharing a flat in London when your dad and I got together,' said Rosalie. 'I was Piers' accompanist for his London recitals. You must have met him then, didn't you, Felix?'

Felix shrugged. 'Might have,' he muttered.

'And this,' said Rosalie, clearly wanting to change the subject, 'is Ian Skair. He's an old friend, a private detective.'

'Oh yeah,' said Nicola. 'Dad has talked about you. You got him and Rosalie back together.'

He had indeed. He'd often wondered if that had been a mistake – for him, obviously not for Rosalie. Or the kids. 'Good to meet you,' he said, noticing her empty plate and passing her a bowl of salad.

'And who's this friendly little person?' she asked.

'It's Lottie,' said Ian. 'She is friendly, particularly to anyone holding a plate of food.'

'Is she a Scottie dog?'

'Quite similar,' said Ian. 'She's a Cairn.'

'Well, she's very sweet, even if she is only after my lunch.'

'What are your plans while you're in Edinburgh?' Ian asked, wondering if she was here for the festival which was starting in a few weeks.

'Dad's fixed up singing lessons with a woman called Clarice Ward. A last-ditch attempt to get me to reconsider a singing career. She's supposed to be one of the best teachers in Europe.'

'She is,' said Rosalie. 'I've played for her a few times when she's had recitals here. She'll work you hard, but it'll be worth it.'

'So you're a singer like your father?' Ian asked.

Nicola screwed up her face. 'Thing is,' she said. 'I'm not sure I actually want to be a singer. I thought Dad would let it drop after I was chucked out of college. But he wants me to have another go.'

'Is Piers very keen for you to do it?' Rosalie asked. 'I suppose being a famous singer himself he'd want you to follow in his footsteps.'

'He wouldn't really mind if I didn't. I just can't think what I want to do instead. And he gets a bit naggy about my lack of direction.'

'Why did you get chucked out of college?' asked Felix, suddenly coming to life and showing an interest for the first time.

'I hacked into the college computer system and changed some exam results. That's why I've been sent over here. I'm blacklisted at every college in New Zealand.'

That's impressive, thought Ian. Not something a father would want to encourage, but all the same she must have some well-developed skills. Perhaps she had a future in the computer industry, or as a spy. 'How long are you staying?' he asked.

'I've got a three-month study visa. I'll need to get a job as well. I can work up to twenty hours a week.'

'Any idea what sort of job you'd like?' asked Rosalie.

'Haven't a clue. Bar work perhaps. Dad said they always need extra people during the festival.'

'No rush,' said Rosalie. 'You'll need to get over the jet lag first.' She started clearing plates. Nicola jumped up to help her. 'We'll leave Ian and Felix to chat. I'll show you your room.'

'Thanks,' said Nicola. 'I could do with a shower as well.'

They left to go inside, and Ian turned back to Felix. He'd had a few moments to think and was still pondering the best way to get going. 'You were about to fetch the postcards,' he said to Felix.

'Yeah,' said Felix, standing up and shambling off.

He wasn't going to be an easy client unless he livened up a bit. Perhaps he was on medication that was slowing him down. Ian looked over the notes he'd made. There was a mass of leads here that he'd need to follow up; police records, newspaper reports, tracking down witnesses. And that was on top of all the other cases waiting for him in his inbox. In the week he'd been back from his holiday he'd taken four new cases besides this one. Not particularly difficult ones. A lot of slogging around the Internet and a few face-to-face visits. He was going to be busy. But that was good, wasn't it? Showed his agency was getting known. Skair Cases was on the map. But he couldn't turn this case down. He'd always promised Rosalie he would be there for her and wasn't planning on disappointing her now.

Felix returned with a leather wallet. 'Rosalie bought me this to keep them in,' he said, laying out five postcards on the table in front of them as if they were precious stones. They seemed to mean a lot to him and Ian wondered if, in his confused state, that was clouding his judgement. They could just be from some well-wisher that Felix had never met. Ian turned them over, picking them up gently by their edges, taking care not to leave any marks on them. There was a single picture on each, no messages and no address. 'How were they sent to you?' he asked.

'These five were forwarded to the clinic by my agent with my other post.' He took one more from the wallet. 'The sixth was sent to me here.' He placed it picture down on the table.

Ian studied it. It was addressed to Felix and the address, which was correct down to the postcode, was where they were right now. It was Rosalie's address. So someone, assuming it was only one person, had been trying to contact Felix for the three months he was at the clinic and had only the address of the agent. But they had discovered Felix was here with Rosalie now. He looked at the postmark. It had been sent here two weeks ago from Glasgow. The first five must have been sent in envelopes. Ian asked Felix if he had kept them.

Felix gathered up the cards and replaced them in the folder. 'A guy at the clinic helped with my correspondence. I think he probably threw them out.'

A pity. It would have been useful to compare the handwriting. 'You seem very sure they are from Jamie,' he said. 'But why?'

Felix looked at him as if the answer was obvious. 'They're all pictures that meant something special to us,' he said. 'Except the last one.'

Fair enough. Ian turned it over and studied the picture. It was a photograph of Glencoe.

'Never been there,' said Felix. 'We never even talked about it.'

'But the others all have some kind of personal memory for both of you?'

Felix nodded.

'And there was no one else who could have known?'

'Why would there be?'

A good question. Ian was still puzzled.

Rosalie returned with a tray of coffee and a biscuit for Lottie, who had been lying under the table asleep since the food was cleared away. She perked up when she sniffed out more food.

'How are you getting on?' she asked. 'Will you take the case?'

Ian hesitated.

'There's no problem with money,' said Rosalie. 'We'll pay your usual fee. Felix has plenty of money. His fees are enormous, and he never spends any. Even the clinic was covered by private insurance.'

'Look,' said Ian. 'I'll do what I can. Begin a few searches and let you know if I think there's any chance of finding this guy.' He got out his phone and took photos of the postcards. 'Could you write down everything you know about Jamie? His full name, date of birth, where he grew up, does he have brothers and sisters, anything you can think of. And email it to me.'

'Is that how you keep in touch?' she asked. 'By email? You won't be coming here?'

'Mostly. I'll start by setting up a shared folder so I can keep you informed as we go along. Are you okay with that, Felix?'

Felix looked puzzled. Not much need for concert pianists to use computers, Ian supposed.

'He can use my laptop,' said Rosalie. 'I'll help him with it. And don't forget we have a hacking whizz staying with us.'

'Have you both looked at my website?' Ian asked. 'It has details of my various contracts and payment methods. I suggest you sign up for the weekly rolling contract.' He was beginning to sound like a mobile phone salesman. But he liked clients to be clear about what they were letting themselves in for. 'It means I send weekly reports and it gives you a chance to assess the progress I've made. It's flexible for both of us and doesn't tie you in to a specified amount of time.'

'You've become very businesslike since we last met,' said Rosalie.

'That was when I was working from Grandad's back bedroom. Now I'm properly qualified and certified and with some high-profile cases under my belt.'

'And you're in demand? That's good.'

It was good. Over the last few months he'd helped the police, tracked down some criminals, met a selection of interesting people and was generally making it onto the map of go-to PIs. His problem now was not worrying about where the next case was coming from, but whether he was taking on too much work.

Felix had nodded off in his chair, so Ian handed Rosalie his latest business card with all his contact details. She took it and read the address. 'I've never been to Greyport,' she said. 'What's it like?'

'Nice little commuter village on the banks of the Tay opposite Dundee. I've set myself up with an office there.'

'You look very well on it,' she said. 'How's your leg these days?'

'Not so bad. Aches a bit when I'm tired, but mostly I don't even think about it.'

She laughed. 'Do you remember how Eric used to try and pair us off?'

'I do. Now I've lost Eric and gained the wife of an ex-colleague whose mission in life is to set me up with unattached women.'

'And has she succeeded?'

'That,' he said, as he picked Lottie up and headed for his car, 'is classified information.'

She waved them off as he pulled out of the drive with Lottie standing on her hind legs wagging her tail. She'd behaved impeccably all day. He'd stop somewhere on the way to give her a good walk. Crail perhaps, where she could feel the sea breeze ruffling her fur.

He set off towards the Forth bridge, trying to sort things out in his head. It would be an interesting case, but God knew how he'd find the time for it. He needed help. He'd been thinking about an assistant for a while. He wouldn't be able to afford anyone full time, maybe a couple of days a week. But where was he going to find one? It could suit a student during the summer, or he could advertise on a website. Then it came to him in a flash. Nicola needed a job. He'd pay her train fare for one day a week to come to Greyport and she could work from Rosalie's house for another day. She could help him with online searches and that was something she had already proved to be good at. He just hoped she would keep it legal.

4

Ian spent the next few days catching up on some of his less exciting cases, clearing the way for his hunt for Jamie. An email arrived from Rosalie. Felix apparently didn't use any kind of technology, but Nick (she preferred Nick, Rosalie told him) was setting him up with an email address and was training him in how to use it. Rosalie had attached details about Jamie. It was a bit like pulling teeth, she told him. Felix's concentration was shot to pieces by the medication he was on, but hopefully he would start to come off it soon and would start making more sense and not fall asleep quite as much.

It's sad, she wrote. *He always used to be so full of energy. He could be bad-tempered and temperamental but that's what had got him to the top. He hadn't been an easy flatmate, but I preferred the way he used to be to the way he is now.*

It must be exhausting for her, Ian thought. It was good that Nick was helping. He clicked reply and wrote:

Must be tough for you. Let me know if there's more I can do to help.

Has Nick found a job yet? If not, ask her to call me if she'd like to be my assistant a couple of days a week.

He clicked send and then opened the document with Jamie's details.

Sorry – this isn't much to go on. Felix is vague about a lot of it and I've made one or two assumptions which I hope are clearly mine rather than Felix's.

Jamie McLeash. Born 1989 in Aberdeen. Parents are local estate agents (Felix doesn't know any more about them than that. He doesn't think Jamie got on well with them).

They were at St Archibald's, a school which Felix thinks was somewhere north of London (sorry, I warned you he was vague). Felix was there briefly in the early nineties. Jamie probably in the early 2000s.

They both had piano lessons with a woman called Dora Meadows.

Jamie studied Hospitality (Felix thinks but isn't sure) at Stirling University. Then he worked as an intern at Lansman International at their Park Lane hotel.

They met while Felix was in London in the spring of 2012. Jamie had finished uni the previous summer and had been working at a hotel somewhere in Scotland (again Felix doesn't remember where). This sounds like some kind of dead-end job and I assume Jamie had jumped at the chance of an internship at a prestigious hotel, which he would have hoped might be a springboard to a career in hotel management. Felix tells me he was staying with a friend in South Kensington but doesn't remember the address or the friend's name – could be an ex-college friend? I think interns only get paid expenses and assume the friend was letting him stay for very low rent, or maybe even for nothing.

Hopefully Felix will start to remember more as his head clears. I'll let you know if there's more to add.

Ian sent her a short email to thank her. He sat back and thought about where to start. As ever, he needed a visual plan. He stood up and rearranged the whiteboard that he had fixed to the wall of his study. He'd had to extend this recently with the new cases that were coming in. He picked up a marker pen and created a new column, writing

Jamie McLeash at the top. Then he printed Rosalie's email and pinned it to the board. Rosalie had been apologetic about the vagueness of Felix's account, but there was a fair bit here that he could get going with. Interesting that Jamie, like Ian, was born in Aberdeen. And only ten years younger than himself. Jamie would have just been starting secondary school when Ian was setting out on his police career. They might have met, although aged eleven and twenty-one, the age gap would have seemed far greater than it did now. Aberdeen was a big city, and he had no recollection of the name McLeash. It might be a good place to start though. He'd drive up there, drop in on his parents at the same time. Not a thought that filled him with joy, but he could keep the visit brief and they might just know something about the family.

It would be worth finding out more about the friend Jamie was staying with. Rosalie had suggested it was someone he knew at university, but it could have been a colleague he met while working at the hotel in Scotland. It was possible that if he could find Jamie's parents in Aberdeen, they might know both the name of the hotel and Jamie's friend.

He started making a to-do list and then his phone rang. It was a number he didn't recognise. He tapped accept.

'Hello?' he said, hoping it wasn't a cold call from someone who wanted to promote his business. He got a lot of those. They always promised staggering results and usually for a staggering amount of money.

'Hi, it's Nick,' said an enthusiastic voice.

'Oh, Nick, thanks for calling back.'

'S'okay,' she said. 'Rosalie said you wanted to talk about a job.'

'That's right.' It was good that she'd called so quickly. Was it a sign that she was keen to work for him? 'What do you think about working for me for a while?' he asked, hoping she wasn't going to laugh in his face.

'Could be cool,' she said. 'What would I be doing?'

'Well, don't expect wall-to-wall excitement.' Might as well start with the downside, he supposed. Or would that just put her off? He wasn't used to being a prospective employer. 'A lot of the work involves trawling the Internet and it sounds like you know your way around that.' He really was making it sound like the dreariest job in the world. 'But I travel around a bit. Could be a chance for you to get to see a bit more of Scotland.'

'You're helping Felix find this Jamie person?'

'That's the idea, but I've other cases as well.'

'Sounds better than bar work.'

'I can't pay much above a minimum hourly rate, but I'll pay your train fare.'

'How many hours would you want me to do?'

'I was thinking one day a week here and another day in Edinburgh, so shall we say sixteen hours? I'm afraid it doesn't quite take you up to twenty.'

'Well,' she said, sounding as if she was pausing to think about it. At least she hadn't turned him down out of hand. 'I can always do one evening a week in a bar. Which days were you thinking?'

'That's up to you. When are your singing lessons?'

'Monday and Thursday.'

'So shall we say Tuesday and Wednesday?'

'Yeah, maybe.'

'Would you like to think about it and let me know in a day or two?'

'No, I don't think so.'

Oh well, it had been a nice thought. It's not something everyone would want to do and she could probably find something much more interesting in Edinburgh. 'Well, it was worth asking,' he said. 'Hope you find something soon.'

'No, I didn't mean that.' He could hear she was laughing. 'I meant I don't want to think about it. I'll do it. When can I start?'

'Tuesday next week? Can you make it for about nine? Are you okay at early mornings? I'm afraid it's an hour on the train from Edinburgh.'

'An hour? That's nothing, and I'm great at early mornings.'

'Even with jetlag?'

'Even better with jetlag. I wake up at about four in the morning.'

'Well, I don't want you that early,' he laughed.

'You're in Dundee, right?'

'I'm across the estuary. Rosalie has the address. You can check it out on Google Earth. But don't go to Dundee. Get out at Leuchars and I'll pick you up there. Parking's easier. Text me from the train so I know what time you're arriving.'

'Great. Do I need to bring anything?'

'Bank details, passport, can't think of anything else.'

'Laptop?'

'That would be a great help.'

'Okay, see you Tuesday. Oh, I'm calling Dad later. Any messages?'

'Ask him if he remembers an evening in MacTavish's whiskey bar.' He assumed Piers would remember that. He'd got decidedly drunk that evening and had told Ian a great deal about himself. About his divorce, his shortcomings as a husband, his time with Rosalie in London and about his daughter, who must have been about eleven then. At the time he hadn't known that Toby even existed.

'Sure, will it embarrass him?'

'It was the evening before he met Toby for the first time.'

'I'm guessing it will then.'

'You can let me know when I see you.'

He ended the call with a good feeling that they were going to get on well. But right now, he needed to sort out his office. He couldn't have her thinking he wasn't organised. He'd never employed anyone before, and his only experience of an assistant was when Anna had spent a day with him a few months ago.

He tidied his desk then stood and looked around the room. She'd need a desk of her own, and he had just the thing upstairs in one of his spare rooms. A nice pine desk that had been dismantled by the removal people when he moved in and never put together again because he didn't know where he wanted it. He climbed the stairs with Lottie skittering behind him. Lottie had never been up here before. Hell, he'd only been up here two or three times himself, and that was to stash away stuff he didn't know what to do with. Climbing stairs had been slow and painful, but arriving at the top he realised that it was a lot easier than it had been a few weeks ago.

Lottie was sniffing around, pouncing on the occasional spider and kicking up dust. He really needed to do something about these upstairs rooms. He'd left them when he first moved in because his leg was still painful, but he didn't have that excuse now. After ten years it was healing at last and gave him little pain. His regular monthly order of painkillers was stacking up in the bathroom because he needed them far less often. He made a mental note to get online and reduce his prescription.

He found the desk, brushed off cobwebs and dust, and carried it downstairs one piece at a time. There was also a chair he'd forgotten about. One that Grandad had owned for years. It had a padded seat and looked as if it could be the right height for an office chair. Lottie was still happily sniffing into the corners of the room, and he stood and watched her for a moment. He believed there was a recurring dream that people had about finding undiscovered rooms in their houses. It felt a bit like that now. He'd lived here for nearly six months and it was time to make use of the space he had. He could turn this room into his bedroom. It had a dormer window with an even better view of the estuary than he had downstairs. If work continued to flood in the way it had over the last couple of months he would need more office space. If things worked out with Nick he'd think of taking on more help. Someone to do some of the legwork, someone else to sit outside hotels. He'd need to look into the legal side of being an employer, but it couldn't be that hard.

Lottie nudged his leg, looking hopefully at the stairs. 'Okay, Lottie,' he said. 'Just a daydream.' For now. But definitely something to think about. He grabbed a table lamp and headed downstairs to reassemble the desk.

He decided to have the desks at right angles and once in place they looked good. Very businesslike. He searched the hall cupboard and emerged with something he thought was called a power socket strip. He supposed Nick would have whatever kind of power lead she needed. He'd no idea what they used in New Zealand, but they could always nip over the bridge and buy an adapter. Then there was the printer. He dragged out a box of cables. The printer he used connected through the Wi-Fi. Hopefully Nick's would be the same, but if not there would probably be a cable in the box that she could use. Why didn't someone invent one kind of cable that could be used for everything? Perhaps they already had and he was just behind the times. Or perhaps cable would soon be a thing of the past because everyone used Bluetooth or Wi-Fi. He suspected that Nick was going to be far more knowledgeable about it than he was.

So what else did an assistant need? The desk looked rather bare and the drawers were all empty. He checked the drawers of his own desk and found paperclips, pens, rubber bands, drawing pins, some Post-Its and sticky tape. Would she need any of those? He took out the Post-Its and a couple of pens and put them on the desk. Still a bit bare. He'd take Lottie for a walk and check out the village shop. He'd buy notebooks and pencils. And coffee, he suddenly realised. Assistants, he was sure, drank a lot of coffee. And if they didn't, well, he drank quite a lot himself, so it wouldn't go to waste.

He attached Lottie to her lead, then called to Lainie over the fence. She spent most of her time in the garden when the weather was as good as this.

'Just off to the village,' he said, and then added, as he usually did, 'Do you need anything?'

'Been cleaning?' she asked. 'Your face is filthy.'

Was it? He should have checked in a mirror. It had been very dusty upstairs. He pulled out a packet of tissues and rubbed at his face.

She tutted at him. 'Bless you,' she said. 'Pass Lottie over while you go in and give it a proper wash.'

He handed Lottie over the fence and went back inside. She was right. He looked at himself in the bathroom mirror and then gave his face and hands a good scrub. *One of the problems of living alone,* he thought. That was probably why everyone he knew tried to marry him off.

He returned outside and retrieved Lottie. 'Thanks for the warning,' he said. 'I've been clearing out for my new assistant.'

'You're getting help?'

'Just a couple of days a week. Daughter of a friend over from New Zealand for a few months.' Was Piers a friend? Close enough. He was hardly going to go into details about employing the daughter of a man on the other side of the world that he had spent a drunken evening with whilst reuniting him with his long-lost love, who also just happened to be Ian's potential girlfriend. No, friend would do.

5

The day before Nick was due to start work, Ian sorted through his ongoing cases and wrote a list of jobs for her to do. One or two for each case would be best. It would give her a chance to see the kind of work he did without becoming too involved in any one thing. She'd be a great help with the admin, sending out invoices, recording receipts and compiling lists of expenses. But he also wanted to involve her with some of the more interesting parts of the job and since she was living in the same house as Felix, that would be a good place for her to start. He wasn't sure himself how he was going to set about the 'Finding Jamie' case, so he sat at his desk and started a list.

The murder of Leopold Lansman - were any arrests ever made? Was the case closed unsolved? Were there any witnesses? Ask Duncan for case notes. Was Jamie a suspect?

Jamie's background – start with the obvious and google him, when was he last seen, where and by whom? Try and find his parents and the friend he stayed with in London.

What is the significance of the postcards? Could they really have been sent by Jamie or is this just Felix's wishful imagination? How reliable is Felix?

He downloaded the photos he'd made of the postcards Felix had received, printed them and pinned them to his board. He'd photographed the back and front of each one but found no information. That was strange, wasn't it? Picture postcards usually had details of the pictures. These were blank with only the printed lines needed to write the address and a square for a stamp. But hardly anyone sent postcards any more, maybe he just didn't remember what they were like. They still had a few dusty ones in the village shop. He should have looked at them. He stared once again at the pictures. There was a bronze statue of a man wearing a hat and overcoat and standing on a small plinth in front of some buildings. One was of a painting; some cows grazing in a field at sunset. There was some kind of monument, a gothic-style structure with a figure of a man seated inside. On closer inspection he could see that the figure was covered in gold. It looked familiar, Ian thought. Then he turned to a photograph of an old-fashioned shop with a brown door on either side of which were tall, curved windows with what Ian thought were called mullions near the top. Then another painting. One he recognised. It was Millais' Ophelia. And then there was the only card with a place identified. A picture of Glencoe with Rosalie's address handwritten, and postmarked Glasgow. Was that last one a message of some sort? Were they all messages, a code perhaps?

He returned to his computer and enlarged the image he thought he recognised. Yes, he'd seen it quite recently from the top deck of a bus. It was the Albert Memorial in Hyde Park. He wrote *Albert Memorial* underneath the picture on his board. He needed to know why Felix thought they all had a connection to Jamie. What was it he said? *All pictures that meant something special to us. Except the last one.* He needed to know why they meant something special. Perhaps there would be a clue about where Jamie went and where he was now. Talking to Felix about it was something Nick could do. She could choose a time when he was at his most lucid and it would save Ian another drive to Edinburgh.

Why was Glencoe significant? Was there a memory Felix had forgotten? A plan to go there together perhaps. Ian had never been there. Call himself a Scot and never been to Glencoe? He should be ashamed of himself. But he knew the scenery well enough from paintings and travel brochures. As bleak as anywhere in Scotland, but popular with ramblers, climbers and wildlife spotters. And of course, ghost enthusiasts. An unlikely spot for a couple of romantic pianists, but who was he to say?

He glanced at his watch. Five-thirty and time to put work aside for the day. Lottie needed a walk, and he needed an evening in the pub. *The beach at St Andrews*, he thought. Lottie enjoyed the dog friendly part of the beach and after he'd given her a walk, followed by a good rub down with a towel because she also enjoyed running in and out of the sea, he'd drop in and see if Duncan fancied joining him for a pint.

It was a pleasantly warm evening, and they stayed an hour on the beach. Lottie was happy running in and out of the water chasing sticks and there was no hurry. It would be light until well after ten o'clock at this time of year, but if he wanted time for a meal at the pub he shouldn't stay too much longer. He called Lottie and led her to a tap in the car park where he hosed her down and rubbed her dry. Full of sea air, they'd both sleep soundly tonight. He called Duncan, who had just come off duty and would welcome the chance of a pint and a chat. 'Just give me time to change,' he said. 'I'll meet you at the Pigeon in half an hour.'

'Not St Andrews?' Ian asked.

'It's Jeanie's night for line dancing in the Greyport village hall,' he said. 'She can pick me up when she's done.'

Ian drove Lottie home and decided to walk to the pub. He wasn't a heavy drinker but it would be good to sink a pint or two without worrying about having to drive home. Good plan. Duncan too would be able to drink. As a police inspector he would never risk drinking and driving, which was why, although they met regularly, they took it in turns to drink in Greyport or St Andrews. In Greyport Duncan stuck to shandies and when they met in St Andrews it was Ian's turn to go easy on the alcohol. Jeanie's sudden enthusiasm for line dancing benefitted both of them. All three of them probably, as it also helped Jeanie to keep in shape.

'Looks like the holiday did you good,' said Duncan as he arrived at the Pigeon, grabbed a chair next to Ian's and sat down with a pint of Fife's best. 'How did it go?'

'A bit damp, but restful. Lottie and I went for long walks and most evenings I ate in the local fish restaurant, so plenty of healthy eating as well.'

'Did you go on your own?' Duncan asked with a wink.

'Just me and Lottie.'

'Caroline not with you? I'm surprised,' he said, grinning.

'She's on a walking holiday with her sister in North Wales,' said Ian, with a twinge of irritation. He and Caroline were friends. The kind of friends that had benefits, so he was told. They weren't joined at the hip. He took a swig of his beer. 'I saw Rosalie a few days ago,' he said. That would get Jeanie's tongue wagging when it got back to her, which it would if he knew Duncan as well as he thought he did.

'Oh yeah, that all starting up again? Bit of two timing?' Duncan grinned at him. 'One of the advantages of being single, I suppose. Lucky devil.'

'Caroline and I are not an item,' he said. 'We're both free to see whoever we like.' He didn't think he'd tell Duncan about red-haired Elsa who lived in Glasgow. He'd had enough nudging and winking for one evening. He didn't want to invite accusations of three timing – was that a thing? It would be too much for Jeanie, who for some reason had made finding a long-term love interest for Ian a mission. 'Actually,' he said. 'I went to see Rosalie because she has a case for me.'

'Mislaid another lover, has she?'

In a way Duncan was right, although not in the way he was suggesting. 'No, Rosalie and Piers are still together.' As much as any couple could be together when they lived on opposite sides of the world. 'She has a friend who wants me to find the lost love of his life.'

'How did he lose her?'

'Him. He disappeared after his boss was murdered. And his boss was this guy's father.'

'You're losing me,' said Duncan.

'It's complicated. Actually you might be able to help. Do you remember the collapse of Lansman International and the murder of its owner?'

'The hotels? Vaguely. That was what, six years ago?'

'About that. Do you know if the case was ever solved?'

'I don't remember that it was. But it was London, wasn't it? Probably wouldn't have got much publicity up here. Do you want me to check for you?'

'If you could. I'm interested in two people who went missing at the time. One was the son of the owner, Franz Lansman, who is the brother of my client, Felix Lansman. The other was a young a man called Jamie McLeash. Felix thinks his brother was probably a suspect and that he escaped to South America. He also thinks that Jamie has been sending him postcards for the last few months.'

'Was he a suspect as well?'

'I don't know. That's why it would help to see the file.'

'You realise that if he was suspected you would have to hand any information you found to the Met? Even if the case has been closed.'

'Yes, of course I know that.'

'So why would he start sending postcards?'

'I have no idea. I don't even know if he has been. It's what Felix thinks but he's, well, he's not in the best state mentally right now. But someone is sending postcards and it's the least I can do to try to find out who and why.'

'I'll see if I can get a copy of the report for you. I'll do it very discreetly – we don't want them to think we're trying to get the case reopened. I'll just say we might have discovered a local connection.'

'Which there is,' said Ian.

They'd just drained their glasses when Jeanie arrived, looking red-cheeked and cheerful. 'Glass of lemonade?' asked Duncan.

'Thank you, darling,' she said, sinking into the chair next to Ian's.

'Nice boots,' said Ian. 'I've always fancied a pair of cowboy boots.'

'You should join us,' she said. 'It's not so different from Scottish dancing.'

'Really? I always thought it was all Dolly Parton lookalikes and blokes in Stetsons.'

'As opposed to blokes in skirts?'

'Shame on you,' he said, laughing. 'I'll have you know that the kilt is a highly respected, ancient and not to say macho piece of clothing.' And at least she hadn't mentioned his love life. Yet.

'How's Caroline?' she asked.

'She's in Wales with her sister.'

'You should grab that one while you've the opportunity.'

Ian smiled. She'd never learn. Not until she had him safely shackled to *a good woman*.

6

Ian was just finishing breakfast when the text arrived.

Train arriving Leuchars 8.55 Nick

He looked at his watch. Nice timing. If he left now, he'd be there when the train arrived. Only a short drive from Greyport, Leuchars station always seemed to Ian to be in a place that no one actually wanted to go to. It had an interesting history, having been burnt to the ground by suffragettes in 1913. Leuchars itself was a small town and RAF base, and the new out-of-town replacement station was used almost entirely by commuters to and from Edinburgh, and by St Andrews students and visitors.

He parked close to the station entrance with Lottie jumping up and down expecting a walk. 'Later,' he told her. 'We have to meet my assistant.' That sounded good. It made him feel he was doing a proper job, not just frittering around pretending to be a detective. Real detectives had assistants.

He watched as the train from Edinburgh pulled in and Nick emerged still wearing her canvas shorts and boots, and with a laptop bag over her shoulder. She waved to him, then bounded up to the car and opened the door.

'Morning,' she said, climbing in and stowing her bag at her feet.

She turned and said, 'Hi Lottie, remember me?' Lottie wagged her tail.

Ian guessed that Lottie remembered the biscuits Nick had fed her when they were at Rosalie's house. 'Right,' he said, starting the engine, 'all ready for work?'

'You bet,' she said. 'Can't wait.'

'It's only about ten minutes away,' he said.

Nick looked around as they drove. 'First time I've been out of Edinburgh,' said Nick. 'It's not really what I expected. I thought there'd be mountains and forests and stuff.'

'*The Land of the Mountain and the Flood.* I guess you're familiar with Hamish MacCunn?'

'I played trombone in the local youth orchestra. That was one of the pieces we did. We were told it was the archetypal Scottish overture.'

'Did they also tell you MacCunn lived in London?'

She laughed. 'Doesn't mean he couldn't love Scotland though.'

'Living in London probably means he loved it more. Did you know they used the overture to introduce a TV series? Years ago in the seventies. Don't remember what it was called, but I think it was probably another idealised view of Scotland.'

'So Hamish made it all up? About the mountains?'

'Not at all. It's all there, just not around here. Fife's not typical. It's mostly farmland, golf courses and pretty fishing villages. You'll have seen some from the train.'

'Yeah, the coast looked nice. And we crossed the Forth Bridge. I've seen pictures of it. Being permanently painted, isn't it?'

'I think that's probably an urban myth from the days when it was done by hand with a paint brush. It was painted a few years ago with some new type of paint and won't need doing for another twenty-five years.'

'Glass flake epoxy paint,' said Nick. 'It's been used in New Zealand.'

'You know about painting bridges?' She was full of surprises.

'I know about all sorts of things. I soak up useless facts, Dad says.'

'Not useless if you have a bridge that needs painting.'

'I'll remember that next time Dad nags about me finding a career.'

'How are the singing lessons going?'

'Okay, I suppose. I like Clarice. She's got style and we laugh a lot. Not sure what she thinks of my voice though. I think she's worked out that my heart's not really in it. She'll probably report back to Dad, and I'll be hauled home for a lecture.'

Somehow he couldn't see the Piers he remembered in a strict father role. 'How is your father?' he asked.

'He's okay. I Skyped him last night and told him about the job.'

'Was he okay with that?'

'Oh yeah, he said you were quite brilliant, a second Sherlock Holmes.'

'Really?'

'No, not really. He said you were a nice guy and that I should work hard and not hack your computer.'

That sounded more like it. Everyone thought he was a nice guy. It got quite tedious after a while. Perhaps he should cultivate a more rugged persona. 'And will you?' he asked.

'Of course,' she grinned at him. 'But I'm not letting on which I'll do.'

This was going to be fun. Nice to have someone to joke with across the top of his desk. 'Look over there to the right and you'll see the Tay Bridge.'

'The one in the poem?'

'No, that was the railway bridge. This is a road bridge opened in 1966.'

'There are a lot of bridges in Scotland,' she said. 'Is that Dundee on the other side?'

'It is, but we're not going there. I live on this side.' He swung round a roundabout and turned onto the road that took them down into Greyport.

He pulled into a parking space. 'That's my house up there,' he said. 'It's a bit of a climb up to it, but you get a stunning view once you're at the top.'

Arriving at his front door, she laughed as she watched him stagger up behind her. 'You do know I've done mountaineering courses in New Zealand?'

He could believe it. She'd galloped up like a mountain goat, barely drawing breath. He unlocked the door and led her into his study, no, not study. From now on it would be the office. 'Right,' he said. 'Let me show you around.' He pointed to the desk he had set up for her. 'You can plug your laptop in down there,' he said, gesturing to the row of sockets. 'The Wi-Fi password is written on your notepad. Up there,' he pointed to the whiteboard, 'are notes about all the cases I'm working on right now. Take a look around while I make coffee.'

By the time he returned with two mugs of coffee she had started up her laptop and was looking at the whiteboard. 'What would you like me to do?' she asked.

'I've set up a shared workspace for us. Details are on your notepad. Your username is Stroppysinger23. Create a password for yourself and when you're in you'll find a list of tasks.'

'Thanks for the username,' she said. 'Can I change it?'

'Nope. I like it. Suits you.'

'Been talking to my dad, have you?'

He ignored that. 'It's mostly checking details that clients have given me. I've added a checklist so when you've verified them you can save the results. They'll show up in my own workspace. That way we'll know where we've both got to. I've given you one for each case, so you get to know your way around what I'm doing.'

'Okay. I'll get going. What are you going to be doing?'

'I've a mate in the local police and I'm hoping he'll have sent me some details about the Lansman murder.' He checked the time. 'We'll work until twelve-thirty then take a break. We can walk down to the village for some lunch and this afternoon we'll talk through the Lansman case and decide on some kind of action plan. I've one or two things I'd like you to check with Felix so we'll make a list, and you can work on that tomorrow. And before you go today, I need to check your visa and bank details.'

He thought that was all she needed to know. He looked across his desk and she seemed to be getting down to work with no problem. He opened his own email and found one from Duncan. *'Info you requested – I've summarised,'* was all the email said, so he clicked on the attachment.

Murder of Leopold Lansman, owner of Lansman International chain of hotels.

The body was discovered by builders at 8am on the morning of 15th July at Lansman Park Lane, which at the time of the incident was closed to guests for minor refurbishment.

Post-mortem revealed the cause of death was a single stab wound to the back of the neck. No weapon was ever found but it was believed to be a kitchen knife. It was the practice of the hotel's kitchen manager to inventory the equipment at the close of business every night. On the night of the murder the kitchen had been closed during the refurbishment of the hotel taking place that week. Kitchen staff were not working that evening and no inventory took place. However, the next morning the kitchen manager was asked to check all equipment and reported that a filleting knife, a narrow blade of twenty centimetres with rivetted handle and used in the prepara-tion of fish, was missing. The pathologist confirmed this as a possible weapon.

Time of death was believed to be between midnight and 2am.

The deceased was a well-built man in his mid-sixties. He was seated at his desk in an antique captain-style leather chesterfield, his head having been pulled back against the curved padding on the back of the chair after death.

Considerable strength and skill would have been needed to inflict the fatal injury. The knife entered at an angle suggesting that the murderer was standing and, taking into account both the height of the victim and the chair, that he was between six feet and six feet two inches tall. Almost certainly a right-handed male, and very likely one who was trained in some form of armed combat. Death was caused by a single thrust of the knife to the back of the neck and would have been instant. It was assumed by detectives to have been a premeditated and carefully planned attack.

The office was on the fourth floor of the building. The only access to the room at the time was through the door. An emergency exit via the window onto a fire escape had been disabled by the building work, the top flight from floors three to four having been temporarily removed.

The only staff on duty that night were members of a security team who patrolled the building in pairs throughout the night but had been instructed by Mr Lansman himself not to interrupt him in his office. It was believed that he was working with his son, Mr Franz Lansman and an intern, twenty-four-year-old Jamie McLeash. Both Franz Lansman and Jamie McLeash were seen around 10pm on July 14th when they received a delivery of coffee and sandwiches from Coffee 2U, a delivery service working in Mayfair. The delivery boy confirmed that Lansman Junior signed for the delivery and that he saw McLeash standing with Lansman in the hotel staff entrance.

The two were seen again by security staff leaving the building through the same entrance at around one a.m. Witnesses said the two seemed to be in a hurry and didn't respond when wished a good night.

The post-mortem revealed that the victim's stomach contained coffee and prawns.

SOCOs have confirmed that apart from a considerable amount of blood around the desk and chair, the room was tidy. They found a handprint in the blood on the desk. No financial papers were found, and a desktop computer had been wiped. Further investigation revealed the company to be in financial trouble and suspected of fraud. At the time of the murder, it was under investigation by the fraud squad in the UK and in Europe.

All fingerprints found at the scene have been traced to employees of the company. DNA was taken from coffee cups. A close match to the victim likely to be that of Franz Lansman. The other believed to be that of McLeash.

Since Lansman's desk faced the door of the office and there was no sign of a struggle, police believe that the attacker must have been known to the victim.

The victim left a wife and younger son who at the time were living in Paris. Both have alibis for that night. Felix Lansman performed at the Olympia Bruno Coquatrix that evening to an audience of over one thousand. This was followed by a reception after which Mr Lansman was driven home in a taxi. Mrs Lansman was seen dining with friends at L'Orangerie in the Four Seasons George V Hotel. She left shortly after 11.30.

Alerts were in place at airports across Europe for Lansman Junior and McLeash, who it is believed may have escaped to South America where Franz Lansman had business colleagues.

Police were unable to make any arrests and the case was closed after the statutory three years.

That pretty much confirmed what Felix had told him. Ian would need to be very careful. There was nothing to stop the police reopening the case if new evidence was found and as Duncan had said, if he made any discoveries that could be relevant to the case, he was obliged to report them. He wondered if Felix realised what a difficult position Ian was now in. He'd need to know all of that, but Ian wondered if he was clear-headed enough to understand. He wanted to help, but not if it was going to end in the arrest of someone Felix cared so much about. He sat tapping his desk with a pencil and gazed out of the window.

Nick looked up from her work. 'You okay?' she asked. 'You're staring out of that window like a cat waiting to pounce.'

'Yeah, sorry.' He stretched. 'Just getting involved in this police report.'

'Felix's dad's murder?'

'That's the one.' He looked at the time on his computer screen. 'Time for a break, I think. How are you getting on?'

'Almost done. Just need to tick off the last couple of boxes and it's all yours.'

'Any problems?'

'No, like you said, all straightforward searches.'

'Not too dull, I hope.'

'Not at all. It's fascinating what you can find out about people.'

'I hope it goes without saying that everything you find stays confidential.'

'Of course. Do you want me to sign some kind of non-disclosure thingy?'

He wondered if she should. He'd check on the IPI website later and see if there was a template he could use. He hadn't given her anything confidential this morning, but he should probably cover himself for things he might want her to look into in the future. 'Let's take a break now for some lunch. We can sort all that admin stuff this afternoon.'

'Should I have brought some sandwiches? I didn't realise you were quite so out of the way.'

'There's a good café down in the village. It's not a complete wilderness. We'll take Lottie and get a bit of fresh air. You'll get a nice view across the estuary.'

'Sounds good. I'm starving.'

'And when we get back we'll make a start on Felix's case. There are one or two things I'd like you to talk to him about.'

'Can I ask you something?' Nick wiped the crumbs from her fingers, having just chomped her way through an enormous cheese and ham panini.

'Ask away,' said Ian, coming to the end of his own tuna baguette.

'Before you found my dad, did you and Rosalie have, you know, a thing together?'

'I didn't really find your dad. We already knew he was in Edinburgh. I just set things up so they could meet again.'

'You haven't answered my question.'

No, he hadn't. That was deliberate, because he didn't really know the answer. They'd been friends, gone on dates, he supposed. He and Toby got on well. And yes, he had to admit that he'd hoped for more. 'Not really,' he said.

'Okay, I get it. You don't want to talk about it.'

She was right. He didn't want to talk about it. 'Was it weird discovering you had a brother you hadn't known about?' he asked.

'Yeah, I suppose. But it didn't mean much at the time. I was eleven and kid brothers weren't that interesting. I liked him when I met him though. He was a good kid and he adored Dad even though he hardly knew him.'

Toby had been four when Ian met him. He'd been desperate for a father, asking every man he met the same question: *Are you my daddy?* So it made sense that when he did meet his father, he adored him. Piers was a good father. Rosalie had been worried that once Piers got over the initial excitement, he'd disappear back to New Zealand and forget Toby. But it hadn't been like that. They'd Skyped regularly and Piers had sent letters and never forgot birthdays. He travelled the world on concert tours and always arranged for Rosalie and Toby to visit whenever he was in Europe. 'How old were you when you met him?' he asked.

'I was nineteen. Tobes was twelve. He'd flown over on his own with one of those airline guardian people keeping an eye on him. I was dead impressed. I'd never really gone anywhere. He's been back every year since then.'

'And Rosalie and your dad are still together, even when divided by ten thousand miles?'

'Yeah. It seems to suit them. Maybe that's the best way. It must be much easier to keep the excitement going when you only see each other a couple of times a year. Probably beats marriage any time.'

'So cynical for one so young,' he laughed.

'My mum and dad knew each other in high school. They were never more than a mile or two apart. And they finished up hating each other.'

She had a point, he supposed. It was not so different from his own marriage to the girl next door. They'd pretty much hated each other from the get-go. Had they? Or was it just distorted memory? There must have been something there to suggest that marriage was a good idea. Apart from parental pressure.

But time was getting on and they had work to do. He paid the bill and they walked back up the hill to his office.

'Right,' he said as he sat down at his desk. 'We need to sort out Felix and his lost love, not to mention the postcards.'

'The pianist, his lover and the postcards. It sounds like one of those art house movies.'

'Don't forget the murder.'

'Okay, film noir then.'

'I got a summary of the police file this morning. Read it through and tell me what you think.'

'Really? I get to work on an actual case?'

'Of course, can't have you getting bored.'

He made some notes while she read it through. 'We have to be very careful,' he warned. 'Felix may be keen to find this guy, but we need to be aware that if we do, he could be investigated for murder. We need to think about why he disappeared in the first place.'

'Why disappear if he wasn't guilty?' Nick said thoughtfully.

'Precisely.' He was enjoying this. Being able to tease out ideas and talk about them.

'He might not have had any choice,' Nick suggested.

'Been abducted? That's one possibility.' Unlikely, Ian thought, unless this was the work of a gang who were able to smuggle him away without being seen. Not impossible but why would they? In any case Jamie had been seen leaving of his own free will with Franz.

'Or threatened because he knew too much,' Nick suggested.

'Definitely.' That was much more likely. Had Jamie been a witness? If so, he would have been in danger.

'Or scared that he'd be suspected and had no way of proving it wasn't him.'

'So do you think he did it?'

Nick thought for a while. 'From what Felix told us, I don't think so. Why would he? He was just a young intern. I can't see what motive he'd have had. It's far more likely that it's something to do with the...

what did the report say? Financial problems and suspected fraud. Isn't it probable that someone did it because of something to do with the money?'

Ian agreed. McLeash was only twenty-four at the time of the murder. A bit young to be involved with international fraud. 'So I think we need to try to prove his innocence before we try to find him.'

'How?' asked Nick. 'We've never met him. We don't even know what he looked like.'

'That's where we have to start,' said Ian. 'We need to know that. If he's a five-foot-nothing weakling he's in the clear.'

'It says the murderer was likely to have been known by the victim, which could mean Jamie was a suspect. But it also says he was tall and probably trained in armed combat.'

'And armed combat probably isn't on Stirling University's Hospitality syllabus.'

Nick laughed. 'Should I check that out?'

'Run a check on the university's clubs and activities. It's probably not in the degree programme but it could be something students are interested in.' That had made him think of Caroline, who took a self-defence course and was quite handy at flooring and detaining violent types. You can put that at the top of your list of things to do tomorrow.'

'Okay,' she said, writing it down. 'What else?'

'Try to catch Felix when he's awake and concentrating. We need him to describe Jamie. Particularly his height and build. All we know so far is that he was sweet and gentle, but that could just be the way Felix likes to remember him.'

'Through rose-tinted glasses?'

'Yeah. If Felix tells us he was also six-foot-two and heavily built we could be in trouble, but we need to know.'

'Okay.' She added that to her list.

'And ask about Franz.'

'Same questions?'

'Yes, a description and also his interests. Was he a gym regular, weightlifter, into violent computer games, contact sports?'

'Fencing?'

'Possibly. He'd know about blades if he was, wouldn't he?'

'What about fishing? You know, handy with a filleting knife.'

'I suppose that might apply to Jamie as well.'

'Okay, got all that. Shall I write it up and upload it to our workspace?'

'Yes, do that. And if you have time left and assuming you still have Felix's attention, see if he remembers anything else about the friend Jamie was staying with in London. And ask him about the postcards. He said they were all places that had meant something special to them both. Ask him what the pictures are. The only one I recognise is the Albert Memorial.'

'Okay. Let's hope tomorrow is one of his more lucid days.'

'And keep a record of the hours you spend doing it. I don't want to exploit you. Stop when you've done your eight hours. I'll set up a time sheet for you.'

'It's so cool being a detective. I'll enjoy doing all of that. What will you be doing?'

'I'm going to Aberdeen to track down Jamie's family. They were probably questioned by the police at the time, and I'm hoping they'll give me more background on Jamie. We need to build up a picture of who we are dealing with.' And he was planning to drop in on his own parents. They were owed a visit, uncomfortable though that might be. And they knew a lot about local businesses. Estate agents, Felix had said. Ian hadn't heard of a McLeash estate agent, so they were either small and local, or running under a different name. His father was a member of the Grand Society of Antlers, an organisation that raised money for charity, but which also had striking similarities and possibly affiliations to the Freemasons. Ian didn't want to belittle its charitable aims, but he always thought it was more about network-ing. His parents were also members of the Royal Aberdeen Golf Club. Another exclusive networking organisation where business deals were signed and sealed over a round of golf. His father would know all there was to know about local businesses, and since the oil boom property would have been, as it were, hot property. If Ian had done what he was supposed to do, he would have risen to the rank of chief inspector. The golf club would be his home from home. He would have become an honoured member of the Antlers and would have attended dinners in full dress uniform. He would also no doubt still be married to Stephanie and the sire of a brood of expensively educated, entitled offspring. No doubt their grandparents' pride and joy. The idea made him shudder. He'd had a lucky escape. Things were much better as they were, he thought, ruffling Lottie's fur and glancing across at his new assistant. He could hear his mother's criticism now. Why can't she dress properly? Why that vulgar accent? Doesn't she want a husband and children? Why can't she get a proper job? It would almost be worth taking her with him for the shock value. Nick would give as good as she got, and fur would fly. But he'd probably come away even more in disgrace than usual and without the valuable information he was after.

The afternoon passed quickly. It had been a good day. They'd got a lot done on the more mundane cases and his fingers were itching to get going on his search for Jamie, problematic though that might be. He had set Nick up with work for the next day and looked forward to seeing her in a week's time. He drove her to the station and waved her off with a slightly guilty hope that she'd impress Rosalie with her day's work. Why? He wondered. Did he expect Rosalie to fall into his arms with gratitude? No, he neither expected it, nor surprisingly, did he want it. Other fish to fry, he thought, not sure that either Caroline or Elsa would find the image flattering.

He fancied a quiet evening at home with Lottie, so having said goodbye to Nick he took a detour and called in at his much-loved farm shop to stock up on some of his favourite food. There was still plenty of daylight for Lottie to have a long walk at Tentsmuir and then for him to cook a steak and eat it in the garden, watching the sunset over the estuary.

7

He'd been invited for lunch. That was a surprise. He was usually only tolerated at family gatherings or for afternoon tea. It must be his new status as a homeowner. Ian's parents were strong believers in the housing ladder and the necessity of being on it. It was a tall ladder with flats and starter homes near the bottom and reaching up to places the size of Balmoral at the top. The owner of a two-bedroom semi-detached probably meant that Ian was a rung or two off the bottom, but he couldn't imagine why he'd want to rise any further. His parents, on the other hand, were still scaling it. The first home Ian remembered was a two-bedroom terraced house on the outskirts of Aberdeen where he'd shared a bedroom with his brother. By the time he was in secondary school they had moved to a detached house with a small garden on a new estate. Shortly after he'd left school his parents' computer software business took off and even though their offspring had fled the nest, they moved to a four-bedroom newbuild a few miles outside the city. Now, with the arrival of grandchildren (his brother's children, not his) they had moved once more, this time into a luxury gated six-bedroom executive home on a sought-after development. At what stage in the hierarchy did a new estate become a *sought-after* development? Ian could only guess. His brother, having made a packet on the oil rigs, had moved his wife and children into a period cottage with authentic details in a village fifteen miles away. So for most of the time five of his parents' bedrooms were unoccupied. 'We need room for the grandchildren to visit,' his mother had told him. Although how two quite small children were going to fill five bedrooms Ian couldn't imagine. After one unfortunate Christmas, Ian's sister-in-law, Freya, who ran a shabby chic furniture business in a purpose built shed at the bottom of their garden, swore she would never spend another night under her in-laws' roof. Ian could sympathise. He felt the same, although he was rarely invited, having grown up to become the family disappointment.

Now he and Lottie were setting out on a seventy-mile drive for lunch followed by a snoop around the city on the lookout for estate agents by the name of McLeash. He'd already established that there was no firm of that name in the city or anywhere else in the county, but the city library might have records of companies that had merged recently. It was also possible, more likely even, that his father would have heard the name. He wasn't sure what people talked about during a round of golf, but with the way Aberdeen had boomed over the last fifty years, property prices would be high on the list of topics.

Arriving at his parents' house, he pulled up at the entrance, tapped in a code and watched as the gates slowly swung open. He parked tidily on the paved drive between two Greek-style urns filled with red geraniums. He climbed out and released Lottie from the back of the car, but kept her on a lead. The door opened and his mother appeared. She'd changed very little over the years; still with her hair expensively bobbed and the same shade of chestnut that he remembered from childhood, although now probably with a bit of help from an upmarket hairdresser. She didn't do casual, even for an informal lunch at home with her son. As ever she was dressed in a tailored skirt and silk blouse. His father appeared at her shoulder in grey flannel trousers and a navy blue blazer with brass buttons.

'Lovely to see you, darling,' his mother said, turning to one side so that he could kiss her cheek and then moving inside and into the living room. Ian picked Lottie up and followed her. His father poured glasses of sherry and then noticed Lottie. 'Stephanie had a dog like that,' he said.

'This was her dog,' said Ian. 'She gave Lottie to me when she moved to America.'

'I hope she's not moulting,' said his mother, with a glance towards the spotless upholstery. 'Such a shame,' she sighed, not for the first time. 'You should have tried harder. Marriage takes work, you know.'

Ian took a swig of sherry, not bothering to point out once again that it was Stephanie who had left *him*. Left him at a time when he was pinned to a hospital bed, his shattered leg immobilised in plaster as he began his slow recovery from the gunshot wound that had ruined his career.

'Don't be too hard on the lad,' said his father. 'Six of one, half a dozen of the other and all that.'

'But Stephanie was such a lovely girl. Her father was a bank manager, you know.'

Yes, he did know, he'd been told that more times than he could remember. And why it should make Stephanie a lovely girl he couldn't imagine. As far as he was concerned it had turned her into a gold digger who had left him for the first passably rich man she came across.

'To what do we owe this visit?' asked his father. 'You don't usually drop in like this.'

'I'm here for work,' said Ian. 'Searching for someone.'

'Oh, your little detective business,' said his mother. 'Still playing at that, are you?'

'Making any money?' asked his father.

'I'm actually doing quite well. I've hired an assistant.'

'But it's not the same as the police, is it? You could have been a chief inspector by now. Such a smart uniform. And you could have joined the golf club, even the Antlers.'

'So who is it you're searching for?' asked his father.

'A family called McLeash. Used to be estate agents in the area. They had a son who disappeared.'

'Can't say I remember the name,' said his father. 'Was he a member of the golf club?'

'I've no idea.' That was a thought though. He might drop in there this afternoon.

'Lunch,' said his mother, standing up. 'A cold buffet. It's all ready in the dining room.'

They had bought an enormous dining room table. Ian supposed a smaller one would look rather silly in a room this size. His mother was always saying she needed a large dining room for entertaining. He piled enthusiastically into a Mediterranean fish salad. His mother had her faults, but she was an excellent cook. Lottie sat at the side of his chair drooling. *Probably leaving a damp patch on the carpet*, he thought hopefully.

As they were starting a dessert of raspberry pavlova the phone rang. 'Excuse me,' said his father. 'I'm expecting a call from Roddy about the charity tournament.'

His mother tutted. She hated to have meals interrupted.

It was a short call and his father was soon back. 'All settled,' he said. 'Oh, and I asked about your McLeash chappie. Roddy remembered him, John McLeash and his wife Andrea. An unfortunate business about the son,' he said. 'Came out, I think they call it these days.'

Ian's mother sighed. 'I don't know how a mother copes with something like that. Thank goodness neither of you two...'

'You have to move with the times, dear. It's all out in the open and acceptable these days.'

'But just imagine, never having grandchildren.'

Ian wasn't going to get involved. He could point out a lot of things about diversity and causing offence, but it would be a waste of words. Interesting though. Remembered for coming out rather than being a suspect in a murder. 'Do they still live in the area?' he asked.

'No idea,' said his father. 'Better left alone if you ask me.'

Ian hadn't asked for an opinion and probably never would. Easy to find out anyway. He had access to voter rolls and now he knew their first names it would be even easier.

Politeness required that he stay for coffee, but then he told them he needed to get on and left with relief. He gave Lottie a walk and then drove to the beach where he used his phone to log in to the voter roll and found an address for John and Andrea McLeash. They lived a few miles to the south of the city. It was on the way home. He'd take a chance and drop in.

He found the house easily. A man was deadheading roses in the front garden. Ian got out of the car and walked over to the gate. 'Mr McLeash?' he asked.

The man looked up and nodded. He was in his early sixties, Ian thought, slightly built, maybe five foot eight or nine, with greyish fair hair and striking blue eyes. Promising, Ian thought, unlikely that he would have a six-foot-two brawny son. He handed McLeash his card. 'I wonder if I could talk to you for a minute?' he asked.

'What about?' Not exactly unfriendly, but not tripping over himself to help.

'About your son, Jamie.'

'Yes, I know my son's name. You'd better come in.' He led him into the house. 'Andrea,' he called. 'Fellow here, detective, asking about Jamie. Better put the kettle on.'

A woman came into the room. She looked tired and sad but smiled at Ian. 'You've got news about Jamie?' she asked, a look of hope in her eyes.

'He left home years ago,' said John McLeash.

'There was an argument. We said things we should never have said, and Jamie left. He'd just finished university.'

'Do you know where he went?' Ian asked.

'He had a... a friend.'

'Can you tell me the friend's name? Or where he lived?'

She shook her head. 'The police came, you know? I thought they'd come to tell us he'd been in an accident, but they just wanted to know where he was. And I couldn't tell them.' She dabbed at her eyes with a tissue.

'You'd better go and make us some tea, love,' said John, not unkindly.

Ian watched as she left the room, wishing he could say something that would comfort her.

'She's never got over him leaving like that,' said John.

'You've not heard from him at all? Not a letter or a phone call?'

'Not a word.'

Andrea came in carrying a tray of tea and biscuits. 'Yes, there was,' she said. 'You remember, dear, just after you retired. A postcard.'

A postcard! Another one. 'When did you retire?' Ian asked.

'Three months ago. I stayed on for the pension, but it was a relief to get out. I started that business forty years ago. I was my own boss but there's no place for small businesses now. It's all big multinationals. I sold out, merged with a bigger company. They kept me on, but it wasn't the same.'

'You were an estate agent?'

'That's right. How did you know?'

'I was told by the man who wants to find Jamie.' That at least was one of Felix's more lucid moments. Ian found it encouraging that Felix's story wasn't an entire fiction.

'This man,' asked Andrea. 'Why does he want to find Jamie? Is he in trouble?'

Ian hesitated. They clearly didn't know about the murder, and he didn't want to upset them with information that might not be true. 'We don't think he's in trouble,' he said. 'But he might have been mixed up with some people who were.'

'I just want to know he's all right,' said Andrea. 'I don't care what he's done. He's still my son.'

'Tell me about the postcard,' said Ian. 'Do you know where it came from?'

'I've still got it,' said Andrea. She left them and returned a few moments later with a wooden box. 'I kept everything of Jamie's.' She flicked through some papers, pulled out a postcard and handed it to Ian.

A painting of an old man with a long white beard in bed. A

younger man with a quiver of arrows was kneeling at his side. And another figure, perhaps a nurse, stood on the other side of the bed. The address was written in black ink, carefully printed in capital letters. Was this the same handwriting as Felix's last postcard? It could be, Ian thought. He'd need to compare them together. 'Do you mind if I take a photograph?' he asked, holding up his phone.

'If you think it might help,' said Andrea.

John looked doubtful and held her hand. 'Don't get your hopes up,' he said. 'It's been a long time.'

'Does the boy in the painting look anything like Jamie?' Ian asked kindly.

'Maybe,' she said. 'A little. He has the same solemn expression. But I've got photos of him.'

She pulled several out of the box; a child playing on a beach, then a little older dressed in school uniform and then a graduation photo. The graduation photo interested him. Ian could see a likeness to his father. No idea how tall he was, of course, but certainly not hefty. Strong enough and tall enough to stab a man in the back? Hard to tell. He took copies on his phone.

Andrea was holding the school photo, still dabbing at her eyes with a tissue. 'We were so proud of him when he went to that school. It was a long way, but he got a music scholarship to go there.'

'He played the piano?'

'Yes, he did.'

'Can you give me the name of the school?' he asked.

She wrote it down for him. St Archibald's in Warwickshire. So once again Felix had been correct. 'Do you think you'll find him?' Andrea asked.

He looked at her kindly and took her hand. 'To be honest,' he said, 'I don't have much to go on. But I'll do my best, I promise.'

'Thank you,' she said.

John was frowning 'This person who wants to find him,' he asked. 'Who is he?'

'Jamie worked for his father,' said Ian, not wanting to disclose too much. If they didn't know about the murder someone would need to break it to them very gently. And now wasn't the time to do it. He didn't think *he* was the person to do it either. Why hadn't the police mentioned it? Was that a sign that perhaps Jamie hadn't been a suspect after all?

'They were close then?' John asked.

'So what if they were?' said Andrea, suddenly angry. 'I don't care. I just want to know he's all right and if, well... just tell him to come home.'

John patted her shoulder. 'She finds it all very emotional,' he said. 'But she's right. Things were said that need to be put right.'

Ian handed them his card. 'I'll keep in touch,' he promised as he left.

8

I t hadn't been the most fun day he could remember. Lunch with his parents – well he hadn't expected much from that but at least he'd got the visit out of the way for another few months. The McLeashes had made him feel sad. He'd driven away worried about what he had stirred up for them. John seemed resigned. Things had gone badly with his son but he seemed to have accepted that there was probably nothing to be done about it. He'd have to live with all his regrets. Andrea was different. She still had hope and Ian was afraid he had fuelled it. He was angry with himself for barging into their lives. He should have considered it more carefully and prepared them with a tactfully worded letter, or at least a phone call.

Then he became snarled up in traffic in Dundee. There had been an accident and he sat for half an hour on the approach to the bridge. He arrived home tired and fed up. He didn't feel like writing up his notes or opening the folder to see what Nick had done. He took Lottie for a short walk. Then he opened a tin of baked beans, heated them up and piled them onto two thick slices of over-buttered toast. Comfort food which he ate in front of the TV watching repeats of ancient and irritating quiz shows.

. . .

It's amazing what a good night's sleep can do. The next morning it all looked a lot more cheerful. He would check over what was in the Felix folder and make sure it was all organised for Nick's next visit. And his new sofa was coming today. He needed to clear a space for it and move things that were cluttering up his hallway. That was overdue anyway. He tended to sling things down whenever he came through the door; coats, scarves, boots, shopping bags, Lottie's ball, all needed to be sorted and cleared away. It was a mindless but not unpleasant task and after he had hung up coats and stacked shoes and boots away, he felt pleased with the way it looked. He ran a vacuum cleaner around the rooms and replaced books on shelves. He gathered up old newspapers, boxes and tins and carried them down to the recycling bin. He was something his mother would never have thought any man could be. He was domesticated. It was time to invite someone to admire his work. He got out his phone and sent a text to Caroline, hoping she was now home from her holiday.

Fancy coming round this evening to sample the new sofa and my cooking?

He'd missed her. Perhaps next time they might take a holiday together.

His phone pinged within seconds, but it wasn't a reply from Caroline. It was a text from John Lewis telling him to expect his delivery in the next fifteen minutes. He called Lainie and asked her to look after Lottie, who didn't take to delivery people. She'd either get trodden on or attack them. Lainie as ever was happy to look after her. 'As long as I get a preview of the sofa when it's in,' she said.

'You can be the first to sit on it,' Ian promised, passing Lottie over the fence just as the van drew up at the bottom of the garden.

It all went much more smoothly than he'd expected. He'd been worried about the steepness and twistiness of his garden path, but the two delivery men were unfazed and carried it up to the house as if they did it every day. It helped that the cushions and feet came separately. Ten minutes and it was safely installed in his living room. He called to Lainie, who carried Lottie in and looked at it admiringly.

'You could do with some cushions in bright colours,' she said. 'I'll crochet some for you, and a blanket for Lottie. You'll not be wanting her dirty paws leaving marks.'

She was right. The room did need a splash of colour. He didn't know that cushions could be crocheted. But Lainie was always doing things with wool. He hoped she'd go for Scandinavian style primary colours. He could curl up with Lottie on cold evenings on his squashy sofa with cosy cushions and be all, what was the word? Hygge?

Lainie left him to sort through her wool and a message arrived from Caroline.

Lovely. I'll be there around eight. I assume Angus is invited as well?

He replied with a thumbs up and started thinking about what he would cook. Two or three hours work and then he would go and see what was on offer at the farm shop.

He went into the office and logged into his computer. He uploaded the photos he'd taken yesterday; three of Jamie and a postcard. Then he typed up a summary of what the McLeashes had told him. *Not a lot for a day's work,* he thought. He wondered if Nick had done any better. He clicked open the folder she had completed and opened some files. One she had named *Postcards*, the other *Descriptions*. Ian opened *Postcards* first.

She had copied in a picture of each card and made numbered notes.

1. *Statue of Bartók. Felix was working on the first piano concerto at the time he met Jamie. The statue is in South Kensington.*

2. *Picture of cows. Felix thinks it's a reference to a romantic picnic they had. He doesn't remember where it was, but they went by train and drank champagne at sunset – presumably in a field with cows.*

3. *The woman in the river – Felix tells me it's Ophelia. The two of them went to an open air performance of Ambroise Thomas' opera* Hamlet *performed in a London park. He doesn't remember which.*

4. *The shop. Felix's mother took Jamie there to buy him a shirt while Felix was practising his Bartók. It was blue Liberty Lawn*

and, according to Felix, made Jamie's eyes look even bluer than
usual.

5. *Albert Memorial. They'd been to some prom concerts just across*
   the road from there.

6. *Glencoe/Glasgow. No apparent connection.*

Interesting but Ian couldn't see how knowing any of that would help
to find Jamie. There must be more to it. There was some kind of
message and he needed to break the code. Perhaps when Felix
became less befuddled with drugs, he might realise what it was.

Next he looked at the *Descriptions* folder.

Jamie – not as tall as Felix, who is five-ten. Slight build – Felix said
wiry. Fair hair and blue eyes (very blue Felix said, see above re shirt). Not
sporty at school and no interest in combat type activities.

Franz – Felix was a bit vague. He was getting tired and just said he
looked like a thug. I took this as subjective rather than a practical descrip-
tion. I'll have another go when he feels better.

The friend – Felix went a bit quiet when I mentioned this – jealous
perhaps? Thinks he might have been called Ricky or Dicky.

Stirling University – there are martial arts and self-defence courses. There
used to be a rifle club, but it was closed after the Dunblane massacre which
was long before Jamie was there. There is also a fishing club but they only
fish for fun – the fish get put back in the river so filleting knives wouldn't be
part of the kit.

Ian clicked the message app and scanned in the photo of Jamie's postcard to his parents. *Good stuff,* he wrote. *And Jamie seems to make a*
habit of sending postcards. Do you recognize this painting? Might be useful
to get some more info on that. Add it to your task list for next week. Not sure

where to take this next. Will concentrate on other cases for the rest of this week and we'll confer on Tuesday.

A reply came quickly. She must have been on the lookout for his comments.

Three bits of news.

1. Felix's mother is flying over to visit next week. I can talk to her, or Rosalie says why don't you come for a meal and meet her.

2. Rosalie has borrowed one of those folding bikes for me that I can take on the train and you won't need to keep driving me.

3. I discovered a novel by a woman called Dora Meadows. I checked it out on Amazon and the author page says she used to be a piano teacher.

He replied. *Well done for all of that. Ask Rosalie when would be a good time for me to visit. I'd like to meet Felix's mum. Re Dora Meadows. We might check her out on FB, but leave that for now. I don't want you to work over your hours.*

They were making progress slowly. But it was time to put work aside and think about tonight's meal. He called Lottie, collected some shopping bags and set off for the farm shop.

He tied Lottie up outside the shop and collected a trolley. However firm his resolutions he always bought more than he intended. He had a dish he hadn't cooked for a long time; lamb and aubergine escallops baked in breadcrumbs and garlic. If he was going to make a habit of inviting people for dinner, he would need to broaden his repertoire, but that would be fine for now. He'd serve them with new potatoes sprinkled with spring onions, and a dish Grandad had taught him – cabbage sautéd in butter with sesame seeds. After that they would have raspberry meringue – a farm shop speciality, Belgian chocolates and coffee. And after that? He'd wait and see.

. . .

'Something smells wonderful,' said Caroline as he opened the door to her a couple of hours later. She handed him a bottle of wine and a bunch of deep red peonies.

'Wow,' said Ian. 'I don't think anyone's ever brought me flowers before.'

'Well, they should have done,' she said, kissing him on the cheek and taking her jacket off in the hall. The two dogs seemed happy enough to see each other and were scampering round the garden together.

'We can leave them out here,' said Ian. 'The garden's secure. I'll see if I've got something for the flowers.' He carried them into the kitchen where he found an earthenware jug that had been Grandad's. He'd almost thrown it out when he moved but he'd always liked it, and now he was glad he'd kept it. He filled it with water and arranged the peonies. He'd probably done it wrong, but they looked nice bunched together. He found a couple of glasses and opened the wine. 'Let's go through to the living room,' he said. 'You can try the new sofa.'

'It's a lovely house,' said Caroline. 'I was wondering when I'd get to see it. I thought you must live in a complete mess or have a mad woman stashed away in your attic.'

'Nothing like that,' he laughed, wondering why he'd never invited her here before.

'Are you going to show me round?' Caroline asked. 'When you've put those flowers down.'

He led her into the living room and put the flowers on the windowsill. 'They were a good choice,' he said. 'They look lovely there.'

'Are you pleased with this?' she asked, sitting on the sofa.

'I think so, but I've not really had a chance to use it much yet. I think they were right about bright accessories. Especially since I've seen how lovely the flowers look. My neighbour is going to knit me some cushions, no not knit, crochet. And a blanket for Lottie. Have I told you about Lainie? She lives next door and looks after Lottie quite a lot. She lives on her own and does a lot of knitting. And washing,' he added. *For God's sake*, he told himself, *stop rambling.* 'How was your holiday?' he asked.

Caroline laughed. 'It was fine. Wet though.'

'Mine too.'

'Come on then,' she said, jumping up. 'Show me the rest of your house.'

He led her through the downstairs rooms; bathroom, bedroom, office.

'What's upstairs?' she asked.

'Just a couple of mad women. Actually I've not really sorted upstairs yet. Two rooms full of junk.'

'I love a bit of junk,' she said, heading towards the stairs.

'I was thinking of moving my bedroom up here,' he said, following her.

'That would be great. There's a stunning view.'

'And I might have the other room turned into a bathroom and use the one downstairs for laundry.' He'd only just thought of that, but it seemed like an excellent idea. 'But right now I think our food should be ready. What about eating in the garden? I inherited a table and some chairs from the last residents. A bit battered but quite functional. The furniture I mean, not the last residents, although as far as I know they're still quite functional.' What on earth was the matter with him? Why didn't he just shut up.

Caroline took his hand. 'Ian, love, am I making you nervous?'

'I'm afraid so,' he said. 'Sorry.'

'Don't be sorry. It's rather sweet. But why?'

'I don't know,' he admitted. His past catching up with him? Memories of both Stephanie and his mother telling him he was a social disaster?

'Let's have another drink,' she said. 'You don't have to drive anywhere. And I'm guessing that if I behave myself, I might not have to either.'

'You can behave as badly as you like,' he said, suddenly feeling more relaxed, and grinning.

. . .

His meal was a success. Cooked to perfection even though he said so himself. One day he might even accept that Stephanie and his mother were wrong about him.

'Any interesting cases at the moment?' Caroline asked.

'One is very interesting and rather baffling. I'm working for a famous concert pianist, Felix Lansman, who wants me to find his lost lover. I'll show you my incident board. But...' he sighed.

'Not going well?'

'I messed up. I was clumsy and tactless and I think I upset two people who have been badly hurt.'

'Tell me,' she said, taking his hand.

He explained a little about the case. 'It's very sensitive,' he said. 'If I find him, I may discover that he's wanted by the police.'

'Was he ever a suspect?'

'Hard to say. The case has been closed for a long time.'

'And there's no way to find out?'

'Duncan got me the case file and he's said that if I find relevant information, I'm obliged to hand it over. On one hand I'm thinking I should keep well out of it, on the other, well, I'd be upsetting people who have been hurt by his disappearance.'

'And the people you say you upset?'

'His parents. They'd reacted badly to his coming out and he left home. This was a while before the murder. I'm not sure they even knew he was involved in it. The police visited them, but it's not clear what they wanted other than to know where he was. I felt I'd opened it all up for them, given them hope when there were no grounds for it.'

'Did they seem upset?'

He considered that for a moment. 'Not really. Shocked perhaps, after all this time. The father I think might just want to put it all behind him. The mother is still hoping he'll come home.'

'Then she was probably really glad you visited. Think about it. She's living with a man who doesn't want to discuss it. She's still missing her son and then you turn up wanting to talk about him.'

'I wouldn't want them to think I was being insensitive.'

'That's the last thing anyone would think.'

He hoped she was right.

'What are these?' she asked, looking at the photos.

'Those are photos of postcards. Six sent to Felix who is sure it's a message from Jamie. They were all sent through his agent except the last one, which was sent to the address he's staying at in Edinburgh. No message on any of them.'

'So why does he think they were from Jamie?'

'All reminders that mean something to both of them, apparently. It could just be wishful thinking. But the parents had one as well.' Ian tapped on the picture of the boy kneeling by the bed. 'And this was on the back.' He turned the card over and pointed to the letter J.

'J for Jamie?'

'That's what they assumed.'

'Why are postmarks always illegible?' she asked, staring at the smudge of letters. 'Do you think he's trying to tell them he's safe?'

'It's what his mother thinks.'

'So why not just write it?'

Ian shook his head. 'The more I get into this the more puzzled I feel. And why would he start sending people mystifying messages after a gap of six years?'

'Because something's changed?' Caroline suggested.

'Possibly. Or could he be feeling his way? Trying to find out how people will react if he suddenly turns up again?'

'But how would he know? He's not there when the cards arrive.' Caroline returned to the picture of the man in bed. 'I know that painting,' she said. 'It's in the Dulwich Picture Gallery in London. It's Isaac blessing his son.'

'Jamie asking for his father's blessing, perhaps?'

'And Ophelia is at Tate Britain. It's by Millais.'

'Ophelia went mad, didn't she?'

Caroline nodded. 'And killed herself.'

'Could that be about my client? He tried to jump off a bridge. Could there be a message for him in that?'

'Maybe, but it's rather gruesome.' She turned and smiled at him.

'You'll keep up the search, won't you? It's exciting. Like a treasure hunt.'

Ian hadn't thought of it like that. Perhaps there would be more clues to follow. It would be an interesting angle. Could he find out if other people had been sent cards?

'I like your office,' Caroline said, looking around. 'You can gaze out at the estuary while you sort out all your clues.'

He laughed. 'I do like the view, but most of the time my computer does the brainwork.'

'Why do you have two desks?'

'Oh, that's new. I've just employed an assistant for two days a week. She's a singing student from New Zealand staying in Edinburgh with a friend of mine, the same friend that Felix is staying with. She's here for three months and can work twenty hours a week.'

'A singer?'

'A reluctant one. I think her real ambitions are more tech related.'

'Your business must be doing well.'

'It is. I was getting more cases than I could handle, and Nick is taking on some of the more time-consuming searches.'

'That's great. Duncan must be pleased. I think he was quite worried about you when you first moved here.'

'He and Jeanie have been keeping an eye on me. And Duncan has passed on one or two things to me.'

'And I bet Jeanie's been feeding you. She did the same for me when I first left London. I've known her since I was at school in Perth. She was a shoulder to cry on when I first left my husband, when I was here in a new job and all on my own. Not sure how I'd have managed without her.'

'Did she try to pair you off with every single man she knew?'

'Oh yes, but that's how *we* met, isn't it?'

'I thought it was because we had similar dogs.'

'Lucky coincidence. Did you say you had raspberry meringues?'

She didn't like to talk about her past. That was the most she'd ever told him, and it was enough for her. She was clamming up with a quick change of subject. He knew that feeling well. 'Raspberry meringues coming up,' he said. 'Shall I make coffee as well?'

'Mm, that would be lovely.'

They took their coffee into the garden and watched the sunset, leaving the two dogs curled up together on Lottie's blanket.

9

It would be Ian's second drive to Edinburgh in less than two weeks, but Felix's mother was only staying a couple of days and he wanted to meet her. They seemed to be a family of colourful characters and he was finding it difficult to picture the matriarch who had raised a possible murderer and a concert pianist. They seemed to him like polar opposites. Ian was different from his own brother, but not that different. In fact they were probably quite alike in many ways. They looked like brothers. Their differences were mainly ones of ambition. Stewart took after their parents; ambitious and aspirational. Ian, well, he just wasn't.

He looked at the clock on his dashboard. He was running late. Twelve-thirty, Rosalie had said. It was now twelve-fifteen and he had just crossed the bridge. Rosalie wouldn't mind, neither would the rest of them, but it annoyed him. It wasn't just a social visit. He was working and this was unprofessional. He'd been held up by one of his neighbours calling round with a petition. He'd greeted Ian, clipboard and pen at the ready, just as he and Lottie were preparing to leave. The man either wanted speed bumps on the main road into the village or he didn't. He'd not been clear. Ian listened to him ramble on for longer than he wanted to and then signed the petition without having paid much attention. It had set him back by about fifteen minutes. He grabbed his phone with the list of questions he had planned. He stuffed a notebook, some pens and some of his cards into his messenger bag while grabbing his jacket and Lottie's lead. He skidded down his garden path, opened up the back of his car and loaded them all in – a jumble of dog, jacket and bag bulging with pens and papers.

Heavy traffic into Edinburgh delayed him even more and he pulled into Rosalie's drive half an hour later than he'd planned. He opened the back of his car and Lottie leapt out, catching her paw in the strap of his bag and dragging it along with his jacket onto the drive. She kicked her leg free and headed towards the road, where a man in an orange hi-vis waistcoat was picking up litter with a long-handled grabber and stuffing it into a black binbag. Lottie bounded towards him trailing her lead. Ian shouted her name and ran after her.

The man dropped his tools and bent down to pick Lottie up. He smiled at her and fondled her ears. 'It's okay,' he said to Ian. 'I've got her.' He gathered up the trailing lead, stepped into Rosalie's drive and handed her to Ian.

'Thanks,' said Ian, wrapping the lead around his wrist as he bent to pick up the contents of his bag, which were now scattered on the ground around his car.

'Here,' said the man, bending to help him and handing Ian some pens and his notebook.

'Thanks,' said Ian. 'I was in too much of a hurry.'

'No worries,' said the man, heading back towards the pavement and resuming his litter gathering.

Ian picked up his jacket, put everything back in his bag and rang Rosalie's doorbell.

'Sorry I'm late,' he said.

'No problem,' she said. 'We're just lazing around this morning. 'Was the traffic bad?'

'That and a Greyport resident obsessed with speedbumps wanting to give me a lecture and sign his petition.'

'Don't worry,' she said, holding the door for him. 'Felix and Véronique are in the sitting room. You know the way. Nick's out somewhere but she'll be back for lunch. I'm just sorting some music books ready for next term. I'll join you in a bit with some coffee.'

Ian found Felix and his mother sitting by the window, watching a robin taking a bath in a stone trough.

'How are you, Felix?' he asked.

'Much the same,' said Felix. 'This is my mother.' He waved vaguely in the direction of a petite, dark-haired woman wearing a purple wool dress with clunky gold jewellery.

'Ah,' she said, holding out her hand. 'You must be Mr Skair. Rosalie has told me all about you.'

'Pleased to meet you,' he said, sitting down next to her.

'And you are going to find Jamie for us,' she said. It wasn't a question, he noticed. 'Such a sweet young man. We went shopping together while Felix was working on his Bartók.'

'This was when you were in London?'

'Yes, Felix had a few weeks between concert tours, so we flew over for a break. Felix doesn't like to do nothing, and I say to him, it's not good for you to work all the time. But he insists he needs to practise Bartók for his next concert. He was rusty, he said, not played it since Moscow. But in London there is a Bartók specialist, a professor at one of the colleges. Felix worked with him in the mornings and I took Jamie shopping.'

A forceful type, Ian was thinking. A son with a reputation and as hard-hearted slave driver giving way to his mother's need to take his intern shopping.

'Jamie didn't have to work?'

'Franz didn't like it. He said Jamie has to work, but I said, Franz, he's working for your mother.'

'Tell me more about Franz,' Ian said.

'Oof, always a naughty boy. Angry like his father. Felix is artistic like me.'

'Have you seen him since your husband...?'

'Since Leopold's murder? No.'

'Do you know where he went?' he asked.

She shook her head. 'He had friends in Colombia. Very dangerous place. But Franz, he can look after himself.'

'Was he wanted by the police here?'

'They think he killed his father,' she said.

That had crossed his mind, and from the police report, they seemed to think he was a suspect. But it was not an easy thing for a mother to consider. 'What do *you* think?' he asked.

'It's likely,' she said. 'They had quarrelled about the money that Leopold was transferring to me. He said to me that Leopold and I were planning to take everything from the hotels and disappear - poof!'

Ian couldn't help laughing. 'And is that what you were planning?'

'No, Leopold was going to divorce me. This money was a monthly payment to keep me quiet so that there wouldn't be any enquiry into his finances.'

If she hadn't been so tiny, probably less than five feet tall, he might have suspected *her* of doing it. There was obviously no love lost between them.

She looked at him quizzically. 'You think *I* did it? When he was paying all that money to me every month?'

She was right, of course. Why kill the goose that was laying monthly golden eggs?

'Was there anyone else there who could have done it?' he asked.

She shrugged. 'I was in Paris. I only know what the police tell me. That the hotel was empty that night. Franz and Jamie were there and the security staff who always worked in pairs.'

Could it have been them? Presumably that was something the police had investigated at the time. No, it kept coming back to Franz and Jamie.

'How tall is Franz?' he asked.

'Taller than Felix, maybe a little taller than his father. Five eleven perhaps.'

Interesting. He supposed the pathologist could have been out by an inch or so. Or perhaps Véronique was wrong. In Ian's mind Franz was still the number one suspect. Everything he'd discovered about Jamie made Ian feel that he couldn't have had anything to do with the killing. So why had he disappeared?

'We don't want to find Franz, do we, Mother?' said Felix, suddenly alert.

Véronique patted his hand. 'Don't upset yourself,' she said. 'He won't be back.'

How did she know that? An image of contract killers crossed his mind, with sums of money making their way from Parisian bank accounts into those of crime cartels. But no. She didn't seem too upset by her husband's death, so going for a bit of expensive retaliation didn't seem likely. He'd just been watching too many crime dramas.

'Do you remember Jamie mentioning a friend?' he asked, watching Felix for a reaction. 'Ricky or Dicky?'

'Nick asked me that,' said Véronique.

'Didn't like him,' Felix muttered under his breath.

'Don't be silly, Felix,' said Véronique. 'He was just a friend who had helped him.'

Ian was about to ask more when the door opened, and Nick arrived with a tray of coffee. She put it down on the table and poured everyone a cup. 'Sorry I wasn't here when you arrived,' she said. 'I went out for a bit of shopping. I've got buns.' She opened a paper bag and passed round pastries.

'I was just asking about Jamie's friend,' said Ian. 'But it seems you got there before me.'

'I'm sorry,' said Véronique. 'I don't remember his name. All I could remember was that he'd been at college with Jamie.'

'Jamie was sleeping on his floor,' Felix volunteered.

'Too expensive, these big cities,' said Véronique. 'Same in Paris. Very difficult for young people. Franz should have given him a room in the hotel. I moved him into our flat while Felix and I were in London.'

'And when you went back to Paris?'

She shrugged. 'Probably back to the floor of his friend.'

This wasn't really getting them anywhere. Jamie had camped out in the flat of an old university pal whose name no one seemed to remember.

Nick swallowed the last of her apricot Danish and brushed some crumbs off her shorts. 'I've found him,' she said. 'At least I think I have.'

Ian looked at her in surprise. 'But we didn't know his name.'

'We knew he was Ricky or Dicky. And we knew he was at college with Jamie. So I got into the alumni lists for those years and searched for similar names.'

'How exactly did you get into alumni lists?' Ian asked, wondering if he would really rather not know.

'Pretty easily,' she said. 'It's not a secure site, just a place for ex-students to check up on each other.'

Not without a username and password, he assumed. 'You didn't change anything when you were in there, did you?'

She looked at him indignantly. 'Of course not. I just looked around a bit.'

'And what did you discover?'

'It's interesting,' she said. 'There's quite a lot of activity for the first year or so after students have finished. Showing off their new jobs, stuff like that. Then there's a dip. Usually for quite a long time. I suppose everyone's busy building careers and families. Then there's quite a lot of activity from the wrinklies, people who wouldn't even have had the system when they were students there. I suppose they feel retirement coming on and get all nostalgic.'

'These people who join, er... later in life, what do they have to do to log in?'

'There's a form to fill in. It just asks the date you were a student there and then you choose a username and password.'

'Then you're in? Just like that. No checking up.'

'Like I said, there's nothing very confidential there. Just people keeping up with each other. It's no harder to get into than Facebook.'

'So how did you sign in? You were never a student there.'

'I signed up as Jenny Brown. I'm seventy-two and studied there from 1967. That's when the first undergrads enrolled. I checked. Didn't want to discover I'd claimed to be somewhere that wasn't there.'

He'd need to have words with her about using false identities. Put together a code of conduct. He didn't suppose in this case she'd broken any laws, but it was pushing the boundaries a bit. It might not be illegal but it was definitely unethical. 'Did you discover anything interesting?' he couldn't help asking.

She looked pleased with herself. 'I went through people who had been there the same time as Jamie and found an entry from a Michael Rickson. He was on the hospitality course. He posted a message at the end of his final year to say he was moving to London to share a flat with a friend in Kensington. There was a contact email, but I thought I'd better not do anything until I asked you about it.'

Well, at least she had *some* scruples. 'Quite right,' he said. 'And I want you to go back in and delete your account. Can you do that?'

She grinned at him. 'I was hoping some old biddy might remember me and get in touch.'

'Don't even think about it,' he said, trying to look stern and wondering what Piers would say if he knew his daughter's job had involved impersonating people on websites.

'Okay, boss,' she said. 'I've made a note of the email though. Do you want me to delete that as well?'

She probably should. On the other hand, people left their emails all over the place. He wasn't going to use it to send out spam, or even try to sell him a sofa. Just one email couldn't hurt, surely? Then he remembered the Data Protection Act. He couldn't risk it. 'Yes,' he told her. 'We'll find a different way to contact him. Delete it.'

'Brompton Gardens,' said Véronique, who had listened to every word. 'That's where they had the flat, wasn't it, Felix?'

'Don't know,' said Felix. 'Never went there.'

'No, that's right, you didn't. I took Jamie there in a taxi to pick up some of his things.'

'I don't suppose you remember the number, do you?'

Véronique took a sip of coffee and gazed out of the window to where the robin had finished his bath and fluttered away, his place having been taken by a blackbird. 'Yes,' she said, clapping her hands. There's a rhyme children sing about blackbirds.'

What was she talking about? Was she, like Felix, away with the fairies? 'I don't quite follow,' he said.

'You must know it. They go in a pie. Four hundred?'

'Lunch is ready,' said Rosalie coming into the room. 'What were you talking about? We're not having pie for lunch.'

Thank goodness for lunch, Ian thought. He was surrounded by computer hackers and people who'd lost touch with reality.

'We're trying to remember a children's song,' said Véronique. 'About blackbirds in a pie.'

'I know it,' said Rosalie, beginning to sing. '*Sing a song of sixpence, a pocket full of rye, four and twenty blackbirds baked in a pie.*'

'That's it,' said Véronique. 'It's me who should be the detective.'

Well, that put him firmly in his place. 'So it was number twenty-four Brompton Gardens?'

'No, no, not twenty-four.'

'Four hundred and twenty?' Nick suggested with a giggle.

'Give me strength,' Ian muttered.

'Forty-two,' said Véronique triumphantly.

'Yeah,' said Felix, emerging from some kind of half-sleep. 'Forty-two Brompton Gardens. That's where Jamie lived.'

A pity he hadn't remembered that a bit sooner. Not that it was going to be very much use. Obviously Jamie wasn't going to be there or the police would have found him six years ago. And people moved around. He could check London addresses, but wasn't optimistic about finding anyone who remembered him. And there were probably hundreds of Michael Ricksons.

'Should I check it out?' Nick asked

'No,' said Ian. 'Not yet. We'll think about what use it might be on Tuesday.'

· · ·

He wasn't sorry to be on his way home again. It was always good to see Rosalie, but what on earth had she got him into this time? Negotiating a meeting with Piers all those years ago had been child's play in comparison.

10

T wo weeks in and Ian wasn't sure that they'd made much progress. He'd traced missing people before. Some missing for even longer than six years. But in the past none of the people he had found had really been missing. They had lost touch with families but had still left trails and clues that he could follow. Finding Jamie was much harder. All Ian had so far was a handful of postcards which might or might not have been sent by someone who might or might not be a suspect in a long-closed murder case.

He looked across his desk at Nick. She looked up at him grumpily. They'd just had the conversation Ian had been dreading. The *don't take things into your own hands* talk. He hadn't wanted to be too heavy, but he did have his reputation to consider.

'But detectives go undercover all the time,' she'd argued.

'Police detectives might, but it's all official. And they don't go off doing their own thing. They discuss it with their seniors first.' Was that what was really bugging him? That she'd gone off and started an investigation on her own? That he hadn't been the one to find the name of Jamie's friend? He had to admit she'd been clever. He didn't want to dampen her enthusiasm, he really didn't. She was bright and energetic and just what he needed. In the end he'd typed up a code of conduct and asked her to sign it. 'You did really well,' he told her. 'Just run it by me first next time, okay?'

'Okay,' she said glumly, and he began to understand why Piers had found her difficult. This morning he'd given her the job of finding out all she could about the school Felix and Jamie had been to. He hoped she'd take it as a sign that he still trusted her.

'How are you getting on?' he asked. He didn't expect much. He'd checked the *official* Stirling Alumni site and found no mention of Jamie. He didn't expect there to be much on the school one either. Jamie appeared to have risen without trace through university. It was likely that school would be the same. Not enough of a star to have made it onto notable alumni lists, and never apparently in the kind of trouble that would have made him notorious. Just like pretty much everyone else. Except that most people didn't vanish into thin air. If it hadn't been for the postcards, Ian would have assumed that he'd either gone abroad to live under an assumed name somewhere or that he'd died, but without leaving a body? Wanting to disappear was one thing. But disappearing and leaving no hint of a trace was, for Ian, frustrating. He was getting impatient. *For God's sake, Jamie, if you want us to know something stop being so bloody mysterious about it.*

'Not a word about Jamie,' said Nick crossly. 'If we didn't have Véronique's word for it, I'd think Felix had made him up.'

'So that was a waste of time then, sorry.'

'Not completely,' she said, smiling for the first time that day. 'I've got quite a lot on Dora Meadows.'

'The piano teacher turned novelist?'

'Yes. There's a bit about her in one of the school magazines.'

'St Archibald's has an online school magazine?'

'It's quite a recent thing. Started by the IT department a couple of years ago. So nothing about Jamie.'

'What does it say about Dora Meadows?'

Nick turned back to her laptop. 'She stopped teaching there last year when her books started making money. There's a farewell piece saying she's leaving to spend more time on her writing. I'll read it to you.

We're sad to say goodbye to Dora Meadows after more than thirty years as our piano teacher,' Nick looked up and grinned at him. 'Thirty years teaching piano in the same place. How grim is that?' She turned back to her screen and continued to read.

'During her time with us Ms Meadows' most notable pupil was our own Felix Lansman, now a world famous concert pianist. Winner of the renowned Rebikov prize held every four years in Moscow. We wish Ms Meadows all the best in her writing career, blah blah blah...'

'It's the right person then. Well done for finding her.' He wasn't sure that it had got them anywhere, though.

'There's more,' said Nick. 'I've found her Facebook page. It looks like she's quite successful. She writes, and I quote, "steamy post-apocalyptic fantasy stories set in an English boarding school".'

'God help us,' said Ian. 'Do people actually read them?'

'Apparently they do. And guess what?'

'She's headlining at the Edinburgh book fair dressed as a unicorn in drag?'

'Better than that. She's doing a reading at Dundee Modern Art Museum the day after tomorrow. Shall we go?'

Looked like she'd cast off her grumpiness and was now back to her usual bouncy self. 'It's not one of your working days,' he said. 'I'd have to go on my own and I'm not sure I'd pass as your average reader of post-apocalyptic fantasy... what was it?'

'You forgot *steamy*. And don't be a spoilsport. I'll change my singing lesson to tomorrow and work Thursday instead. We can buy one of her books and get her to sign it while telling us about Felix and Jamie.'

Well, they weren't making much progress with anyone else. 'Oh, why not?' he said. 'If nothing else you'll get to see a bit of Dundee. I'll show you the Discovery.'

'You'll have to explain,' she said. 'I'm just an Antipodean hick, remember?'

'The Discovery is a ship, an Antarctic explorer. It probably stopped off in New Zealand. It's on the waterfront and just a short walk from the gallery.'

'Okay,' she laughed. 'I can tell Dad you're educating me as well as employing me.'

Thursday was wet and Ian picked Nick up at Dundee station, glad that he'd saved her a ride over the bridge in driving rain. The gallery was a short drive from the station and had its own car park. Even so, they arrived with damp coats and dripping umbrellas, which they were asked to leave in a cloakroom. 'They probably don't want to risk Dora being attacked with umbrellas,' Nick whispered to him as they handed over their coats.

'Don't judge her until you've heard her,' said Ian, trying not to laugh. 'She might be very good.'

'Want to bet on that?'

He didn't.

They chose seats near the back of the room and Ian looked round at the thirty or so other people who had turned up for the reading. It was free and he wondered how many of the audience were there just to keep out of the rain.

There was a stack of books on a table at the entrance. An over-optimistic stack, Ian thought, feeling obliged to fork out £10.99 to buy one. He looked at the cover, which shouted 'steamy fantasy' with a picture of a scantily dressed woman with flowing hair and pixie ears against a background of hills and the purple ruin of a school. Or he assumed it was a school since that was what the book promised. It could have been any vaguely gothic building. Its ruin no doubt the result of whatever apocalyptic disaster had occurred. He knew one shouldn't judge a book by its cover but was finding it very hard not to judge this one.

'How long do book readings last?' he asked Nick.

'Not long,' she said. 'She'll read a bit then everyone will line up to buy a copy and get it signed.'

Ian looked at his watch. Only a couple of minutes to go, assuming book readings began on time. He noticed a man slip into a seat close to where they were sitting. A slightly built man wearing a navy-blue hoodie. It was warm in the room and he pushed the hood away from his face, revealing shoulder length black hair and a beard. Was this your average reader of fantasy fiction? Hard to say. There were all types here, but most of them were young, late teens and early twenties. This man and Ian himself were the only over thirties in the room. He couldn't even be sure that the man sitting a few seats away *was* over thirty. Beards were quite aging.

There was a hush as Dora was escorted into the room and introduced. If Ian had had an idea in his head of what a steamy fantasy writer would look like, he would have come up with something very like the woman who was standing in front of them right now. She'd done her best to look like the figure on the front of her book, with the same flowing hair and low-cut purple dress. No pixie ears though. Probably just as well. Nick was biting back giggles and Dora hadn't even started reading yet. And once she did start reading, Ian found himself clenching his fists in an effort not to laugh out loud.

'Any questions?' Dora asked as she finished her reading and closed the book. She took a sip from a glass of something fizzy and pink, and smiled hopefully at the audience. Everyone went quiet. It was like a stand-up show Ian had been to once when everyone huddled back into their chairs in case the comedian picked on them. Ian felt sorry for her. How far had she come for people not to ask her any questions? He shifted in his seat.

'Don't you dare,' Nick hissed at him.

And then to his relief several people had their hands up. Just as well. He had no idea what he'd have asked her. Nick was no help. They should have read the book first and come armed with questions. The first was one that Ian assumed was probably the kind of question most authors got asked.

'Where do you get your ideas from?'

Nightmares or hallucinatory drugs passed though Ian's mind.

Dora wafted her hands in the air. 'They just come to me,' she said. 'Sometimes in dreams.'

There you go, he thought. Nightmares, dreams, pretty much the same thing. She hadn't mentioned mind-altering substances though.

She'd have been in good company. Coleridge had spent half his time high on laudanum and he was probably not the only one. Berlioz, he knew, had experimented. He was a musician, but the creative process was much the same. Or at least he supposed it was. He had little personal experience.

'Are your characters based on real people?'

Ian really hoped not. He'd be seriously worried if he knew people like the characters in her book.

'My friends always assume I've based my characters on them,' she said. 'But mostly they're not.'

Mostly? She must have some really odd friends.

'Is it autobiographical?' someone asked.

What!

'Well,' Dora answered. 'I used to work in a boarding school, so I guess there is an autobiographical element.'

Really? Felix might have some fascinating tales to tell them.

At this point the man in the hoodie stood up and left. Ian didn't blame him. He glanced out of the window and saw that the rain had stopped, and guessed quite a few of the audience would take that as a signal to leave. He'd leave himself if he didn't have a job to do.

The questions quickly dried up and Dora sat down behind a table as people queued up with their books.

'We'll sit here and join the back of the queue,' he told Nick. 'That way she'll have time to chat to us.

It didn't take long to work their way to the front of the queue. Dora smiled up at them as Ian handed her his book. 'Is there a special message you'd like me to write?' she asked.

Ian had a sudden flash of inspiration. 'We're actually here for a friend,' he said. 'Would you write *To Felix Lansman?*'

She looked up in surprise, took off her glasses and wiped her eyes. 'Felix? But I taught him for a while. He's a friend of yours?'

Ian nodded. Client, friend, not so different.

'That's so amazing,' she said. 'After all these years and he's done so well. How is he?'

'He's not been well,' said Ian, 'or I'm sure he'd be here himself.'

Well, how was he to know that Felix wasn't an avid reader of steamy fantasy, post-apocalyptic or otherwise?

'I'm so sorry to hear that,' she said. 'Do give him my very best wishes when you see him.' She picked up a pink and purple fountain pen and scribbled something in the book with a flourish. Then she snapped the book shut and handed it to him. 'I didn't teach him for very long. He was way too good for me. He was so talented. I'm flattered that he remembers me.'

The room was almost empty now. They didn't have very long. Ian pulled up a chair and sat down next to her. 'I gather you taught Jamie McLeash as well.'

She gazed dreamily into the distance and sighed. *At least Jamie had made an impression on someone,* Ian thought. 'I taught him for several years,' said Dora. 'Such a sweet boy. Do you know him as well?'

'I haven't met him,' said Ian. 'Felix mentioned him.'

Mention of Felix had brought her down to earth and she frowned. Ian imagined that he might not have been the most tractable pupil.

'I taught Felix's brother too,' she said. 'Not for long though. He didn't really take to it.'

'That was Franz?' he asked, surprised. What he knew so far of Franz hadn't suggested he was into anything artistic.

'That's right. It's a pity he gave it up. Left-handers usually do quite well as pianists. Their brains have learnt to deal with all the difficulties that right-handed people don't have. It makes them much better at the kind of co-ordination needed for the piano.'

He was speechless. That really messed up their theory.

'Franz is left-handed?' asked Nick, sounding as surprised as he felt but thankfully jumping in and avoiding an awkward silence. 'Are you absolutely sure?'

'Of course. I wouldn't forget something like that.'

A gallery official was hovering behind them. 'I'm sorry,' he said. 'We have another event about to start. Ms Meadows, we have reserved a table for you in the restaurant.' He looked at Ian and Nick. 'Will your guests be joining you?'

'No, no. I'm sorry we've kept you talking for too long,' said Ian.

They'd got an interesting snippet of information. The last thing he wanted was to sit through a meal with her.

Dora stood up and shook his hand. 'Thank you so much for coming,' she said. She collected a carpet bag from underneath the table, opened it and removed a shawl which she wrapped with a flourish around her shoulders. Then she gathered up the unsold books and hefted them into the carpet bag. 'Do remember me to Felix when you see him.'

'We will,' Ian promised.

'Nice bag,' said Nick. Ian held her firmly by the elbow and led her away, not wanting to hold things up by getting into a girly chat about bags. He needed lunch and guessed that Dora did as well.

'I know just the place,' Ian said as they emerged onto the wet pavement which was now sparkling in the sunshine. There was a small café a short walk away and close to the shopping centre. He'd been there with Caroline the day they'd met and set out together to find Lottie, who'd gone missing – believed kidnapped.

He opened the door for Nick and led the way down to the basement where they found an empty table. 'Well,' he said, having read the menu. 'That knocks out our prime suspect. He's left-handed.'

'We already knew he was only five eleven,' said Nick.

Yes, Véronique had told them that. Ian had hoped she might have been wrong, or that the police had made a mistake. Did two or three inches really make such a difference? But he had to reluctantly agree that the pathologist was probably right. They needed to find a six-foot-two right-hander.

'But Jamie is sweet natured and slight,' Nick continued. 'So he probably didn't do it either. Do we know how tall he is?'

'No, but both his parents are quite small. I'm guessing Jamie is as well, but we can confirm that with Felix.'

'What next?' she asked.

'I wish I knew. We've ruled out both suspects named by the police.'

'So there must have been someone else there.'

He nodded. 'A third person in the room may have killed Leopold, but it doesn't mean the other two weren't accessories. And if the police didn't have another suspect six years ago, I don't see how we're going to find one now.'

'Do we still try to find Jamie?' Nick asked.

'I think we have to, for Felix. But what we should focus on is what has changed for Jamie. Why has he started reaching out to people?'

'You're sure that's what he's doing?' Nick asked.

'Yes, the card to his parents persuaded me. It's too similar to the way he sent Felix those pictures. And it's all we've got at the moment. I just wish he wasn't being so obscure about it.'

'Something's changed but he's still frightened,' Nick mused. 'Are you saying something has happened to make him feel ready to face his family and Felix again, but there's still someone threatening him?'

'I think that's exactly what I'm saying. We've got to hope he keeps sending things until we've worked it out.'

Nick cleared her plate and studied the dessert menu. They ordered toffee fudge cake. 'How about we take another look at the pictures?' she said as the dessert arrived, and she dug her spoon into it. 'See if we can work out if there's a code.'

'Good plan. We could also see where they came from. They're not photos he's taken, are they?'

'I don't think so. I'm guessing he used images he found on Google.'

'So let's start there and see if we can find them as well. Try and crack the code, assuming there is one. That sounds like something you might be good at.'

'I'm on it,' she said. 'I'll start tomorrow.'

'No,' he said firmly. 'I want to be in on this and not have you going free range again. We'll work on it together next Tuesday.'

'Okay, cool it. You're the boss.'

'And don't you forget it. And seriously, I don't want you to work too many hours,' said Ian. 'You'll go over your twenty and I can't afford to pay you for more than that.'

She grinned at him. 'Then just pay the same and I'll work as a volunteer for the rest. This is way too interesting to just drop.'

'It may be, but you need to take time out or you'll become obsessed. I've got other cases that need my attention, and you should get out and see a bit of Edinburgh. Spend a few days doing some tourist stuff. Believe me, you'll come back to it with fresh ideas. Thinking about other things is when your brain really engages. You'll be surprised. And now,' he said, scraping his plate for the last of his toffee fudge cake, 'we're taking the afternoon off. Time you saw a bit of Scottish history.'

'That ship you were talking about?'

'The Discovery. Yup. Just down the road.'

They strolled down to the Discovery Pier. Ian bought tickets and they wandered through the visitor centre and then onto the ship itself.

Nick studied her guidebook. 'It says here there were about forty people on board and the first voyage took over three years. And,' she said, bumping her head on a low doorway, 'it's tiny.'

'People were smaller then,' said Ian, studying an Antarctic suit in a display cabinet.

'Not that much smaller. And they had sheep and chickens on board. Can you imagine the smell?'

'I don't suppose the livestock lasted further than the coast of North Africa. They probably relied on dried stuff after that. Although they stopped off along the way to restock.'

'And then ninety days in the ice. My God, they must have smelt horrible by the time they got home.'

'Hard to imagine it, isn't it? Six months just to get to New Zealand.'

Half an hour later they emerged from the ship and sat watching traffic pound past them on its way out of the city, over the bridge or out towards Perth.

'Enjoy it?' Ian asked.

'It was great,' she said. 'But I think I'm glad we've got aeroplanes. Imagine having to shovel coal for six months.'

'Now we've done the educational bit, how about an ice cream?'

'I'll get them,' said Nick. 'They're selling them over there.' She pointed to an ice cream van on the other side of the visitor centre. 'Won't be long.'

'Take some money,' said Ian, searching his pockets.

'Nah, my treat,' she said, bounding away from him and merging into a crowd of schoolchildren all with the same idea.

Ian found a bench and sat down to wait for her. He got out his notebook and wrote down the details of Dora's conversation. He needed to find the third man, he thought with a smile. Was there always a third man? His thoughts turned to Kim Philby and then to post-war Vienna. Or could it be a woman? A third person. Assassins weren't always men. There was Charlotte Corday and the woman who tried to kill Mussolini. He couldn't remember her name. And in fiction there was Villanelle. She was an innocent-looking blonde and not six foot two, but she had an extensive repertoire of ways to finish people off. He couldn't remember whether or not she was left-handed.

He returned to his notebook. *Concentrate*, he told himself. It was his job to find Jamie, not to start looking for a killer. There had to be a clue in the postcards. He opened his notebook and wrote *postcards*, underlining it several times. Then he wrote *Jamie's friend*. He wasn't sure why. He snapped the book shut and put it back in his pocket. Nick was taking her time. He glanced over at the ice cream van and noted the length of the queue. But it didn't matter. It was pleasant sitting here in the sun and it wasn't as if they were making great progress in the office.

A couple of benches further along sat the man who'd been at the book signing. He had crossed his arms and pulled his hoodie around him. Was he cold? Ian wondered. It was now a warm afternoon, but he could have been caught in the rain and soaked this morning. From the little Ian could see of his face, he was pale. Skinny as well. Ian wondered if he was also homeless. Should he offer to help? He'd be happy to pay for a hot drink or a night somewhere under cover. He was never sure what to do. He was caught between wanting to be kind and a fear of doing the wrong thing. Of trampling on someone's dignity or just getting it wrong. Perhaps the guy was happily married, a homeowner with four children and a pretty wife. Ian caught his eye and smiled but the man ignored him. He stood up and walked away, up the road and back into the town.

Nick returned with two ice creams in cones. 'Chocolate or strawberry?' she asked.

'Whichever,' he said, not feeling like ice cream at all.

She handed him the strawberry one. 'Anything wrong?' she asked.

'No, someone just walked over my grave.'

'They what?'

'It's something we say. It means a sudden shivery feeling.'

'You're feeling cold?'

'No, it's more of a premonition. Sorry, can't really explain it. Forget it.' He licked his ice cream. It was good and cheered him up. *No one can help everyone*, he thought sadly. 'Come on,' he said, jumping up. 'Time for you to get back to Edinburgh and for me to go home and walk Lottie.' And maybe an evening in the pub would help his mood. Thursday evening meant bangers and mash at the Pigeon.

11

'Time to go deeper into these postcards,' said Ian five days later. He tapped his pen against the picture of the Albert Memorial. He'd cleared his desk and made a pot of coffee by the time Nick arrived. They could get down to work right away, hopefully with some fresh ideas.

'There's got to be something here that we're missing,' he said. The last few days since the book reading, he'd spent catching up on other cases to make sure that on Nick's next working day they could really get down to it and crack what he was becoming certain was a message.

'So where do we start?' Nick asked as she turned on her laptop.

'We'll make notes on all of the postcards. Where they are, details of the artists or makers, where would he have bought them and how he did he know where Felix was, anything we can find.' He unpinned them and rearranged them, spreading them out on the board, leaving room for notes. 'It's a pity we don't know the order they were sent. All we know is which one arrived last.'

'Apart from the one he sent to his parents, that last one is the only proper postcard,' said Nick. 'The others are not actually postcards, are they?'

'I'm not sure what you're getting at,' said Ian. They looked like postcards. Missing some details about the pictures perhaps, but still postcards.

'There's nothing written on them. Postcards usually have info about artists, or where they were sold, or what they're of. These are blank apart from the pictures.' She studied the plain side of the card again. 'There's some tiny writing at the bottom,' she said. 'Do you have a magnifying glass?'

He thought he did. Grandad had used one for reading small print. He ran upstairs and rifled through some boxes, eventually finding it. It was a small strip of glass, useful for moving down lines when reading, not a round one on a handle that normally appeared in cartoons of detectives. But it would do.

Nick took it from him and studied the text. 'It's a website,' she said.

'So what does that tell us? That he bought them online?'

'Yes, and I think he had them made himself.'

'Ian tapped the URL into his browser. 'Looks like you're right,' he said. 'You upload your photo, and they make it into any kind of card you want.'

'And then what? They send it to you by post?' she asked.

'Or you can have it sent to whatever address you give them. You get a choice.'

'So he sent a picture of the Albert Memorial but it doesn't mean he was there,' she said. 'That's going to make it harder, not easier.'

'Not necessarily. It means he's telling us something about the pictures themselves, not that he was at these places when he sent them.'

'But we already know they all mean something special to Felix,' said Nick.

'Let's assume he's not sent them just to make Felix feel nostalgic. There must be something else he's trying to say. Let's go through them one by one. We'll start with the Albert Memorial. It's the only one I know anything about.'

'Designed by Giles Gilbert Scott and unveiled in 1872,' Nick read from the Royal Parks website. 'Lots of allusions to the Great Exhibition and the Empire. Based on the Eleanor Cross and similar to others found at Charing Cross and in Edinburgh and Manchester.'

Ian made notes next to the picture with marker pens and stared at them. 'Fascinating stuff,' he said. 'But I don't see how it helps us.'

'We should go through all of them and see if there's a connection. I've found the shop,' she continued. 'Brian Bell Bespoke Shirts. It's in Jermyn Street.'

'In London?'

'Just off Piccadilly,' she said, typing busily. 'Known for expensive shirts apparently.'

'Okay,' said Ian, writing it all down. 'What about Ophelia? It's at Tate Britain, isn't it?' Caroline had told him that. 'Remind me about the opera they went to.'

Nick looked at her notes again. 'Hamlet by Ambroise Thomas. Open air performance in Holland Park. There's a review here. It ran for a couple of weeks the summer Felix and Jamie were in London. Shall I print it?'

'Just bookmark it for now. What about Bartók?'

'Designed by Imre Varga. Installed outside South Kensington underground station in 2004.'

'Jamie lived in South Kensington. Check if it's anywhere near Brompton Gardens.'

Nick opened up Google Maps. 'A couple of blocks away,' she said. 'That statue is about midway between Brompton Gardens and the Tube station.'

'That gives us two connections. Felix was working on Bartók while he was in London.' Ian yawned. 'What have we got left?'

'Just the landscape, Glencoe and the painting sent to Jamie's parents.'

'Okay. We'll do those then go and get some lunch.'

'Right,' said Nick. 'Give me a mo. I'll have to do an image search.'

Ian gazed at the notes he'd made. He hoped the two paintings would reveal something. They didn't have much to go on at the moment. Apart from making Felix misty-eyed, he couldn't see any connection at all.

'Right,' said Nick. 'The landscape is called *Landscape with Cattle*. It's by Daubigny and is in the National Gallery.'

'Do we know where they went for their picnic?'

Nick checked the notes she'd made. 'We just know they went by train,' she said.

'Somewhere with cows a short train ride from central London,' he said. 'That could be any number of places.'

'They might have been to the National Gallery, seen the painting and decided a sunset picnic would be nice. I've found the other painting. It's by Gerrit Horst and is in the Dulwich Picture Gallery.'

Ian groaned. If there was any connection he couldn't see it. 'The subject?' he asked.

'It's Isaac blessing Jacob.' Yes, of course. Caroline had known that as well. Probably not connected to Felix at all then. Just Jamie asking his father's forgiveness.

All places in or near London except Glencoe. Was Jamie making a map? Ian opened a street map of London and dropped pins into all the places they'd found so far: National Gallery, Albert Hall, South Kensington, Jermyn Street, Dulwich, and Holland Park. He sat and stared at it. Then he dropped another pin into Park Lane where the hotel was. He tried drawing lines from one place to another. Meaningless. It didn't lead them anywhere. Apart from an upmarket tourist trail, it told him nothing. It wasn't useful at all. They should try a completely different tack. But right now they both needed a break.

'Let's think about Glencoe while we have lunch,' he said. He called Lottie and they walked down to the waterside. It was a warm day, so they bought sandwiches and lemonade and ate them sitting on the harbour wall. Ian broke off a bit of sandwich and fed it to Lottie. *Why Glencoe?* he wondered. *Come on, Jamie, you need to give us a bit more than that.* Apart from all the climbers and hikers, what most people remembered about Glencoe was the massacre. Campbells and MacDonalds. His memory of Scottish history was dreadful. He should be ashamed. Who had slaughtered who? He got out his phone and checked. The MacDonald clan had been murdered by the Campbells who had been billeted on them at the time. He searched his brain for some hidden message from Jamie. The Glencoe card was the only real postcard in that it had been bought from a shop rather than created on a website. But Glencoe was a famous tourist spot. You could buy pictures of it all over Scotland. It had a Glasgow postmark which narrowed it down although not very much. They could hardly roam around Glasgow with a six-year-old photo and hope to find Jamie.

Nick finished her sandwich and threw the wrapper into a bin. 'What next?' she asked.

'Wish I knew,' Ian sighed. 'Let's go and take another look at what we've got.'

They strolled back up the hill, Lottie the only one of the three showing much enthusiasm.

When they arrived back, Ian made coffee and pulled up two chairs in front of the pictures. 'Come on, Nick,' he said. 'The answer's got to be here somewhere.'

'We've been concentrating on the pictures themselves and where they are. Apart from the Felix link they don't have much else in common. We should look for a different way of connecting them.'

'You're right,' he said. 'As pictures they don't have anything in common. My map idea didn't work. So what are we left with?' He thought of a TV quiz he sometimes watched. It involved making connections between an obscure series of words, pictures, even pieces of music. It was notoriously difficult. He felt pleased with himself if he got two or three correct answers. It required lateral thinking, something he always thought he was quite good at. He was okay at connecting objects and occasionally pieces of music. The problem he had was with words because he found it difficult to disconnect the words from their meanings. 'I wonder if it's a word puzzle,' he said.

Nick stared for a moment. She tore some pages out of her notebook and re-wrote her list, jumbling the words and writing them at odd angles. She pinned each one to the board and stood back. Then she jumped up and tapped the Horst painting. 'Jacob, right?'

Ian nodded. She picked up a pen and circled a letter in each note she'd made. Ian watched. Intrigued at first and then excited. She had circled the letters C for Cattle, B for Bartok, A for Albert, J for Jermyn Street and O for Ophelia. 'Any good at anagrams?' she asked with a grin. Ian took the pen from her. He rearranged the pictures in a row with the shop on the left, then Albert Hall, the landscape, Ophelia and finally Bartók. He wrote a letter under each picture. J A C O B.

'We're looking for a guy calling himself Jacob,' he grinned at her. 'And more than that. Remember what I told you about Glencoe?'

'Campbells and MacDonalds? Oh my God. We're looking for Jacob Campbell or Jacob MacDonald. But which?'

A good question. Jamie – or should he think of him as Jacob now? – had set a complicated puzzle. He wouldn't have gone to all that trouble unless he expected a reply. The other odd thing was that he had sent Felix the puzzle and his parents the answer. How did he expect them to get together? They had nothing in common. Where did people who had no knowledge of each other get together? He had an idea and wondered if Nick thought the same. 'What would you do if you wanted people to get in touch with you but wanted to keep under the radar?' Ian asked.

'You mean somewhere that both Jamie's parents and Felix might look?'

'Yes, I'm wondering if he's been keeping an eye on them, but without revealing himself.'

'He might be able to on Facebook. Everyone's heard of it, and you can create an account without giving much away about yourself if you're careful.'

'I agree,' said Ian. 'A good place to start. We need to know if Jamie's parents have a Facebook page. I already know Felix has but when I looked it wasn't much more than a list of concerts. We'll start with Jacob. You take MacDonalds and I'll do Campbells. Make a list of any possibles and we'll go through them together.'

It was a long, back-breaking afternoon. Even fortified with

multiple cups of tea and a quick trip down to the shop for pastries, by five o'clock they were both exhausted. And they both had very long lists. 'Who'd have thought there'd be so many?' Ian said. 'Where do we start? We can't send them all friend requests.'

'Hardly,' said Nick. *'Are you the Jacob who used to be Jamie?* Great. He'd promptly disappear and we'd never hear from him again.'

Ian laughed. 'And we'd have wasted a great deal of hard work and brain stretching. What do you suggest?'

'There must be a lot we can rule out straight away. We should start with names in the UK, and chuck out all the rest,' said Nick. 'And we can probably eliminate users who post a lot. Assuming he's just set up a page for a few trusted people to find him there's going to be very little activity on it.'

'Could you do that tomorrow?' Ian asked. 'Make a short list and we'll decide the best way to contact them.'

Ian thought about the postcards again. Had Jamie only sent them to Felix and his parents? He wondered fleetingly about Dicky or Ricky or whoever he was. If Jamie had trusted him in the past, he might well try to contact him now. But they had enough to do right now without adding to it. 'Let's check it from the other end,' he said. 'Run a search on John and Andrea McLeash. And I'll check out Felix's page again.'

'His agent might have set it up for him,' said Nick.

'Good point,' said Ian, tapping Felix's name into the search bar. The name appeared at the top of the list. A public page listing concerts and reviews. Nothing added in the last three months. 'Have a word with Felix,' he said. 'Get him to start using it. You may need to change his settings. Ask him to contact the agent if necessary. He can tell them he only wants it for personal use until he kickstarts his career again.'

'Shall I tell him our theory about Jacob?'

Ian wasn't sure. But Felix was his client and he should know anything he had discovered. 'Tell him it's only a theory at the moment. Don't let him put it on Facebook. Just get him to post an update about his health or how much he likes Edinburgh. Casual chatty sort of stuff. It's possible Jacob will come back with a message to him.' If he did, Ian hoped it wouldn't be something in an obscure code.

'I'll do it tomorrow, and monitor what he posts. Shouldn't be difficult. He'll probably get me to do it anyway. I'll keep an eye on all the likes and friend requests as well.'

'Have you found the McLeashes?'

'Andrea McLeash has a page but it's very private. Should I send a friend request?'

'I'll do it,' said Ian. 'She knows me, and I told her I'd keep in touch. I'll give her a call first and let her know what I'm doing.'

'What are we going to do about all the Jacob pages we've found? There'll still be quite a few even if after all the ones I've crossed off.'

'Not sure yet. Any ideas?'

'How about we get Felix to message the likely ones. Something a bit enigmatic. Just to say he gets the code in the postcards.'

'Sounds like a plan. But don't let Felix try to contact him on his own. We'll work out what he's going to post together. And don't let him accept any friend requests until we've monitored them.'

Nick stretched. 'It's been a good day,' she said.

'It has. I think we've actually got somewhere.'

He watched as she jumped on to her bike and pedalled off to the station. She waved and shouted, 'Catch up tomorrow.'

Ian smiled. It was great having an assistant. She had some good ideas and was fun company. It was useful for this particular case that she also had easy access to their client.

He and Lottie walked down to the village. He'd have a pie and a pint and sit on the harbour wall watching boats. As he walked, he wondered if they'd got a bit carried away. It was all rather boy detective, finding names hidden in codes. They could be way off the mark. But he supposed there would be no harm done trying to contact people on Facebook. If it was a complete red herring he could just back away. His only concern was that it might get Felix's hopes up. Those of the McLeashes as well. He'd be quite open with them and say that it was a long shot. He was sure that they would be happy for him to try anything. He must think very carefully about the message they asked Felix to send. No mention of the murder, no use of Jamie's real name. Just a 'catching up with old friends' type message perhaps. No harm in Felix using *his* name. *Hi, Jacob. Do you remember me from school?* Something like that. If one of the Jacobs was really Jamie, he'd recognise Felix's name. Any of the others would just assume it was a case of mistaken identity and either ignore it or politely reply that they weren't the Jacob he was looking for. Probably best not to mention the name of the school. He'd get Nick to monitor any incoming messages very carefully. Felix was, or had been, famous. They didn't want a rush of posts from clamouring classical music fans. How long did it take for concert pianists to drop off the radar? Longer, he suspected, than pop musicians. But they had a bit of wiggle room to think about a strategy. It would be a day or two before Nick had sorted things out with the agent. She was going to call and tell them that Felix was only going to use it for close friends for a while. It would probably just involve handing over login details and changing whatever email had been used to set it up. Nick was going to know a lot more about it than he did. Another reason he was glad to have her on his team. *Team*, he thought, liking the idea. He hadn't been part of a team since his police days. He'd missed it.

12

The next morning, woken again by Lottie yapping at the postman, he shambled sleepily to the door and picked up the post. As usual there was a mixture of flyers and begging letters. And then at the bottom of the pile was one that was different. One that made him drop all the others in surprise. It was a postcard. Probably just from a friend on holiday. The light in the hall was gloomy so he carried it into the office and pulled back the shutters. It wasn't from a friend on holiday. There was no message. Just his address printed in black ink with a postage stamp and postmarked Dundee. *What the hell?* He felt a chill run down his spine. He examined the handwriting. Was it the same? He took it to the board and compared it with the two others. One to Felix, the other to Jamie's parents. He was as sure as one could be from a printed address, that it was from the same person. Once again black ink and block capitals. He felt as if he had joined a slightly sinister club. An elite group of those who had been sent postcards by Jamie McLeash. But Jamie had known his parents (obviously) and Felix. Ian was a total stranger. So how the hell had Jamie known his address? How had he known Ian's role in the case? He turned the card over, expecting another well-known artwork. Another clue in an increasingly complex puzzle. He was disappointed. All he'd been sent was a picture of some sandwiches and a sheep. *Oh, Jamie or Jacob or whoever you are, we've only just worked out your last puzzle. Are you starting something quite new? And why me?*

He scanned it and emailed it to Nick. *What do you make of this?* he wrote. Two possibilities crossed his mind. Either Felix had jumped the gun and announced to the world via his Facebook page that he was employing Ian as a private investigator. Or Andrea McLeash had mentioned him in a Facebook post of her own. The first seemed unlikely. Felix was barely capable of sending an email, never mind uploading a post to Facebook. And Nick had promised to keep an eye on him and stop him doing anything like that. He tapped open Andrea's Facebook page, but of course he couldn't see anything she had posted recently because of her high level of security. If she had posted it, was it possible Jacob could have seen it? Had Andrea accepted a friend request from someone called Jacob? She had the postcard with the painting of Jacob and she seemed like an intelligent woman who would put the two together. He was planning to call her later anyway and could ask her.

He took his usual morning walk with Lottie, waving to Lainie on his way out. She was dressed up today. 'Just waiting for a taxi,' she told him. 'I'm off to Dundee for my knit and natter morning. I'll be working on that blanket for Lottie,' she said with a grin. 'Can't concentrate on complicated patterns with all that chatter.'

That made sense. He couldn't imagine the concentration needed to create anything other than a tangle of multicoloured yarns. But he'd never tried knitting. It hadn't been encouraged when he was young. Particularly for boys. Dog blankets, he assumed, were square so probably straightforward for a knitter of Lainie's experience with or without conversation. He had an idea she'd said she was going to crochet Lottie's blanket, but perhaps that was the same thing. 'I'm sure Lottie's going to love it,' he told her.

. . .

Back from the village with his usual bag of warm croissants, he decided to call Andrea McLeash. He was on edge about his postcard and hoped this would clear it up. He made coffee, settled at his desk and tapped her number. She answered at once and he explained who he was, hoping that she'd remember him. She knew as soon as he told her his name and he noticed a note of hope in her voice. He must keep this low key. He'd hate to build up her hopes only to have to dash them again. He told her he had found her Facebook page and asked if she would accept a friend request from him.

'All right,' she said, sounding puzzled. 'We don't use it very much. Just a few holiday snaps, keeping up with people John used to work with, that sort of thing. But I'd be very happy for you to see them if you're interested.' Then she hesitated. 'Is it...is it something to do with Jamie?'

'I'm not sure yet. Has he contacted you through Facebook?'

'No,' she said and sighed. 'I only wish he had.'

'Have you had a request from someone calling themselves Jacob?'

'No,' she paused for a moment. 'Is that the name Jamie's using now? Like the painting he sent us.'

'It's possible,' he said. 'It could be nothing, but... well, maybe keep a lookout for any contact from a Jacob. We think he might be calling himself Jacob Campbell or Jacob MacDonald.'

'That would be just like Jamie,' she said. 'He used to love history and stories. And he was always making up names for himself.'

'Did he enjoy puzzles, quizzes, that sort of thing?'

'Oh yes. He used to write long complicated messages in code and send them out to sea in bottles. I think that's why he loved music. He saw it as a kind of cipher that he could crack and turn into some magical sounds.'

That sounds like our man, he thought. 'Will you let me know if you hear from him?'

'Of course,' she said. 'I'll check our Facebook every day. I don't need to go public, or whatever they call it, do I?'

'No, definitely not. Keep it as private as you can. Just accept my invitation. And I'm going to ask you to accept one from a man called Felix Lansman.'

'The pianist?'

Of course, she'd know about Felix. He'd been at the same school as Jamie and now he was famous. 'Yes,' he said. 'Just accept his invitation and invite him back. Don't get into any kind of communication with him.'

'Is he your client? The one who wants to find Jamie?'

'I'm sorry, I can't tell you that. And please, this is just a vague idea that I had. It might be nothing and I'd hate you to be disappointed again.'

'And your settings, are they private too? I'm not going to be tagged all over Facebook, am I?'

'They are,' he assured her.

'I'm sorry,' she said, sounding upset. 'I don't understand how this can help. I don't want to be contacted by just anyone, but if it helps Jamie then shouldn't I be a bit more public?'

'I know how difficult this is for you, but just trust me for now. I promise if we have any contact with him, I'll let you know.'

'Even if he says he wants nothing to do with us, could you just let me know he's safe?'

'Of course.' He really wanted to be able to do that. 'Have you had any more postcards?' he asked.

'No,' she said. 'Nothing.'

'Would you let me know if you do?' Could he tell her more than that? Yes, he felt he must. 'We're thinking he might be setting some kind of puzzle. That all the cards are linked in some way.'

'Other people have had them?'

'Just a couple.'

'Then yes, of course. I'll let you know at once.'

'Email me, or call me,' he said.

'So nothing on Facebook?'

'No,' he said. 'Just use it for your usual stuff. Don't upload the postcard.'

She laughed. 'I wouldn't know how to do that anyway,' she said. 'But all this secrecy, you don't think Jamie's in any danger, do you?'

Take care, he told himself. 'I've no reason to think so at the moment,' he said cautiously. 'But we shouldn't take any chances.' If it was Jamie, they didn't want to frighten him away. And if it was not Jamie there could be someone quite dangerous out there. Either way, he didn't feel the time was right to point that out to Andrea. He'd given her a little bit of hope. He didn't want to dash it by suggesting anything more sinister. Particularly as he didn't know himself what it was all about. He ended the call and felt that shiver of unease again. Was someone stalking them? He didn't think sending anonymous postcards was actually classed as stalking, but it was a long way from normal friendly communication.

He turned once more to the card that had arrived that morning. It must be part of the puzzle but who knew he was involved? Nick? No, she was way too open and honest in spite of her hacking history. And she'd not even been in the country when Felix's cards had arrived. Rosalie? Hardly. She cared far too much for Felix to play tricks on him. Felix himself? At some point he may have been delusional enough to send himself postcards but there was no way he'd have taken himself off to Glasgow and Dundee without Rosalie knowing. The McLeashes? Very unlikely. What motive did they have? So who else was there? Only Jamie or, and this *was* a chilling thought, the actual murderer.

His thoughts were interrupted by a call from Nick. 'How's it going?' Ian asked.

'You got a postcard,' she said, not answering his question. 'How did he know about you?'

'I can't imagine. It feels a bit creepy. I don't suppose you have any idea? Not someone playing tricks on me, is it?' He hated himself for asking that. But he did need to ask. He'd not known her for very long and she had a history of being troublesome. All the same, he hoped he hadn't offended her.

She laughed. 'Oh, believe me, if I fancied playing tricks I'd have thought of something far cleverer than that.'

And probably a lot more scary. 'Sorry,' he said. 'I had to ask.'

'It's okay. I have done some pretty stupid things in the past. But honestly, I promise I didn't do that.'

'Good,' he said. 'I didn't really think you had. I'm all over the place right now. Even thought it might have been from Lottie.'

'Well, food and sheep, definitely things with Lottie appeal. She'd have had trouble with the handwriting though.'

'We'll rule her out then. Have you had time to do anything today?'

'I've done a bit of research. Not sure any of it helps much though. The sandwiches were from a recipe site. *Ways to spice up packed lunches.*'

'With sandwiches?'

'Spicy fillings. It's a pun.'

'Yeah, I get that. What about the sheep? Mutton sandwiches?'

'It's a Jacob sheep.'

'Interesting.'

'Possibly the oldest sheep breed in the world. Kind of black and white blotchy with big horns.'

'And that helps us how?'

'It doesn't, except for the Jacob connection.'

'Okay. Any thoughts about how he's connecting me with it all?'

'Might need to work on that.'

'I talked to Andrea and she's not had anything from him. She's going to accept a friend request from Felix, so make sure he sends one. It's just an idea I have that if Jacob sees Felix and his mother are friends, he might just open up a bit.'

'Good thinking,' she said.

'We'll come back to it next week and see if there's been any response. How is Felix? Did you talk to him about Facebook?'

'Yes, he got quite animated. Although that might be because they've started to cut down on his medication. We called the agent and they agreed to hand over management of the Facebook page. They were a bit grudging about it, but we said they could have it back once Felix starts performing again.'

'And you know what to do with it? All the techie stuff?'

'Yeah, no problem. Have you thought what you want Felix to post?'

'Leave it for now. I might do something from my own page since Jacob seems to have discovered me.'

'Sure. Anything else?'

'Can't think of anything. We'll go over it all on Tuesday and think about what to do next. In the meantime, I've got to do some work on an untrustworthy boyfriend. I can't ignore my other cases.'

'Can I do anything to help with that?'

'No, go and do some singing practice.'

'Spoilsport. You sound like my dad.'

13

'You need a day out,' Caroline had told him. It was Saturday morning and Ian was having trouble with the *up to no good* boyfriend. His client, the girl's father, had told him the lad worked at a garden centre on Perth Road. 'And,' the client had told him, 'he's also up to no good with a girl called Belinda, who works in the tropical fish centre which is right next door.' Also, the man had told him, and this was far more worrying, his daughter was only fifteen and the boyfriend in question was a lot older. How much older, his client hadn't been able to say. Ian didn't know much about fifteen-year-old girls, but he probably knew enough to know that being told by her father not to see her boyfriend wasn't likely to be well received. He'd visited the garden centre where the boyfriend was easily identified by a badge, which proclaimed his name as Howie, pinned to his shirtfront. Having established through some careful questioning of the girl on the checkout that only one Howie was employed at the garden centre, Ian agreed with his client that this was not a partnership made in heaven. He estimated Howie's age to be mid-thirties and even that was being generous. He could well be ten years older. He'd popped into the tropical fish centre and discovered that Belinda was a formidable lady in her late twenties. He'd been in luck. As he feigned a sudden interest in a tankful of peaceful-looking Japanese fighting fish, he eavesdropped a conversation Belinda was having with one of her customers about a double date planned for the weekend. Howie's name had cropped up in the conversation as someone who couldn't be trusted as the designated driver for the evening. *And that's not all he can't be trusted with,* Ian thought.

He reported all of this to his client and then spent the next half-hour dissuading him from hoofing it down Perth Road with a pitch-fork to 'give the little toerag what he deserved'.

'So what do you suggest?' the client had asked. A reasonable enough question. All Ian could offer was setting up surveillance. He'd sit in his car, camera at the ready, and wait for an elicit tryst of some kind between the two buildings. He'd even spotted a promising over-grown path conveniently sited close to the side entrances of both buildings. He didn't plan to spend all day there. It was most likely they would contrive simultaneous lunch breaks and meet for a quick cuddle and sandwich somewhere between the hours of twelve and two. And not having much to do postcard-wise until Nick's next visit on Tuesday, he had planned to do it this very Saturday, hoping to have it all wrapped up by the beginning of the week.

'I've just got back from holiday,' Ian objected. *And I have suspicious boyfriends to spy on.*

'Your holiday was several weeks ago,' said Caroline. 'I repeat. You need a day off. And you don't work on Saturdays. We can take the dogs and I'll make a picnic.'

True. He didn't usually work on Saturdays. The prospect of a day with Caroline was way more pleasant than a couple of hours sitting in his car waiting for something that might or might not happen. In any case, it was no less likely to happen on Monday. Maybe it was even more likely to happen on Monday. A day when garden centres were quiet after the weekend. 'A picnic where?' he asked.

'There's a new sculpture trail at Clampton Castle.'

'Never heard of it.'

'It's only an hour's drive. A few miles north of Perth. The grounds open to the public every couple of years. It's really lovely. Heather just coming into flower, beautiful views over the five hills, quiet corners for picnics.'

He was coming round to the idea and it sounded like good dog walking territory. 'Did you say it was a sculpture trail?' he asked.

'It's all put on by Glasgow art students to raise money for a drug rehab centre.'

That was it really. He was a sucker for a good cause. Howie and Belinda would have to wait. It was a pity Nick didn't drive. It was the kind of job he could delegate to an assistant. When Nick returned to New Zealand he would think about contracting someone with a car for jobs like that.

So there they were, wandering around in a steady drizzle looking at scary objects made out of old car parts, rolled up barbed wire fencing, lumps of concrete and redundant railway sleepers. They stopped to look at a huge target mown into the grass on the side of a hill. He quite liked that. Art and nature hand in hand rather than locked in some kind of combat. It would look good seen from a distance. He looked across the valley, wondering if a climb up the hill opposite would be too far to walk. Maybe he'd suggest it after lunch. A view from a small plane or, even better, a hot air balloon would be good. He'd seen balloons flying over Greyport. There must be a hot air balloon place nearby. That would be a wonderful day out. He might look into it before the end of the summer.

A little further on, they came to a series of treehouses almost hidden in a small thicket. It was hard to tell where the trees ended and the sculptor had taken over. Kids would love this. He thought of the small residents that a child's imagination might conjure up.

They strolled down the hill to the bank of a river. It was hard to believe this was the Tay. Here it was just a stream where a couple of children had kicked off shoes and socks and were fishing for tiddlers with jam jars, paddling warily across slippery stones. Only half a day's drive away the river was a wide estuary, deep enough for oil tankers and cargo ships.

The dogs ran ahead of them and plunged in. Angus knocked one of the jars over. 'Sorry,' Ian said to the children. 'Had you caught many?' Should he offer to remove his shoes and socks and replace their catch?

'S'okay,' said one of the children. 'Our mam won't let us take them home anyway. She says they're happier in the river.' The children abandoned their fishing and started throwing sticks into the water, laughing when the dogs dived in to fetch them. This was a game that could last for quite a while.

He turned back to look at the castle. Not a patch on Drumlychtoun, it was more of a manor house. But an attractive one, particularly now the sun had come out.

'Told you the weather would turn,' said Caroline, taking off her jacket and spreading it out so they could sit on a grassy part of the riverbank.

She had laughed when he loaded up the car with waterproofs and wellies. But this was Scotland, and it could turn back any minute to the damp drizzly day it had been an hour ago. 'We should have our picnic while the sun's still shining,' he said, sliding the bag off his shoulder and finding a flat rock near the water.

'It's nothing elaborate,' said Caroline, unzipping the bag. She spread out a red and white checked tablecloth and took the lids off plastic boxes. 'Just a few sandwiches, Scotch eggs and some fruit.'

'It looks splendid,' said Ian, biting into a Scotch egg. 'These are delicious.'

'From your favourite farm shop,' she told him. 'I'm afraid they made the sandwiches as well, which is horribly lazy of me considering it's the school holidays.'

'Don't you have any work in the holidays?' he asked enviously. There were some perks to being a teacher.

'I do. Loads to prepare for next year. But nothing that involves wrangling classes of hormone-ridden teenagers.'

Long summer holidays were a bit of a myth then. Not that he'd ever fancied being a teacher. 'What's in the sandwiches?' he asked.

'It's a farm shop lucky dip,' she said. 'All kinds. Try one.'

He took a bite. Beef and mustard. It was delicious and the beef was no doubt local. Probably the mustard as well. The Arran Islands were famous for it. The only problem with sandwiches from the farm shop, he decided, was that they didn't make them big enough. He reached for another. Salmon this time. Again local and even more delicious. This picnic had definitely been a good idea. Parked outside the garden centre the best he could have managed would have been a plastic wrapped cheese roll from the nearest petrol station.

He stopped mid bite as something stirred in his brain. He stared at the river wondering what the hell it was.

'Is that one nasty?' Caroline asked.

'Not at all, it's delicious.' He took another bite.

'Only you seem to have gone off into one of your daydreams.'

Yeah, he did that. 'Sorry,' he said. 'It was the salmon.'

'Daydreams about salmon?' she laughed. 'You had me worried there for a moment. I thought it might be something weird. Are you thinking the contents of your sandwich might have mates right here in the river?'

'No, nothing like that.'

'I bet it's something to do with a case.'

'On a lovely day out like this? Of course not.' All the same. Salmon, sandwiches, fishing... No, he wouldn't spoil this afternoon. Although the moment he got home he needed to check his notes. But there was no hurry. He sat back while Caroline fed him grapes. Sometimes life was pretty much perfect. A sunny afternoon picnic by the river. The drive back to Caroline's house for a relaxed evening and where he was pretty sure she'd suggest phoning out for a meal. And then what? A few rather nice images came to mind. Checking his notes could wait. If necessary, they could wait until tomorrow.

He was almost nodding off when Lottie and Angus scampered up from the river where they had been splashing around together, and shook themselves all over him. Why did dogs always do that? Why couldn't they shake a few feet away from people who were wearing clothes. He looked down at his trousers. Oh well, they'd soon dry in the sun.

As he had hoped, it was Sunday morning before he and Lottie returned home. He glanced at his watch. It was, in fact, only just Sunday morning. He hoped he had left food in the fridge. The village shop closed at twelve. Oh well, he'd eaten splendidly yesterday and there was always the pub for an evening meal. Tesco in Dundee was open pretty much all the time, but he wasn't in the mood for that. What he felt right now was a very nice sense of wellbeing. Nothing like a trek round Tesco to ruin the effects of a lovely day out in the sun with good food and a best friend for company. The pub it would be then. But first he had work to do.

He turned on his computer and googled Coffee 2U. Amazingly it was still in business, although he supposed six years wasn't so long. It was a family firm run by a father and son. The son had only recently joined the business. There was a photograph of him and his father wearing green and white striped aprons and grinning into the camera. They still delivered coffee and sandwiches around Mayfair but were now proudly 'going green' with brown paper sandwich bags instead of the the old style plastic boxes. *Our delivery personnel now ride the latest retro bikes to cut down on pollution.* There was a photo of a hipsterish looking young man riding one of them. Ian wondered how bikes could be the latest and also retro but that wasn't something he really needed to dwell on. He sat back in his chair concocting a story for himself. Nothing dubious that involved a false identity. *Practise what you preach,* he thought, remembering the talk he'd delivered to Nick just a day or two ago. His cover in place, he opened up his email.

I realise this is a long shot, he wrote, *but I'm based in Scotland and I'm doing some research into an unsolved crime in London.* Did that sound believable? It was probably plausible enough, and basically true. He wasn't expecting this to be a lasting partnership. *I believe you deliver to hotels in Mayfair and I'm interested in a delivery you made to Lansman*

International on the evening of July 14th six years ago. Like I said, a long shot, but if you happen to have a record of the order that night it would assist me greatly in my research.

He used his personal email, not his business one and fired it off hoping that he just sounded like some slightly nutty, vicarious crime freak. Most likely he'd never hear from them, but this was about the only lead he had, and he was clinging to it like a life raft. Jamie, or should he call him Jacob, had sent him a picture of four sandwiches. That confirmed his theory that there had been *four* people in the office that night. Why had the police only looked for two of them? One, obviously, was dead. Two were seen leaving. And he had been sent a picture of *four* sandwiches.

He clicked send and shut down his computer, rounded up Lottie and strolled down to the pub. He and Lottie were regulars at the Pigeon where they did good plain food, but he thought a change would be nice this evening. They'd go to the Thistle and Stone, which was moving in a rather gastro direction. Dogs were not allowed inside but it was a nice evening and there were chairs and tables in a very pleasant garden. He tied Lottie to the leg of a heavy wrought-iron bench and went inside to order a pint and look at the menu which was chalked up on a blackboard.

'Nice bit of salmon tonight,' said a woman behind the bar.

For some reason he didn't fancy salmon and ordered lamb fillets with peas. He bought a packet of crisps and went back outside where he found Lottie making friends with a woman who was sitting at a nearby table reading with a marker pen in her hand. He untied Lottie and settled at his own table. The woman looked up from her book and smiled at him. 'Lovely evening,' she said.

He agreed that it was. 'Good book?' he asked, as she closed the book and put it down on the table next to her.

She blushed. 'Actually, I shouldn't offer an opinion. You see, I wrote it so it would be biased.'

That would be the second author he'd spoken to in a few days. 'What kind of book is it?' he asked, sincerely hoping it wouldn't be any kind of fantasy, apocalyptic kind of thing. He wasn't sure he could take another one of those. Not if he was expected to be polite about it.

'Crime,' she said. 'It's a murder set in St Andrews. It's not actually published yet. This is a proof copy.'

'Have you written a lot?' he asked. He was genuinely interested. He enjoyed a good crime story. And he wondered if constructing the plot of a crime novel was anything like solving the kind of cases he was involved with, although his current one was his first murder. *Her* stories probably contained several murders each.

'It's book four of a series,' she said.

'So I could read the other three?'

'Oh, please do. They're all on Amazon or in the book shop in St Andrews if you prefer a real book.'

'I'll do that. Do you live round here? Perhaps if we meet again you would sign it for me.'

'I'm just up the river from here. I've a nice little house with a stunning view of the estuary.'

'Me too,' he said. 'Although my house is in the village here.'

'And what do you do?' she asked. 'If I'm not being nosy. I'm afraid if I ask people questions, they'll think I'm going to write them into one of my novels.'

'And do you?'

'Very rarely. Although I do pick up ideas from what people tell me. And you didn't tell me what you do. Are you afraid I'll turn you into a character?'

'I'm a private investigator. But believe me, it's way too dull to be any use to a novelist.'

She laughed. 'You'd be surprised.'

'I'd rather not be.'

'Don't worry.' She put the book in her bag and stood up. 'All my characters live strictly in my head.' She held out her hand. 'I hope we meet again soon,' she said.

His food arrived and Lottie perked up and gave him one of her *I'm a poor starving dog* looks. 'Good luck with the book,' he said. 'I'll look out for book signings.'

'There'll be one at the art gallery in a couple of months. But I come here quite a lot when the weather's good.'

'Then I'll look forward to seeing you again.'

She left before he remembered to ask her name. And he really did intend buying one of her books. But for heaven's sake. He was a detective. It couldn't be too hard to find a crime novelist living on the banks of the Tay. And since he was a detective with an assistant, he'd get Nick onto it on Tuesday. That was if they weren't too bogged down by sandwiches.

It was cooling down now and the midges were beginning to bite. He didn't want to spend the night scratching so he put Lottie on her lead and walked home.

14

As he had assumed, Mondays were quiet at the garden centre. Ian had filled a flask with coffee and stopped off at the village shop for some sandwiches. It could be a long, boring, and possibly fruitless wait. But he was used to that. A large part of his job, particularly when he was starting out, had been sitting outside various workplaces and hotels waiting for people to provide him with evidence that would prove their misbehaviour to whoever it was that had hired him. The biggest problem was staying awake, hence the flask of coffee – strong and black, that he could consume in small quantities meaning that he didn't need to leave his post to use the toilet.

This Monday morning the car park was nearly empty. He chose a spot where he had a good view of both side entrances and the path between the buildings. He sat back, sipping his first cup of coffee, hoping that Belinda and Howie were early on the lunch break roster and he could get home again and get stuck into tasks that were way more interesting. He turned on the radio and listened to a comedy programme. *A bad description,* he thought. It didn't make him laugh, or even raise a smirk. It was about a trio of very stupid women with high-pitched voices, all apparently pursuing the same man. The man in question was a weak-willed, dithering type who was unwilling to express an opinion. He allowed himself to be led into ludicrously unlikely, and definitely unfunny situations by each woman in turn. Ian should have switched channels, but it had a kind of dire fascination and he sat it out to the end. It was followed by a fifteen-minute reading from a novel. He was just getting interested when the fifteen minutes were up. If he wanted to find what happened next, he would have to tune in at the same time tomorrow to find out. Or, he supposed, he could buy the book. But he probably wouldn't. It wasn't that good. After that came a consumer programme with people who had returned from disastrous holidays only to find themselves unable to claim compensation because they hadn't read the small print on their booking forms or failed to take the necessary photos of the squalor they'd found in their hotels.

Then at last, just as the one o'clock news was starting, the couple appeared. They paused at the entrance to the path, concealed from passing pedestrians, but from Ian's position in the car park and with the help of a zoom lens fitted to his camera, he was able to take a clear photograph as they hurled themselves into each other's arms in an incriminating clinch. He checked the picture and, satisfied that he had the evidence he needed, packed away his camera and headed for home.

Once home, he downloaded the photograph and sent it off to his client. He hoped that would be the end of it, at least as far as he was concerned. He could only hope that his client would use a degree of tact and that his daughter's heart would not be broken beyond repair.

He was about the save the photo to the client's folder, when something caught his eye. A moment before he took the picture, a flatbed truck had drawn up at the side entrance to the garden centre. It appeared on the right-hand side of his photograph, as clearly in focus as the snogging couple. Two men were unloading boxes of plants. Such an everyday occurrence at a garden centre that Ian had barely registered it. Now though, he took a closer look, zooming in and enlarging the picture even more to study the two men. One was a sturdy type dressed in a boiler suit. The other was slight and wearing a navy blue hoodie. Ian noticed that some of his long hair had escaped from the hoodie and that he also had a beard. *Interesting*, he thought. It could be the man they had seen at the book reading and again at the Discovery Pier. No reason why someone from a plant nursery shouldn't be interested in fantasy novels, Ian supposed. He looked at the picture again and had an uncanny feeling, the same feeling he'd had that day at the art gallery, that he'd seen this man before.

He shifted the picture to the left and looked along the side of the truck. There was some lettering, but even with his high-spec lens, it was too blurred to read. Why did it even matter? He'd seen someone two, or maybe three times. Dundee wasn't a huge city. He'd probably see a lot of people more than once. But something was bothering him. He remembered the furtive look the man had given him that day on the pier, before he disappeared into the throng of people making their way to the city centre.

Another day. Another postcard. A grisly one. A young man holding an older man by the hair and brandishing a long-bladed knife. Ian passed it across to Nick, who looked at it and frowned. 'Not very nice, is it?'

'Enough to give me nightmares,' said Ian. 'Can you find out what it is?'

Nick scanned it onto her phone. 'It's David with the head of Goliath,' she said, Ian once again marvelling at how quickly she could find things. 'By Caravaggio,' she added. 'In a gallery in Rome. You can't really see that it's only a head. It just looks like he's attacking him from behind.'

'Is there an obvious message here? Is Jamie or Jacob or whoever he is trying to tell us he's guilty?'

'Why would he? Isn't it more likely he's telling us something about the murderer?'

'Like what?' Ian asked, tapping his pen on the desk.

'Well, it doesn't look like Franz. Not from the description we've got of him.'

She was right, but at the moment he was more worried that it looked like Jamie himself. 'What about the artist? What do we know about him?'

She tapped at her keyboard for a few minutes. 'He worked in Rome but fled to Naples after being accused of murder.'

'Did he do it?'

'Never proved. It was the result of a drunken brawl. There's a chalk portrait of him here. Looks a bit like Felix. Oh, and he was probably gay and likely to have been murdered himself.'

'Quite a few messages in there then. But why the hell is he sending them to me? How can he possibly know my connection to the case? I get this scary feeling that he's watching me.' It made him feel restless and unable to concentrate. He went and made them both coffee, opened a packet of biscuits, put some on a plate and fed one to Lottie. What the hell. One biscuit wouldn't hurt. They could go for a long walk later.

Returning to his desk he found an email. To his surprise it was from Coffee 2U. Probably just to tell him he was wasting his time trying to discover anything about something that had happened six years ago. But he clicked it open.

You're having a laugh, right? How could we forget? It was that murder that made us. So much publicity Dad had to take on extra staff to cope with it all. He kept the order from that night and framed it. I'm attaching a copy. Good luck. Drop in if your research brings you to London. Regards, Steve.

He opened the attachment. *God bless businesses who keep their records straight.* The order had been phoned in at ten on the night of the murder and carefully recorded. Coffee 2U used a system that allowed whoever took the order to tick off details on a pre-set up form which then either took credit card details or added the amount to an account. On this occasion it had been added to Lansman's account, details of which had probably disappeared into the vaults of the international fraud squad. But that didn't matter. This gave him the information he needed. The order had been for four rounds of

sandwiches, two cappuccinos, a latté and a flat white. Ian was beginning to see where Jamie's messages were heading.

'Four rounds of sandwiches,' he said aloud.

'Feeling hungry?' Nick asked, grinning.

'The night of the murder the police believed there were three
people in the room. The victim and two suspects. So why order four
rounds of sandwiches?'

'Perhaps one of them was extra hungry.'

'And four coffees?'

She looked at him in surprise. 'You think there were four people
in the room?'

He nodded. 'Leopold, now deceased. Franz, who was left-handed
and not tall enough, and Jamie, who by all accounts was a blue-eyed
sweetheart who'd never hurt a fly.'

'And also not tall enough,' Nick added.

'And I think there could have been one more - the actual murderer.' Why hadn't he thought of that before? And why hadn't the police?
Had they taken the three coffee cups and three rounds of sandwiches
as evidence that there were three people in the room?

'But the police report said they found three empty sandwich
packs and coffee mugs,' said Nick. 'And the only fingerprints and
DNA they found belonged to employees.'

'Perhaps the murderer *was* an employee. Or perhaps he wore
gloves.'

'And only two men were seen leaving the hotel. There were security staff at the back entrance all night. All the other exits were sealed
off by the builders.'

There must have been another way out. The building was
searched from top to bottom as soon as the body was discovered. It
was still a puzzle, but it did feel a bit like progress. Thanks to Caroline and her picnic. He'd let his thoughts settle for now. There were
other things to get on with. 'How's the Facebook thing going?' he
asked.

'Felix and Andrea are now friends. Have you friended them as
well?'

'I haven't done it yet. So that can't be how Jacob found me.'

'With the high privacy settings, he won't see who they friended unless he does as well. And Felix would have told us if he'd made contact.'

'Give him time,' said Ian, reluctant to let go of his theory. 'How many likely Jacobs have we got now?'

'Five in the UK and a couple more who are concealing where they are.'

'Okay, let's get Felix to send his message. Have you got one ready?'

'I thought something very bland, like *were you the Jacob MacDonald, or Campbell, I was at school with?*'

'What's in Felix's profile? We don't want people accepting just because they've heard of him.'

'I took off anything that would make him stand out and changed his photo to a sheep.'

'Good thinking.' Ian was impressed with that. 'A Jacob sheep?'

'Of course. So what do you think? Shall I send it now?'

'You have his password?'

'Yes, he said he'd leave it all to me.'

Not very ethical, but probably necessary knowing Felix's state of mind and lack of IT skills. And he had given his permission.

Nick sent off five messages, making notes of who she'd sent them to. Ian sat back and wondered what to do next. A plan was beginning to take shape in his head. He would go and talk to the police.

The next morning he called Duncan. He was never sure where he would find him and didn't want to spend the day driving around all the police stations in north-east Fife looking for him. He was in Arbroath apparently. Way out of his patch and Ian wondered why. On the other hand, Arbroath meant a nice drive and possibly a lunch of fresh fish. Duncan seemed pleasantly surprised when Ian suggested it.

He prepared carefully, printing out the email from Coffee 2U and highlighting the references to sandwiches and coffee cups in the police notes. He had no intention of taking any of the postcards.

Arriving at the police station in Arbroath, he was shown into an office where Duncan was sitting with a cup of coffee. He was not on his own. Sitting opposite him was Kezia Wallace, Ian's nemesis. She'd been quite keen to have him arrested on suspicion of fraud at the end of the Drumlychtoun case. Completely unjustified in his opinion. He'd simply been checking up on what he thought was a vulnerable elderly lady. How was he to know she was in fact an experienced embezzler of online funds? He had sent Kezia a hefty file about his own case and hadn't even received an acknowledgment. She been decidedly dismissive of his work and treated him as the lowest of the low in detection terms. Ian couldn't have hoped for anyone better to hear what he had to say right now. He got out his notes and laid them out in front of them both. He explained his theory of the sandwiches in great length. Duncan gave him a look that suggested he should get back to spying on adulterers and Kezia sighed crossly and scowled at him.

'Ian,' said Duncan, not unkindly. 'I know how much you miss police work, but really there's nothing here to go on.'

'You did say I should reveal anything I found out.'

Duncan nodded. 'I did, but I meant real evidence, not some theory about sandwiches.'

'Total waste of police time,' said Kezia. 'That's an offence, you know.'

So charge me. He stopped himself from saying that out loud.

But she hadn't finished. 'I remember the case. I was only a sergeant at the time. If there'd been anything to discover, the Met would have found it. The case was closed and handed over to Interpol and even they drew a blank. So the best thing you can do is push off and stop wasting our valuable time.'

'But thank you for being so conscientious,' said Duncan.

Ian hoped he looked suitably crestfallen. It couldn't have gone better. He'd obediently reported what he knew, and they'd rejected it. He could now continue his search safe in the knowledge that they thought he was just an interfering nuisance. He only hoped that Duncan would forgive him if it turned out that there really was enough evidence to reopen the case. For now, his concern was to find Jamie, and not just for Felix. The more he got into this case the more he felt that Jamie needed to prove his innocence. All these coded messages told him that this was a guy who needed his help. What he needed to find out now was why he had waited six years to reach out. As Nick had said, something must have changed. And Ian needed to find out what it was.

Lottie had been well behaved but not all that welcome. She was usually a popular visitor at police stations where she got thoroughly spoiled. Perhaps Kezia Wallace wasn't a dog person. That wouldn't surprise Ian. She was probably more of a tarantula type. She'd have a house full of tanks containing deadly spiders, possibly snakes as well. But he shouldn't be spiteful. Finding her with Duncan had been a stroke of luck. And they'd both reacted just as he'd hoped they would. He bought some fish and chips and sat on the harbour wall to eat them, carefully peeling batter off small pieces of fish and feeding them to Lottie.

They watched boats coming and going. Once they would have been fishing boats but now there were more small holiday yachts, the scruffier herring fishers having been confined to the far end of the harbour. It was nice to see families out enjoying their holidays. A short season, he supposed. No one would go out in a small boat for fun once the autumn set in.

He scrunched up his fish and chip wrapper, threw it into a bin and headed back to his car, Lottie trotting obediently at his side. Home in half an hour and time to plan a message to what he hoped would be Jamie's Facebook page. He'd be ready to fire it off the moment Felix had a reply to his message. Something told Ian he wouldn't have to wait long, assuming, of course, that they'd reached out to the right person.

It was there wating for him when he arrived home. He'd heard the ping on his phone while he was driving but couldn't to stop to read it. He read Nick's message as he climbed the path to his door. Four of the five Jacobs had replied. Two said they were sorry, but they weren't who Felix was looking for. One hadn't replied at all and the fifth had sent him a picture of a bird. Ian had been a boy scout and had earned his birdwatching badge. This was a nightingale. He recalled a struggle he'd had at school with a poem they'd read in an English literature class. It was about a nightingale and didn't have any obvious appeal for teenage boys. One of them had asked why a poem about a nightingale was titled *Philomela*. The answer had stuck in his mind. Philomela, he was told, had been the victim of a violent crime. She'd had her tongue cut out to silence her and as consolation she'd been turned into a bird with a beautiful voice. The significance, as well as the heartbreak, hit him between the eyes.

15

It was time for Ian to send Jacob a message of his own. Nick had sent him the link to Jacob's page. It seemed he was using MacDonald as his last name, which made sense as the MacDonalds had been the victims of the massacre not the perpetrators.

Ian wasn't a great user of Facebook. He only had ten friends and one of those was Stephanie. He wouldn't have described Stephanie and himself as friends but at some stage they must have accepted requests from each other. She had posted a picture of her new house in America, which looked pretty much like the house she had lived in in Scotland. A house, in his opinion, that oozed new money and lack of taste. She'd also got herself a new dog. A bichon frise which looked like a pimped-up version of Lottie with fluffy white fur. He bent down and patted Lottie's head. 'You've been replaced,' he told her. 'With a tarted-up model.' Not unlike himself really. But at least it meant Stephanie wasn't going to demand that he give Lottie back. He'd have resisted that with lawsuits if necessary.

He'd uploaded some photos of his holiday, as had Caroline, and they had liked each other's pictures. His had three other likes and Caroline had fifty. *Which says a lot*, he thought.

There were some new photos from Anna; St Andrews student, his one-day assistant and recently discovered heir to the Drumlychtoun estate. She was having a great time with her family and boyfriend in the South of France and her recent upload had been rewarded with over three hundred likes. Strange, he'd thought that Facebook wasn't much used by the young. But Anna had friends who were not young, himself for one, so it seemed like a good way for her to keep up with them. The pictures made him long for a retry at his own youth. A chance to do it better. Anna and her twin sisters, all with the same unruly fair curls and all wearing shorts and skimpy striped tops, playing on the sand with a coloured beachball. It was a clever photo. A small white dog with its fur tied in a topknot on its head with a red bow – Fifi, he remembered – was caught in mid-air making a dive for the ball. A woman, Anna's mother he assumed, wearing enormous sunglasses and an elegant black one-piece swimming costume was on a lounger at the side of a pool sipping something from a glass. And then a picture of what must be Anna's stepfather, Mathias, suntanned and wearing a pair of spotless white shorts, linen shirt and boat shoes, his hair casually, and probably expensively, brushed back from his face. And finally, a selfie of Anna and her boyfriend, Robin, sharing an ice cream sundae. A mass of fruit, cream and chocolate wafers in a tall glass with a paper umbrella and spoons long enough to reach the bottom. He was pleased to see them looking so happy. Anna and her mother must have had a rough few years after the death of her father. It was all so different from his own rain-sodden holiday. Next year perhaps he would travel to somewhere that had guaranteed sun and sea warm enough to swim in.

Stop daydreaming, he told himself. He checked the details Nick had sent him, signed in as Felix – guiltily, although Nick had assured him Felix was perfectly happy for him to do it, and took a look at Jacob's Facebook page. If he'd thought *he* was low key on Facebook he was far outstripped by Jacob. There was nothing – no pictures, no posts. Jacob had two friends – his mother and Felix. Ian had expected that and hoped he was about to make himself the third. He was hazy about how it all worked. He needed a training session with Nick, but he supposed it was possible to lock down everything. Although in that case there didn't seem to be much point being on Facebook at all unless it was to hide in the background and keep tabs on what other people were up to. Which was exactly what Jacob seemed to be doing. The only thing clickable on Jacob's page was Messenger and Ian clicked it. He'd thought long and hard about what to say to Jacob. He wanted to let him know that he knew who he was, but without frightening him back into his six-year-long silence. He would love to have sent a message that said, 'How the hell do you know about me and why are you sending me pictures of sandwiches and grisly murders?' But that could wait. For now, he wanted to send something that was reassuring and that showed he was beginning to understand the message in the pictures. He downloaded Coffee 2U's menu and created a nice little image of his own with four cups of coffee, onto one of which he posted a shot of their logo. He copied it into Messenger and typed, *Would you accept a friend request?* Then he clicked send and tried to get on with some work, every now and then casting anxious glances at his phone. Stupid thing to do. How many people sat gazing into screens waiting for messages to pop up? Apart from himself, of course.

He pushed the phone to the far side of his desk and returned to the police report. Three people in the room, it said. One dead and two seen leaving by the only entrance that wasn't sealed by the builders. So how does a six-foot-two assassin, presumably armed with a fish gutting knife, a cup of coffee and a pack of sandwiches, escape? The obvious answer was the fire escape, but that had been removed for pointing work on the outside of the fourth floor. Was it too far to jump? What was the distance between floors? If only part of the fire escape had been removed what would remain? He searched Google for images of London fire escapes. They seemed fairly standard in design, zig-zagging their way up the side of buildings with platforms strategically placed close to windows. So perhaps the killer left the room after the murder and made his way down to the next floor. He assumed that in a hotel, fire exits would be carefully signposted, probably lit up. The police had found the door to the office locked, a simple matter of the murderer slipping the lock on his way out if the hotel had the kind of doors that would lock automatically. Or would he have needed a key? And how could Ian find out? And how had he got in? There were three possibilities. First, he might have been known to Leopold and just knocked on the door. Second, he could have arrived at the same time as Franz and Jamie, which would make both of them accessories. And third, he could have had his own key and been waiting inside the room before the meeting started. One key was found in Leopold's pocket. An emergency key was kept in the security office and was used the following morning when Leopold failed to respond to calls. Franz would probably have had one, which would explain why he was the prime suspect. Did interns have keys? Probably not. Definitely not to the boss' office. So Franz and Jamie must have gone into the room together after taking delivery of the coffee and sandwiches. The two of them were seen at the back entrance then and no one else was seen going into the building after that. They were spotted again leaving later that night, but again only the two of them. That meant that if there was someone else, he must have been inside the building already and have left a different way. Had the three of them planned it between them? Ian had learnt enough about Franz for that to be a possibility. Hired an assassin perhaps. But didn't assassins usually have their own weapons? And what was Jamie doing there? If Franz wanted his father dead, wouldn't it have been easier to escape on his own rather than in the company of a blameless intern? *Come on, Jamie. I get that you're scared but I need a bit more than a few postcards.*

He closed down everything and called Lottie. All this could wait. It had waited six years. A few more hours weren't going to make a difference. He'd go for a walk. Shake the cobwebs from his head and get something to eat.

Arriving home again he found Lainie trying to prune a bush in her garden. 'Wonderful scent,' she said. 'But it's growing across the living room window and blocking the light.' She'd managed to cut a few branches but at five-foot-one a six-foot-tall plant was too much for her. 'Do you have a stepladder I could borrow?'

He didn't and that was just as well. There was no way he could watch an elderly lady climb up a ladder. 'Let me,' he said, holding out his hands for the shears.

'Oh, I couldn't let you do it.' He hoped she wasn't about to suggest that he was incapable because of his leg. 'You're far too busy,' she said.

'Not at all,' he said, smiling at her. He really must learn not to be so sensitive. 'Just tell me which bits you'd like me to cut off.'

They made a good team. He'd soon cleared her window and they gathered up the branches he'd cut off. Lainie sifted out some that still had flowers. 'It's pretty much finished flowering now,' she said. 'But there are still a few here. Take them for your house. It will make it smell wonderful.'

Ian laughed. 'Are you suggesting my house is smelly?'

'Get along with you,' she said. 'I wasn't meaning that at all. Even yon dog smells fragrant. Y've no worries there.'

He was pleased to hear it. Living alone one never knew about things like that. And it was the second time he'd been given flowers recently. Things were looking up.

'You'll come in for a wee cup of tea?' she asked. 'I've baked a cake.'

He nodded. 'Love to,' he said. Lainie was always baking. Someone had to eat it. It would be rude to refuse.

Lottie padded into the house. She knew it almost as well as their own. Lainie poured her a bowl of water and fed her a small piece of cake. 'You've not been for a sleepover for a while,' she said to Lottie, who managed to gaze at her soulfully, while not taking her eyes off the cake. 'No more trips to London?'

Actually, that was exactly what Ian had been thinking. He could take Ailish up on her invitation and stay with her for a couple of nights. He'd take a look at escape routes from London hotels and accept the invitation to drop in on Coffee 2U. Get a feel for the crime scene. Then he might call in at 42 Brompton Gardens and see if there was anyone still there who remembered Jamie, or his friend. Tricky,

Mickey or Dicky. He couldn't remember. He needed to check his notes, some homework to do before he left. He would call Ailish right now and see when she was free. 'If you're sure,' he told Lainie, 'it would really help me if you could have her for a couple of nights sometime soon.'

'Of course, just let me know when.'

Before he called Ailish he checked out Park Lane hotels. Lansman International in Park Lane had been bought up by another hotel chain and was now calling itself The Serpentine View. Ian checked its website. It had recreated itself as an upmarket business centre with conference rooms and a gym in the basement. The actual building, though, didn't look as if it had changed very much. Its grey stone Georgian frontage, he learnt, was listed so it wouldn't have been allowed to change. He wasn't sure if that went for the rest of the building but how much could you change the upper floors of a hotel? They still needed bedrooms and fire escapes. The hotel boasted a range of eating opportunities. He'd take Ailish there for lunch and see if he could poke around its more domestic areas.

He called Ailish and she was delighted to hear from him. 'It's been a bit quiet since I left Drumlychtoun,' she told him. 'You're just what I need to liven up my life again.'

Really? He'd never seen himself as a livener up of anyone's life. Ailish had led a far more colourful life than he had. Even in his younger days as a copper in a rough part of Edinburgh. 'How would this weekend suit you? Saturday to Monday?' In spite of Caroline's insistence that he should take Saturdays off, in this instance a weekend would suit him well. He would be able to talk over any discoveries he made with Nick the next day. Perhaps he would take Friday off. Drive himself and Caroline up to Loch Lomond for a couple of days for some dog walking and good food.

'What are you planning to do?' Ailish asked. 'Is it a case?'

'In a way,' he said. 'A kind of field trip for a bit of background. I'm planning on nosing round a hotel.'

'Any particular hotel?'

'The Serpentine View in Park Lane.'

'You're just going to drop in and ask if you can nose around?' She was laughing.

'I'll need cover,' he said. 'Can I buy you lunch there on Sunday?'

'Not dinner? I could dress up in my finery and cause a diversion.'

'No, sorry about the finery but if I'm poking around behind hotels, I'd rather do it in daylight. I'm sure you could cause a diversion though.'

'Fair enough. Shall I book us a table? I believe the Queen Mother Brasserie does a very good lunch.'

'Excellent. And we'll take coffee at a little place a few streets away.'

'A particular place or do you just fancy a stroll round the streets?'

'A place called Coffee 2U. I've been promised a free coffee there.'

'Saturday afternoon then. Perhaps you'd allow me to buy you dinner on Saturday evening. Will you be taking the train?'

'I think I'll fly this time.' It would be quicker, and he could park in Rosalie's drive and catch up with Felix before he left. He hoped Felix's head would be clearer than the last time they'd met, and he'd be able to tell him a little about the geography of the hotel.

He called Nick and told her about his plan. Then he gave her a short account of his visit to the police, which made her laugh. 'Devious bastard, aren't you?' she said, sounding impressed.

'Not at all. I was merely passing on evidence. Just being a good citizen.'

'And getting them to say exactly what you wanted. Just enough to get you off the hook and get on with your own enquiry unhindered.'

She was right, of course. He'd impressed himself with the success of his plan. He just hoped it wouldn't all come back to haunt him. 'See if you can catch Felix in a lucid moment and get him to draw me a plan of the hotel as he remembers it. And if Rosalie's there, can I have a word?' He was sure she wouldn't mind him using her drive as a car park, but it would be polite to ask her in person.

· · ·

Everything was falling into place. Lunch with Rosalie, a chance to talk to Felix and Nick before he left and then a short tram ride to catch his afternoon flight.

He handed an enthusiastic, tail-wagging Lottie over to Lainie and set off for Edinburgh. This time he was not held up by petition-wielding neighbours and traffic was lighter than he expected. He arrived in plenty of time for lunch. Felix met him at the door. He looked like a different person, greeting Ian with a warm handshake. 'You're looking well, Felix,' said Ian, as they went inside.

'I'm much better,' said Felix. 'They reduced my medication, so I feel less as if my brain's made of cotton wool.'

'That's good,' said Ian. He remembered that drugged up feeling. In his case it had been painkillers, but the effect, he guessed, was much the same.

'I've drawn the plan you asked for,' said Felix, leading him into Rosalie's living room. The lid of the piano was open and there were piles of sheet music on the floor.

'Are you playing again?' Ian asked, hoping this wasn't a sensitive question.

'Thanks to Rosalie's lovely piano,' he said.

Ian ran his fingers over the gold letters of the maker's name. 'It was her grandmother's, wasn't it?'

'That's right. When Adele died Rosalie thought she would be selling the house. The estate agent suggested she should send the piano for scrap. The man should have been shot. But I think that's one reason she decided to stay. Her grandmother had loved her Stein-way. And she was right. It's a beauty.'

'She was a pianist herself, wasn't she?'

'Adele? I believe she was quite well known in her day. Gave it all up when she married, of course. It's what women did in those days.'

A portrait of Adele beamed down at them from the wall above the piano. Ian smiled up at it. 'She'd be pleased to see it being used now,' he said, wondering if Adele's ghost was hovering around up there willing Felix to start playing again. Not that he believed in ghosts.

'It was a tough time for Rosalie,' said Felix. 'Adele died suddenly from a stroke, I was away in Moscow for the Rebikov competition and Piers had just left her pregnant with Toby.' He spread his plan out on the table. 'This is how I remember the hotel. Offices and our flat on the top floor. Probably not changed much. The ground floor reception rooms will be different, but probably cosmetic changes rather than structural ones. Nick and I did some research and there are restrictions about how much you can change listed buildings. I'm guessing things like kitchens and staff entrances will still be the same.'

It was an impressive plan. 'Did you do this?' Ian asked.

'No,' Felix laughed. 'It's some software Nick found on the Internet. I just told her where things were, and she typed them in. She's got me using Facebook as well and...' He hesitated. 'You've found Jamie.'

'Not exactly,' said Ian. 'We think we know the name he's using and that he's using Facebook to make contact. But we've no idea where he's living.'

'It's a good start though?'

'Yes, but Felix, we must be very, very careful. We don't want the police to get involved and we don't want to frighten Jamie. We can't have him disappearing without trace for another six years.'

'I get it, I think.'

'So watch your Facebook page, but don't do anything without consulting Nick. Just... just don't get impatient.'

'I understand,' said Felix sadly. 'I'll do as I'm told and not interfere.'

16

Ian could count the number of times he'd been to London on his fingers. A few visits when he was a child; going to the zoo or one of the museums. Once during his training at Kincardine he had visited an old school friend in Tower Hamlets. They had gone on a weekend long pub crawl. Ian had arrived back at the police college with a monumental hangover and received an earful from his supervisor. His most recent visit had been brief. He'd done the whole trip from Dundee and back in a single day, spending a total of five hours actually in London. That was just a few months ago. He'd taken the train, which was more or less on his doorstep, but it had meant a very long day. He actually spent twice as long on the train as he had in London, which when he thought about it was stupid. He'd not had time to see anything of London. And it had meant leaving Lottie with Lainie for two nights. The first because of his early start. The second because he was very late getting home. Not that either of them objected. Lainie loved the company and Lottie enjoyed the extra titbits of food that came her way.

This time, and with a twinge of guilt about his carbon footprint, he was doing it in style and flying. Not only that. He was staying for a couple of nights in an upmarket flat in Kensington. He was going up in the world and that would be one in the eye for his parents, not that he was going to tell them. It was probably too late to persuade them that he was anything other than a lost cause. He was the one member of the family who was quite decidedly not upwardly mobile. Not that he was downwardly mobile either. At least not since the shooting. That had downward qualities, but strangely he remembered it now as a calm, satisfying period of his life. It had been a time of recovering from his injuries. The physical results of a bullet in the leg and the emotional ones of a messy divorce. He had moved in with his grandfather who needed a carer, but there had been an equal amount of caring on both sides. Grandad was the one person who had realised the trauma he had been through. Everyone else thought he should just pull himself together and get on with life. Grandad would have chuckled at the idea of arriving in London ninety minutes after leaving Edinburgh. 'Why the hurry?' he would have asked, probably bemoaning the fact that Ian wouldn't have enough time to pair himself off with one of the cabin crew. But Grandad and his friends barely left Edinburgh in their later years. They had been a lively bunch but apart from a few excursions around the castles and gardens of Scotland, possibly taking in the odd whiskey distillery on the way, their activities were all within a few miles of home.

Ian had a window seat and watched the buildings of Edinburgh disappear under a blanket of cloud as the plane took off. An hour later, it began to descend over London on its approach to Heathrow. He watched as they floated above the Olympic Park and Millennium Dome, then flying along the river, westwards out of London before descending bumpily onto the runway at Heathrow. Domestic flights had none of the hassle of customs and baggage checks and within minutes Ian was on a train hurtling into central London. Then a quick tube ride and he emerged into High Street Kensington which was bustling with early evening drinkers and diners. Five minutes from the station and he was at Hibernia Mansions ringing Ailish's doorbell. This was very different from the last time he was here, his first meeting with Ailish and the start of an exciting few months.

This time they were friends and Ailish bustled him in, showing him to his room and then serving chilled white wine and olives on the balcony.

'It's so good to see you again,' said Ailish. 'I hope this is going to be a social visit as well as work.'

'I am working on a case,' he said, grinning at her. 'But it's really just an excuse to come and see you again.'

'That's the spirit,' she said, draining her glass. 'Like I said, you're welcome any time you're in London. And we had such fun at Drum-lychtoun.'

Attacking a dangerous criminal with a grappling hook wouldn't be everyone's idea of fun but it had brought the family together and, he supposed, he had been the one to set it all into motion. He felt a moment's satisfaction for a job well done.

'Do you have a plan?' Ailish asked. 'Apart from lunch tomorrow and creeping round the grimier areas of a posh hotel. I don't suppose you can tell me much about the case.' She obviously hoped he would let something drop about that.

'I can't tell you about my clients,' he said. 'But I'm here to look into a historic murder case.'

Ailish looked at him with a gleam in her eye as he knew she would. She'd always been one for a bit of excitement. Even now in her seventies she was up for anything. 'Interesting,' she said. 'Is it something to do with the Serpentine View?'

'It is, but at the time I'm investigating it was still Lansman International. I'm hoping to have a snoop around, although I expect it's changed a lot.'

'I remember it. Joshua and I went there often. It used to be old-fashioned and traditional. Excellent service, of course. But I hear it's become a bit corporate recently.'

She was right. The new management was chasing quite a different clientele. It would be all mobile phones and global communications. Less about comfortable leather chairs and good old-fashioned deferential service, and quite a lot of dodgy financial stuff going on behind closed doors. 'The public rooms have been completely rebuilt,' he told her. 'But I'm hoping the basic layout hasn't changed. I want to take a look at the fire escape.'

She raised an eyebrow at him. 'I'm sure you have your reasons so I won't pry.'

He unfolded the map Felix and Nick had made. 'This is a plan of the hotel as it was six years ago. I'm hoping it's accurate. It was made from memory but it should be enough for me to find my way. I might need you to cause a bit of a diversion while I slip away and have a nose around.'

'I'm sure that can be arranged,' she chuckled. 'But what about this evening? Do you have any plans?'

He hadn't really. But then he had an idea. 'I'd like to walk around a bit and take a few photos. The Albert Memorial and then a walk down to South Kensington and the Bartók statue.' And he'd call in at 42 Brompton Gardens to enquire about Michael Rickson. Someone might remember him although it was probably too much to hope that he still lived there.

'May I join you? We could find a bite to eat at the same time.'

'I'd like that. Do you have anywhere in mind?'

'Lots of good eating places in South Ken. We'll decide when we get there.'

They walked through the park and Ian took his first photo of the Albert Memorial, glinting in the setting sun. He wasn't sure why he'd taken it. A record of his current enquiry perhaps. Or a chance to cover some of the same ground as Felix and Jamie. People were queuing outside the Albert Hall for a concert and Ian took a photo of them. Felix would have performed there, he supposed. If Ian could solve this case for him, perhaps he would again. Or was that just wishful thinking? Felix would be very happy if Jamie was found but Ian could hardly credit himself for the rescue of his career.

They crossed the road and walked down past the Science Museum, turning into the Cromwell Road and crossing again outside the Natural History Museum. 'Why were so many museums built in the same place?' he asked Ailish, relieved to have safely negotiated six lanes of fast-moving traffic. It reminded him of the way traffic belted along the Perth Road on the Dundee waterfront, but there it only went in one direction. This was way busier.

'Something to do with Albert and the Great Exhibition, I think,' said Ailish.

It was quieter in the roads around the underground station. They found Bartók. He was smaller than Ian had expected, a rather dapper little man in a smart overcoat and a trilby hat that Ian fancied might suit himself. He should get one. It would make him look like a real detective. The kind one found on the cover of novels and film noir posters. He took a photograph of Bartók, then checked the distance to Brompton Gardens. A four minute walk, his phone told him.

Number 42 was a white, three-storey house in a terrace. They walked up some steps to a front door where three doorbells told them it was converted into flats. Ian read the names on the bells. None of them said Rickson, but he had expected that. He dithered for a moment about which one to try. Then he went for the one that had two names on it.

'Hi,' said the young man who opened the door. He was around twenty-five and wearing a spotless white T-shirt and tight black jeans. 'I'm Al. Are you here for the party?'

'No,' said Ian. Ailish, he thought, looked disappointed. 'I'm sorry to bother you—'

'Particularly if you're having a party,' Ailish chipped in.

Was she hoping to be invited? 'I'm just making some enquiries,' said Ian, handing Al one of his cards. 'It's about someone who lived here, maybe six years ago.'

'I've only been here a year,' he said. 'That's what the party's about. Celebrating our anniversary. But come in. You can ask my partner. He was here six years ago.'

He led them into an immaculately tidy living room with a polished wood floor and white walls with black and white photographs of flowers. Ailish walked up to one of them and studied it. 'They're beautiful,' she said, turning to Al. 'Don't you think so, Ian?'

He nodded, surprised at how effective flowers looked in black and white. The detail of texture was extraordinary.

'They're Tommie's,' said Al. 'He's a photographer. Fashion shoots mostly. These are more of a hobby. Here he is now,' he said as a door opened and another man came in carrying a tray with a cut glass bowl of punch and some glasses.

'Oh,' he said in surprise, putting his tray on a table. He smiled at them. 'Do we know you?' he asked.

'It's okay, Tommie,' said Al. 'They haven't come for the party. They're detectives and they want to ask you some questions.'

Ailish swept forward and held out her hand. 'I'm so sorry,' she said. 'We didn't mean to gatecrash your party. I'm not a detective but my friend Ian here is.'

'Have I done something bad?' asked Tommie, with a laugh.

'No,' said Ian. 'Not at all. I'm not a police detective. I'm trying to trace someone who stayed here a few years ago. I'm told he was sofa surfing with a friend. Michael Rickson?'

'Mickey Rix! Yeah, we were living together. We split up a couple of years ago. He was a great guy. We just weren't, you know, life partners.'

'Do you remember his friend, Jamie McLeash?'

Tommie shook his head. 'Mickey was always taking pity on people and letting them stay here. I don't remember any names.'

'Do you know where Mickey is now?'

'We kept in touch for a bit after he left. He was working at the Dorchester for a while. Then he was left a bit of money. He was going back to Scotland to open a place of his own. I haven't heard from him since he left.'

'What sort of place?' Ian asked.

'Small hotel I suppose. He'd trained in hospitality.'

'Do you have any idea which part of Scotland?'

Tommie shrugged. 'Not sure, Inver-something, I think.'

'Inverness?' suggested Ailish.

'No, I don't think so. Sorry. It was somewhere near Glasgow.'

'Never mind,' said Ian. There must be registers of people who ran hotels in Scotland. He could get Nick onto it next week. And it probably wasn't important. It sounded as if Mickey's friends came and went at speed and if he only left London a couple of years ago, he'd hardly be sheltering Jamie now.

'So sorry to have disturbed you,' said Ailish as Al reappeared with a tray of canapés. 'We'll leave you to your party.'

'No problem,' said Tommie. 'Would you like to join us?'

'Another time perhaps,' said Ailish as she and Ian moved towards the door.

They said goodbye and headed back to the street.

'Would you like to have stayed?' Ian asked. He didn't want to cramp Ailish's style. She'd have enjoyed a party surrounded, probably, by beautiful young men. It wouldn't have been his cup of tea, but he'd have been happy enough exploring Kensington on his own.

'Of course not,' she said. 'I can gatecrash a party any day. I've only got you for the weekend. Now, let's find somewhere to eat and you can tell me all about this Jamie McLeash. That is if it's not too confidential.'

They walked back to the underground station and then Ailish stopped suddenly. 'I know just the place,' she said. 'There's a quiet little bistro just around the corner.'

She had lived in London most of her adult life and probably knew of many bistros around many corners, Ian thought. 'It's Saturday evening. Shouldn't we have booked somewhere?' he asked.

'This is run by a friend of mine. He'll always find room for me,' she said, turning abruptly into a narrow side street and descending into a gloomy basement.

Ian expected an opium den populated by the likes of Sherlock Holmes, but he was wrong. They arrived in a small room with candles in bottles and red and white checked tablecloths, where Ailish was greeted like an old friend. Well, she probably was. She only lived a short walk away.

The proprietor, Jean Paul, greeted her with a kiss on the cheek and showed them to a table. 'Darling,' she said. 'What's on the menu tonight?'

'We have Carcassonne Duck Cassoulet,' he said as he fussed around with sliver cutlery, wiping tumblers and spreading napkins on their laps. Not a menu in sight, Ian noticed.

'Lovely,' said Ailish, winking at Ian. 'What about a drink?' she asked.

'May I suggest a Lillet Blanc to clear the palate,' said Jean Paul. 'And with the cassoulet a red Marcillac?'

'You always know best,' said Ailish with what Ian thought was uncharacteristic acquiescence. 'Don't look so surprised,' she said. 'Choice is not always such a good thing. When you're in the hands of someone like Jean Paul, you don't argue.'

'You make him sound like the Mafia,' said Ian, laughing.

'You're not far wrong. I heard a customer once asked him to leave garlic out of one of his dishes. I believe he was never heard of again.'

Their drinks arrived with a dish of pistachios and buttered radishes. 'Tell me about your search for this young man,' said Ailish.

'Jamie McLeash. He was working at Lansman International six years ago. The owner was murdered and Jamie disappeared. The police case was closed but Jamie's friends want him back.'

'Did he do it?'

'From what I've learnt of him so far, I think it's very unlikely. But...'

'I know. You're not at liberty to tell me more.'

He nodded and their main course arrived. The duck was delicious and drove any thoughts of murderers out of his head. It was an unusual wine. Ian was no expert but he thought, although it was very dry, it had a slight taste of blackcurrants. He read the label on the bottle. 'Is this from anywhere near Anna's family vineyard?' he asked.

'A little further west, I think,' said Ailish. The Languedoc is better known for its white grapes. But if you like this, I'm sure Anna can arrange to have a case sent to you. Her family are very grateful for the way you looked after her.'

'You've heard from her recently?'

'Oh, yes. She sent me pictures and she's determined to chum me up with her mother.'

'She sent me photos as well. It looks idyllic.' He took another sip of his wine. 'And she could be right,' he suggested cautiously. 'Her mother was married to your son after all.'

Ailish toyed with the last of her duck. 'Anna's planning to spend a couple of weeks with me in the autumn before her term starts. She's hoping her mother will come as well. She's been tempting her with London shops so it could be a way for us to bond. And Xander wants us all to go to Drumlychtoun for Christmas.'

'He's invited Anna's family as well?'

'He has. So it looks as if it's going to happen. But I suppose they're right, both of them. It's time to bury the past.'

She gazed sadly into her wine glass and Ian reached across the table and squeezed her hand. 'They *are* right. They've forgiven you and I'm sure your son would have as well. Isn't it time to forgive *yourself*? There's no way you could have changed what happened to Pete. He died doing what he loved and I'm sure he'd want to see the family reunited.'

She nodded. 'You're a good detective,' she said. 'And very wise.'

He wasn't sure about any of that but he was prepared to bask in it for the moment.

They rounded off the meal with crème brûlée and walked back to Ailish's flat. It had been a long day with good food and excellent company, not to mention expensive wine. Ian was going to sleep well. But first he opened Facebook on his phone. There was nothing from Jacob. Was he refusing his friend request? Or did they have the wrong Jacob? No, Felix's nightingale proved they had the correct person. He tapped to open Messenger, uploaded the photos he'd taken of Bartók and the Albert Memorial and sent them to Jacob.

· · ·

Ailish was obviously not an early riser and a quick look around her kitchen told Ian she was not an eater of breakfast either. He was incapable of starting the day without breakfast; a cup of strong coffee and a few calories were the very least he needed to kick his day into action. He would miss his early morning walk with Lottie as well. But there was no law against going for a walk without a dog. This was something he had never considered doing before he had Lottie. In fact, any kind of walk was not something he had considered very often. But since he'd had Lottie, he'd lost weight and gained energy, and missing his morning walk left him lethargic and with a feeling that the best he could do was go back to bed. But it was Sunday morning, and he had an hour or two to spare in the most famous city in the world. The least he could do was go and look at some of it. He grabbed his jacket and strolled out of Ailish's flat away from Hibernia Mansions and into Kensington High Street which, considering the early hour, was surprisingly bustling. He walked along past the station, past an arcade of shops and a wholefood supermarket, which reminded him he hadn't yet found breakfast. He discovered a baker's shop where he bought a bag of pastries and a cup of coffee. He was now opposite the entrance to Kensington Gardens so he crossed the road and walked through the park looking for a bench where he could sit and enjoy the caffeine and sugar rush that would set him up for the day. Strolling towards the Serpentine, he passed small children on scooters, dog walkers with dogs of all sizes from the kind that you could slip into a pocket to the sort that needed a restraining order. There were joggers, skateboarders and rollerbladers, and young lads with footballs. He found a bench under a tree where he watched bright green parakeets flitting in the branches. Parakeets in the middle of London? That was something he'd not expected. But no one else seemed surprised. He didn't think they'd ever been seen in Scotland. They were probably used to warmer climates, although if they were, London didn't seem like an obvious choice. He took a picture and sent it to Caroline. *Taking time out for an al fresco breakfast,* he texted in case she started nagging him about working at weekends.

He finished his breakfast and brushed some crumbs from his trousers. Then he walked back the way he had come, pausing outside Kensington Palace to take a photo which he sent to Lainie. He couldn't remember who lived in the palace, but Lainie would know that. He sent a short message hoping that Lottie was behaving and telling her he would be home tomorrow afternoon in time for him to drive her down to the pub for a meal. She'd enjoy that, he thought.

When he got back to the flat, he found Ailish getting ready for their lunch at the Serpentine View. She looked spectacular in orange silk and a black jacket with a design of yellow hummingbirds. She knew how to attract attention. She'd been turning heads all her life and it didn't look as if she was about to stop now. They had planned it all the previous night. He wanted her to attract attention and if anyone knew how to cause a diversion it was Ailish. No one would notice her very ordinary companion, and that was exactly how he wanted it.

Ailish called for a taxi. Not the usual black cab. This one was from a car hire company she used often. She had ordered a chauffeur-driven Daimler. The hotel wasn't far but, as she pointed out, anyone could walk into a hotel unnoticed. This way they would make more of an entrance. Everyone, from the doormen and concierge, to the dining room staff, would treat her like royalty. That suited Ian well. The more they gawped at Ailish the less attention they would pay to him. He planned on being dull and unmemorable.

As the car drew up outside the hotel, Ian glanced up at the fourth floor. According to Felix's plan, Leopold's office was at the back of the building. It was immediately opposite the private apartment that he and his family used. Anyone using the flat would have been able to look out at the traffic in Park Lane and across to the park, as would any hotel guests with rooms at the front of the building. Did the police search the apartment? There was no mention of it in the report, but they must have done. It would have been the first door they knocked on after the body was discovered. During the refurbishment the front of the building was probably covered in scaffolding, so could that have been an escape route? It seemed unlikely. Park Lane was busy twenty-four-seven. Someone climbing down scaffolding would have been noticed.

The Queen Mother Brasserie, even on Sunday, was full of people in business suits with phones clamped to their ears shouting in a language that Ian found incomprehensible and paying little attention to the waiting staff. Ailish was a breath of fresh air and was immediately descended upon by people with menus and escorted to one of the best tables in the room with a view of the park. 'I'd prefer that one over there,' she said, pointing to another table. They seemed surprised but fingers were snapped and the table hastily prepared. 'This is much better placed for our plan,' she whispered to him as they sat down. She was right, and he liked that it was *our* plan, not just his. This table was ideally placed for it, to the right of the service entrance where any waiting staff would have their back to the kitchen door. They fussed around her, taking very little notice of Ian as he glanced around and planned his next move. He unfolded Felix's plan and studied it behind his menu, which was fortunately a very large one. He pretended to scrutinise every dish before he made his choice. He'd already decided on a simple salad. Once Ailish had involved as many of the staff as possible in her own choice of meal, he would slip away. He needed to find the back entrance, and having studied the layout from the plan he knew where he needed to go. It was actually very simple. If he could just slip unnoticed into the kitchen there was a service door just inside which would lead him straight to where he wanted to be. All he needed was for Ailish to engage as many of the waiting staff as she could. A task she was managing with practised skill and, he suspected, loving every minute. She was explaining that she was on an extremely restrictive diet and needed to know every detail of the ingredients. They couldn't do too much for her and eventually the kitchen manager was called. This was Ian's chance. He faked a fit of coughing, stood up with his napkin - luckily a large damask one over his mouth, headed in the direction of the kitchen and slipped unnoticed out into the service road at the back of the hotel. Momentarily surprised to discover that Felix's plan was precise down to the last window, he found himself gazing up at five storeys of fire escape. A study of the structure told him that each level was bolted onto a supporting platform, and he calculated that the removal of a section would happen at the base. The rooms on the upper floors looked smaller than lower down, which would also mean they had lower ceilings. It was, he estimated, about fifteen feet from the fourth-floor windows down to the third-floor platform. For a man of over six feet that would mean a drop of around seven feet. Dangerous when landing on an iron platform but not impossible. He could have stashed the knife up his sleeve and stuffed the sandwich wrapping and coffee cup into his pocket. Once on the fire escape there was a descent down four flights of stairs and then a short walk across the service yard into the street. A quiet back street with little activity at that time of night.

So why hadn't the police worked that out and searched the service yard? Because they were looking for two men who had left by the back entrance which was around the corner. They had focussed on Franz and Jamie, who aroused suspicion by leaving hurriedly and furtively, not even pausing to say goodnight to the two security guards at the entrance.

The yard itself was a bleak, unattractive place; a dump for empty crates, broken furniture and cigarette butts. It needed a good clean. It probably hadn't been swept in the last six years and Ian wondered if was worth sifting through the rubbish for clues. But what kind of clues? The murderer would hardly have left the knife here, and sandwich packs and coffee cups would have been rat food long ago. He wondered if the hotel prices reflected the different views from bedroom windows. If so, any overlooking this yard would be very much cheaper than those at the front of the building – the public face of the hotel which oozed grandeur and opulence. Perhaps the rooms on this side were offices and storerooms. He looked up at what he imagined had been Leopold's office but the windows there didn't look any different from the others on this side of the hotel. It was hard to tell what hotel rooms were like inside just from looking at the windows from the outside. He should know. He had spent many hours sitting outside hotels watching for signs of life inside rooms and rarely seeing any. Occasional shadowy figures passing flimsily curtained windows, but nothing that really gave any idea of what was going on. And hotels like this didn't have flimsy curtains. They had heavy brocade drapes or blinds.

He took some photos and was putting his phone away when he heard a cough behind him.

17

Ian turned around and saw a man in dirty overalls with a bucket and a mop that looked as if it had seen long service. Quite possibly it was the only mop the man had ever used. It was one of those wooden-handled ones with straggling cords instead of bristles. White once, but now a murky sludge colour. Ian looked from the mop to the man himself. He looked extremely old. Even older than Grandad had looked in his later years. But then Grandad had led a comfortable life. The only menial work he had ever done was cleaning his car once a week or brushing leaves from his drive, and that only for a few weeks a year. This man should be sitting in front of a fire somewhere, in slippers and sucking Werther's Originals. He shouldn't be scrubbing grimy areas of hotels with an inadequate mop.

How long had he been standing there? Had he seen Ian photographing the fire escape? And how had he crept up behind him so quietly that Ian hadn't even noticed he was there? Was Ian about to be accused of trespassing and dragged in front of the hotel management to explain himself? Probably not. This guy couldn't drag anyone anywhere, especially someone of Ian's size. A small child perhaps, but Ian was nearly six feet tall and stocky. And in any case the old man was grinning at him. 'Got a thing for fire escapes, have you?' he asked. 'Or are you one of them murder tourists?'

'Murder tourist?'

'Yeah, we've had a good few since then. Not so many recently though.'

'You were here when the murder happened?'

'I've been here since long before that. Used to be a doorman. Had a nice black coat and a bowler hat. But when the new management came, they pensioned me off. Got younger blokes and ponced them up in red coats with gold braid. All they do is whistle for taxis and hand guests over to the concierge team. Concierge, I ask you. What happened to good old-fashioned doormen and porters?'

'But you still work here?'

'Yeah. Couldn't afford to retire so they gave me a few hours cleaning. Only round the back mind, where I'm out of sight.' He pushed the mop into the bucket and leant them against a wall. Then he sat down on the fire escape and pulled out a packet of cigarettes.

He offered one to Ian who shook his head. 'Thanks, but I don't smoke.'

'No more should I. Doc says I must give up or I'll be dead in a few years. But I reckon I'm going to be dead anyway in a few years. Might as well enjoy what's left.' He took a drag of the cigarette and coughed.

Ian sat down next to him. 'What do you remember about the murder?' he asked.

'Well, I weren't working that night. None of us were. Given the week off while they repointed the brickwork and tarted up some of the bedrooms a bit. Full pay. Old Lansman treated us right. More than you can say for that thug of a son of his. He'd have had us all on zero hours contracts.'

'So both Lansmans worked here all the time?'

'Franz ran the London hotel. His dad popped over three or four times a year. He was in overall control, the dad. Reckon that's the reason Franz bumped him off.'

'You think Franz was the murderer?'

'That's what we all thought. Reckon the police did too, but he escaped. Fled the country before they could catch him'

'Why would Franz want his father dead?'

'It was the money, wasn't it? It's always about the money. Rumour was that Franz had squirreled it all into an account in South America without his dad knowing. That's why the hotel finances were in such a mess. He skedaddled off somewhere and the hotel closed. Mind you, the new people moved in smartish. Had the whole place done up and open again within weeks.'

'And they changed the name to Serpentine View?'

The old man laughed wheezily. 'Stupid bloody name. You'd need to be standing on the roof with binoculars to see the Serpentine.'

'So what was it like in the days after the murder? Were you kept off work?'

'Nah, they had us back a couple of days later. Soon as the SOCOs had cleared off. No guests obviously, but they had us cleaning and moving stuff out ready for the new owners.' He looked around him. 'I had to clear up this bit. Right mess it was. Bits of brick, plaster dust, broken bottles, old sandwich wrappers, even smashed up old ladders and some rope.'

'Any coffee mugs?'

'Probably. Don't remember but the restaurants were closed that week so the security guys would have gone round the corner for coffee, or called out for a delivery.'

'Do you remember the intern? Jamie McLeash.'

'Young lad? Yes, I remember him.'

'What was he like?'

'Seemed nice enough. Quiet. And very polite. I remember that. Very nice manners, always a kind word for everyone.'

'Do you think he was involved in the murder?'

'The police thought so, kept asking if we knew where he was.'

'What do you think?'

'Can't see it myself. Nice gentle lad like that. And nothing to gain was there? Bit of a favourite with old Leopold. Franz bullied him for that.'

'Did you meet the other son?'

'Felix? Met him when he was here with his mum. I used to carry her shopping up to the flat for her. Always shopping, she was. Now you mention it I think Felix and young Jamie were friends. Always off out somewhere together.' He chuckled. 'Franz didn't like that. Not one bit. But there was nothing he could do, was there? Mrs Lansman took him from right under Franz's nose. Jamie was working for her, she told him.'

'And what did Leopold say about that?'

'He wasn't here then. Franz was supposed to be in charge. But if you ask me it was his mother that was really the boss. Bugged Franz something horrible, that did. And he took it out on the lad after they left. Wouldn't let him use the family flat any more.'

Interesting, Ian thought. But not a motive for murder. Franz was hardly going to have his father stabbed in the back out of jealousy. But if the old man was right and Franz was after the money, there would definitely be a reason for incriminating Jamie as some kind of cover.

He looked at his watch and wondered how Ailish was getting on and whether he had been missed yet. He should get back to her before someone became suspicious about his absence and started searching for him. He stood up and held out his hand. 'It's been good talking,' he said. 'But I'll let you get back to work.'

The old man stayed where he was and lit another cigarette.

Ian slipped back inside and found the gents. He turned on taps and made as much noise as he could with the hand dryers. Then he strolled casually back into the brasserie where Ailish was still holding court to a group of young people wearing the hotel uniform and who were hovering around her with glasses of water, napkins and cutlery, and a bottle of chilled white wine. Ian sat down just as a waiter appeared with their lunch. He put Ian's salad down in front of him then turned to Ailish, adjusting the jacket she had slung over the back of her chair, replacing her water tumbler with a clean one and lovingly placing her plate of food in front of her. 'I hope everything is to your satisfaction,' he said, refolding a spotless white napkin over his arm and smoothing out an invisible wrinkle. 'Is there anything else I can get you? A little mustard, perhaps?'

'It all looks perfectly splendid,' said Ailish. 'Please pass on my compliments to your kitchen staff.'

'With pleasure, madam,' he said, retreating noiselessly away from their table.

Ailish poured Ian a glass of wine. 'They have an excellent wine list,' she said. 'I took the liberty of ordering a bottle of three-year-old Clos le Brun. I hoped it would interest you.'

'Le Brun? Anna's stepfather?' Ian asked, taking a sip. 'It's delicious.'

'I believe it's quite a small, rather specialised *domaine*. And an interesting name.'

'Le Brun?' he asked, puzzled. It didn't sound all that unusual.

'No, the name Clos. It used to mean a walled vineyard. A lot of the monks who were also vintners enclosed the vines inside a wall to prevent theft, but then discovered that it also produced a distinctive flavour in the grapes.'

Ian smiled. 'If I was Anna, I would have taken a photo of the bottle and sent it to all my friends.'

She laughed. 'You were the one photographing everything in sight last night.'

'That was work,' he said, grinning at her.

'And did you find what you were looking for here? I hope my diversion was sufficient.'

'Couldn't have been better. Anyone would think you were experienced at it.'

'How do you know I'm not?' she said with a wink.

Yeah, she probably did it all the time. 'I picked up some useful scraps from a man who's been working here a long time.'

'And no doubt used your camera?'

'Okay. I'm just as bad as Anna,' he said, tucking into his meal.

.   .   .

To the disappointment of the attendants Ailish had manged to attract around her, they declined a dessert and coffee. A discreet black folder appeared silently at his side, and yet another waiter appeared with a machine into which he inserted his card and tapped in his PIN. Ailish graciously accepted a small posy of violets and help to put on her jacket, and they walked out into the street.

'I hope this coffee shop of yours does cakes,' said Ailish.

He not taken her for a cake type, although she had tucked into crème brûlée last night. 'If they don't, I'll buy you an ice cream in the park,' he said, getting out his phone. He tapped on a link and guided them through the streets to Coffee 2U where he introduced himself.

'Ah, the researcher from Edinburgh,' said the young man behind the counter. 'I'm Steve.'

'You promised me a coffee if I came to London,' said Ian.

'We did indeed. I hope we'll get a mention in your book.'

Ailish raised an eyebrow.

'If it gets that far,' said Ian, deliberately avoiding her gaze and ordering a cappuccino for himself and a decaf latte for Ailish, who although happily sinking gin in large quantities, never drank caffeine.

Ian watched as a delivery was dispatched by bike. A young man in a helmet was stowing six coffee mugs in a cardboard tray and a brown paper bag, presumably containing snacks, into an old-fashioned wicker basket on the front of the bike. It reminded him of Orwell's vision of old maids bicycling to Holy Communion through the morning mist. He doubted whether the lad on the bike would find that a flattering image, or even understand it, as he cycled through the fumes of London traffic to deliver his goods.

Steve served their coffee and his father appeared with two slices of cheesecake. 'On the house,' he said, instantly making Ian feel guilty. Perhaps he really would have to write a book. Had he just misled two perfectly nice coffee shop owners? Had he acquired coffee and cakes by fraudulently claiming to be writing a book? But he'd never mentioned a book, only that he was researching an unsolved murder. That thought made him feel a little better. And if he did ever write a book, he'd make sure he mentioned them. And send them a complimentary copy.

Steve's dad pulled up a chair and sat down next to them. Ian took out his notebook and tried to look like someone researching for a book. Not an easy task as he had no idea what people looked like when researching books. What had he said? Something about studying unsolved crimes in London. 'Do you remember anything about the night of the murder?' he asked.

Steve's father shook his head. 'Police everywhere. Our delivery boy questioned. That's it really.'

'Did you know the Lansmans?'

'Nah, too high and mighty for the likes of us.'

Interesting. Both Franz and Jamie had been at the entrance to collect their delivery. Why? Wasn't that the type of job one left to an intern to do on his own? It was hardly something that needed supervising.

This was still puzzling him as he and Ailish walked back through Hyde Park. Ailish pointed out an ice cream kiosk and Ian bought them both cornets filled with swirls of Italian ice cream. They found a bench and sat watching ducks who, Lottie-like, surrounded them with determinedly hungry expressions. They obviously hadn't read the sign placed very close to where he and Ailish were sitting which said, *Do not feed the ducks.*

'Has today been useful?' Ailish asked. 'You've gone very quiet.'

He'd picked up some useful information, but something was bothering him. 'Why would the boss of a big hotel chain trek down four flights of stairs with his intern to pick up a coffee delivery? Why not just send the intern? You saw the lad leave on the bike. He was carrying a much bigger order with no trouble at all.'

'Well,' said Ailish. 'You're the detective, but perhaps he needed to go outside for a smoke.'

Unlikely. Franz didn't sound like the type to meekly leave the building for a smoke. If he wanted one, he'd just do it. Even if it irritated his father or maybe especially if it irritated his father. And the police report hadn't mentioned cigarettes or ashtrays in the office so he'd no reason to think either of them smoked. There had to be a reason why Franz wanted the two of them to be seen together. But why before *and* after the murder? Something to think about, but maybe not right now. 'Have you any plans for this evening?' he asked Ailish.

'There's a concert in the park,' she said. 'No one well known, just a local amateur band. There'll be deck chairs and a stall selling food.' She looked at her watch. 'Starts at six, I think. Time for a gentle walk through the park and get there before all the chairs are taken. I don't want to sit on the grass. Not in this dress.'

They walked through the park, stopping to look at the Princess Diana Fountain where Ian took a photo to send to Lainie. Then across the carriage drive into Kensington Gardens. The bandstand was close to the round pond where children were sailing boats. There were a few deckchairs scattered around and people sitting on rugs with picnics. Ian bought some falafels from the stall, and they sat and ate them while the band tuned up. He wasn't sure that this really counted as a concert. He'd expected a stage and screaming fans. This was just a small jazz group and an audience of around twenty-five. It was perfect. A lazy evening in the sun listening to gentle music. Ian sat back and listened drowsily. Murder and missing interns very far from his mind.

18

Ian was standing in front of his board when Nick arrived on the Tuesday after his London trip. It was beginning to look like an art gallery. A small one, admittedly, but more colourful than his usual lists and timetables. He shuffled them into groups; six post-cards and a nightingale sent to Felix, a postcard sent to Jamie's family, four sandwiches and a sheep, and the grisly killing of Goliath sent to Ian himself. He printed out the photos he'd taken in London and pinned them up as well. Now all he needed to do was decide how the hell he was going to use them.

He turned as Nick bounced through the door, stripping off her cycling helmet and hi-vis gilet. 'Hiya,' she said, slapping a book down on the table. 'They had this in the Waverley bookshop.'

It was book one of the St Andrews murder series. 'Thank you so much,' he said.

'Wasn't hard to find,' she said. 'I just checked out local authors. Let me know if you want book two and I'll pick it up for you. What are we doing today?'

'We're going to be busy,' he said. 'I've a quite a lot to tell you, and a nice little task for you.'

'Better make some coffee then,' she said, tossing her things onto a chair and heading for the kitchen with Lottie following in her wake.

She returned five minutes later, handed Ian a coffee and perched a plate of biscuits on his desk, tossing one to Lottie as she did so. 'Here you go, Lots,' she said. Ian raised an eyebrow at her. 'I know, you're worried about her weight. But if she doesn't get a bikkie, you'll need to worry more about the puddle of drool she's going to leave on your nice antique floorboards.'

She had a point and actually Lottie was looking quite svelte right now. She'd been getting plenty of exercise recently, as had he. He reached for a biscuit and bit into it.

'How was your London trip?' Nick asked.

'Good,' said Ian. 'I took some photos. These,' he said, tapping Bartók and Prince Albert. 'I sent them to Jacob with another friend request.'

'Did he respond?'

'No, not yet.' He moved along the board. 'These I took at the back of the hotel.'

'Lansman's,' she said, wide-eyed. 'The crime scene?'

'That,' he said, pointing at a window on the fourth floor, 'is, I think, the window of the office. These close-ups of the fire escape are just to show which sections are likely to have been removed.' He drew a circle around what he assumed had been the removed section.

'And who is this?' She pointed to the picture of the old man.

'He works there. Used to be a doorman but was moved to maintenance when the new management took over. The fire escape leads down to a small courtyard with an alley to the road. He's the one who cleared up after the SOCOs moved out.'

'Exciting,' she said. 'Did he find any useful evidence? No, stupid question. It would have been in the police report if he had.'

'He told me there was a lot of rubbish.'

'Any coffee cups or sandwich wrappers?'

'Way too long ago for him to remember. He said there was builders' rubble, some broken furniture, a smashed up bucket or two and some old rope.'

'Rope? The kind of thing climbers use?'

'He didn't say. Does it matter?'

'Have you got these on your computer?' she asked, pointing to the photos. He nodded and opened the file. 'Zoom in on the window.' He did as she asked. 'Damn,' she said. 'Those are new windows. The kind hotels use now to stop people throwing themselves out. They only open a few inches.'

'What are you thinking?' Ian asked.

'I'm just remembering about a summer school Dad sent me to when I was going through a fit of teenage rebellion.'

'Grown out of that now, have you?'

She ignored him. 'We weren't allowed out after curfew. We did all the shoving your pillow into your bed stuff because they patrolled the rooms at night. We used to climb out and go to parties and because we couldn't leave the window open, bit of a giveaway you see, we stayed out all night and strolled back in for breakfast looking like we'd just been out for an early morning walk.'

His own teenage years had really been quite dull. 'Fascinating,' he said. 'Your point being?'

She went over to the window. 'Sash windows,' she said. 'If they're a bit old, like these, they don't stay open. You have to wedge something in to stop them dropping down.' She opened the window a few inches and it gradually slid back shut once she'd let go.

'Okay, so our murderer climbs out of the window, somehow hoiking out whatever he's used to wedge it open, then abseils down to the next level on a rope. But he would have had to fasten it to the windowsill somehow and the police would have found it.'

'You're forgetting the ingenuity of teenage girls in confined spaces. Got any rope?'

He found some that had been used to tie up boxes when he'd moved in. 'It's not very strong,' he said.

'That's okay. I don't need it to take my weight.' She went into the kitchen and returned with a wooden chopping board which she turned on its side and wedged into the window leaving enough space for her to climb out. She made a loop in the rope and tied it loosely around the chopping board. Then she looped the remaining rope round a radiator. After that, she climbed out of the window holding on to the two ends of rope in her hands. Once outside she tugged one end of the rope which dislodged the chopping board, and pulled it and the remaining rope out with her. The window slid gently shut. It was ingenious. They were on the ground floor, but it would work just as well if she climbed out of a window higher up. They could try it from one of his upstairs rooms but perhaps it was best not to risk that. He didn't want her filing for an injury claim. It was fine as a theory for now. It was the kind of thing he and his brother might have tried if they'd ever needed to escape from upstairs bedrooms. But as children they had led an easy-going life and had been able to come and go pretty much as they pleased. During his police training there had been various exercises in escaping from and entering buildings, some of which involved climbing up or down ropes. It had been fun but wasn't a skill he'd ever had to put into practice. And they hadn't learnt how to close windows behind them. Nick had a far more colourful and clearly disreputable past. He wondered if Caroline had pulled stunts like that when she was a girl guide. Images of Caroline dangling on a rope passed through his mind. But, back to the case. 'We don't know if the hotel had sash windows then,' he said. He hoped they did. It was an excellent theory.

'Scroll down and see what the lower floor windows were like. They might only have replaced the upper floor ones. People don't usually commit suicide by jumping out of first-floor windows.'

He enlarged some of the lower floor windows, but it looked as if they had all been replaced.

'I could ask Felix,' Nick suggested.

'You could, but I doubt if Felix would know the difference between a sash window and a portcullis. Concert pianists don't need to know a lot about architecture.'

'You're probably right. Although he knows a lot about floors.'

Nick had this way of finding out odd little details about people. 'Why?' Ian asked.

'Apparently it can affect the way a piano responds. Felix was telling me about a pianist he knew, can't remember the name, who travelled with a suitcase full of wooden blocks of different sizes that he could put under the feet of whatever piano he was about to perform on, because even a slight angle could change the timbre.'

Ian thought about Rosalie's piano, a great lumbering thing with an iron frame, and that wasn't even a concert-size grand. 'Do they have to train as weightlifters as well?' he asked.

'I think there'd probably be people to do the lifting for them. Performers don't even open the piano lid for themselves.'

'Your dad's life must be a lot easier,' said Ian. 'All he has to do is open his mouth.'

'Singers have other problems,' said Nick. 'You should see all the throat sprays and lozenges we have to carry around with us.'

'Still, compared to a suitcase full of wood...' He was allowing himself to be distracted. Again. 'But back to the windows.'

'Felix would have been way too busy practising the piano and falling for Jamie to be interested in windows. Perhaps Véronique would remember. They had a flat there. She probably opened the windows occasionally.'

It was a good theory. Not one he felt was necessary to share with the police. Not with his reputation for producing trivial facts about sandwiches. But if they ever managed to piece it all together it could be another fragment in the jigsaw.

'Wouldn't it be great if we could solve the murder?' Nick said excitedly. 'My first case.'

Just then there was a ping on Ian's phone. Jacob had accepted his friend request and sent him a message. Just one word. *Grosvenor.*

He sighed and showed it to Nick. 'I'd love to help him,' he said. 'I just wish he was a bit less obstruse about everything. What do you make of that?'

Nick was already typing Grosvenor into Google. 'Grosvenor Street, Grosvenor Mansions and Grosvenor Park, several hotels and that's just in London. Several thousand people called Grosvenor.'

Ian groaned. 'Leave it for now. I'd like to try and trace Jamie's friend.'

'Ricky, or Dicky, I don't remember his name.' said Nick.

'Michael Rickson, known to his friends as Mickey Rix. I talked to the guy he used to live with. Mickey left London a year or so ago to start up his own business.'

'Do you think he'll know what happened to Jamie?'

'Bit of a long shot, but I think they were quite close. Mickey let Jamie sleep on his floor when he was in London. And that was around the time he'd fallen out with his parents.'

'You think Mickey could have been a sympathetic shoulder to cry on?'

'Possibly. They were at Stirling at the same time both studying Hospitality. If Jamie had a bad experience coming out to his parents, Mickey sounds like the type he might well have gone to for support.'

'So where should I start looking? Do you have any idea where he went or what kind of business he was starting?'

'He'd been working at the Dorchester so it's possible he was opening a hotel of his own. And it was at a place called Inver-something near Glasgow.'

He googled Michael Rickson, Glasgow. But found nothing. It was going to be a long and tedious slog. They'd share it. 'I suggest you start finding hotels and I'll call them.'

After two hours of phoning what seemed like every hotel and restaurant in the Glasgow area, and several more with Inver as the start of the name, they found nothing. No one had heard of Michael Rickson or Mickey Rix.

'This is going nowhere,' said Ian, yawning. 'Let's go and get some lunch.' Nothing like a breath of air, a pint and a plate of sandwiches to get the brain going. 'Then we'll come back and make a timeline for the murder. We'll put Mickey aside for now.'

'I'll bring a notebook,' said Nick. 'We can do it over lunch.'

Good to have an assistant who was so keen. A working lunch? Well, he'd take time off this evening. Settle down with a whiskey and Netflix.

.   .   .

Ian ordered beer and sandwiches while Nick found a table in the garden. 'I've made a list,' she said, biting into a sandwich. She read:

Meeting in office – Leopold, Franz, Jamie and A.N. Other.

10 o'clock they get hungry and phone out for coffee and sandwiches.

Franz and Jamie are seen at the back entrance when they are delivered, and again leaving the building around 12.30.

Murderer left by the window sometime after 12.

Security check finds the body at 8am the next morning.

The building is empty apart from security teams who all vouched for each other.

'Do we know anything else?'

Ian shook his head. 'Write down what we *need* to know.'

'Okay. We don't know when Leopold arrived.'

'No,' said Ian. 'But we do know that he told security staff he wasn't to be disturbed. We can probably assume that Franz and Jamie were also seen working there earlier in the day.'

'So how and when does the murderer arrive?'

'It could be any time,' said Ian. 'There were other people working in the building all day. We know the office staff were there until around six. They all came forward for fingerprinting and have alibis for the evening.'

'All of them? Are you sure?'

'Good point. Can we assume the murderer was working there as well? That he was there during the day?'

'Perhaps he used one of the empty bedrooms,' Nick suggested. 'After the others had left.'

'Or,' said Ian. 'He was someone Leopold knew and spent the early part of the evening with him.'

Nick wrote that down. 'When did he get the knife from the kitchen? And what did he do with it afterwards?'

'He could have picked it up at any time. Remember the kitchen was closed all that day. And he must have taken it with him after the murder.'

'When he climbed out of the window?'

'My guess would be that he wrapped it in something and hid it up his sleeve. That way he'd have left his hands free.'

'Do we have anything that puts Jamie in the clear?'

'Only that he is around five eight, but the police could argue that he was standing on something.'

Nick drained her drink. 'Let's get back and do a reconstruction,' she said. 'It's what they do on crime programmes on the telly.'

Couldn't do any harm, he supposed. It would be better than fruitless phone calls to hotels. 'We'll give Lottie a bit of a run in the park first,' he said. 'Then I'm all yours.'

'Right,' said Nick as they arrived back at the office. 'You sit here behind the desk and pretend to be Leopold.' She moved three chairs to the other side of the table, sat Lottie on one of them and put her bag on the one in the middle. Then she sat down on the third. 'Lottie's Franz and my bag is Jamie. I'm the murderer. Franz has sat Jamie in the middle because what he's about to see is going to terrify him and Franz doesn't want him to leg it. Franz and I have planned this together. He keeps his father chatting and I pretend to get fidgety so I stand up, pick up my coffee and sandwich and stroll to the window. Maybe open it because it's getting hot. Then while Franz keeps Leopold distracted. I chuck my coffee and sandwich out because I know it's going to be evidence. Then I slip the knife out of my sleeve, creep round behind Leopold and stab him in the neck.'

'I don't think it's all that easy to kill someone with a single stab. This guy must have known what he was doing.'

'Who would know something like that?'

'A doctor, perhaps. Or a wrestler. Don't they have to know about pressure points or whatever they're called?'

'Or someone from a family of assassins,' said Nick.

'Family of assassins? What kind of world do you live in?'

'Same one as the Godfather or the Sopranos.'

'I hate to break it to you, Nick, but they're fictional characters.'

'The Kray twins then.'

'Or how about someone who's been in something like the SAS or MI6?'

'There you go,' said Nick. 'Loads of possibilities.'

'And how do you suggest we find the right one?'

'You're the detective,' she said. 'Perhaps Jacob is about to tell you.'

That was their only hope. If he went to the police with crazed theories about East End gangsters and wrestlers, they'd assume he was even more unhinged than they had last time. He got out his phone. Nothing else from Jacob. Perhaps he'd never hear from him again. Right now, he wouldn't be too sorry. But then he thought of Felix's broken heart and Rosalie's shortly to be destroyed opinion of him.

19

It had been an interesting day. Ian and Nick had some useful ideas, but they'd also wasted a great deal of time trying to find Mickey Rix. Did they really need to do that? Mickey had taken Jamie in when he'd first arrived in London, which suggested they were already close. Did he have any reason to think Mickey had helped him again after the murder? Ian stared into his pint, threw Lottie a handful of crisps and looked around. There were several other people in the pub garden this evening, but not the crime novelist. He hadn't particularly expected her to be here but had brought her book just in case. He opened it now and started reading it. He read the first three chapters and they gave him an idea. The main character was a woman detective inspector, a very much pleasanter character than Kezia Wallace. Perhaps he would send Kezia a copy. She might use this character as a role model. One that would hopefully be nicer to private investigators. At the end of chapter one the DI had found her first body, a nameless character, probably a tourist, discovered murdered in a St Andrews B&B. She had spent chapter two mulling over ways of tracking the victim's final days. By chapter three she had made the decision to check other B&Bs on the assumption that visitors moved from one to another as they visited the tourist high spots of Scotland. But Scotland has hundreds, if not thousands of B&Bs. Police resources were stretched and she didn't have the manpower to visit all of them. She made what Ian thought was the very sensible decision to consult the owner of the B&B where the body had been found on the assumption that B&B owners networked in the same way as everyone else. In other words, the best way to find out about B&Bs was to consult someone who ran one.

He closed the book, put it in his pocket and started to walk home, thinking about Mickey Rix. Mickey may have worked at the Dorchester but perhaps, as a first business venture, he had set his sights on something smaller. Unless he'd been left a fortune, and as Tommie had only mentioned a sum of money, not an eye-wateringly large sum, he probably wouldn't have started with a large luxury establishment. Maybe not even a smaller hotel. Perhaps, Ian thought, he'd start with a B&B. And if he lived in or near Glasgow...

He started to walk faster, pulling Lottie away from a particularly interesting smell that she seemed determined to spend some time on. 'Sorry, Lottie,' he said. 'I need to make a phone call.'

Elsa Curran. Red-haired Elsa with whom Ian had shared a couple of very nice meals recently. She ran a B&B in Glasgow. If the fictional DI was to be believed she would be networking like mad with other B&B owners around Glasgow.

Elsa answered immediately, which could mean either that she was thrilled to hear from him, or that she wanted to get rid of him as quickly as possible.

'Ian, how lovely. I was just thinking about you.'

Really? He wasn't going to ask why. He asked how she was instead. Unoriginal, but safe.

'I'm fine. It's so nice to hear from you,' she said.

'I was wondering if you could help me,' he said cautiously.

'Of course, if I can.'

'I'm looking for someone who might own a B&B somewhere in or around Glasgow.'

'Well. There are plenty of us. Can you give me a bit more detail?'

'A guy called Michael Rickson. He probably moved here a couple of years ago.'

'It doesn't ring any bells, I'm afraid. Do you know any more than that?'

'He's known to his friends as Mickey Rix.'

'Oh,' she said. 'Why didn't you say? Of course I know Mickey Rix. Never think of him as a Michael.'

'Another B&B owner?'

'He'd hate it to be called that. He has this quirky little place called Inverbank. It's up on the edge of the National Park, just a few miles north of Callander.'

'So if it's not a B&B, what is it?'

'It's a boutique hotel. It's not been open long. Mickey worked in Glasgow for a while before he found the right place. That's how I met him. He spent a lot of time dropping in on people like me, asking questions.'

'What sort of questions?'

'All sorts, everything from the best designers to which websites to get onto. I went to some viewings with him and I was there when he fell in love with Inverbank.'

'So you know him quite well. What's he like?'

'Lively, quirky, stubborn. Are you hoping I'll introduce you?'

'It would be a great help if you could. He was a close friend of someone I'm searching for.' This was far more than he'd expected. He and Nick had spent a whole morning searching unsuccessfully for this guy. Elsa had been a sudden last-minute idea. Clutching at straws before he gave the whole thing up. He thought that at best Elsa might have heard of him. To find he was a friend, quite a close one it seemed, was a real bonus. And yes, he really wanted to meet him. He sounded exactly like the kind of person who might shelter a close friend who was suspected of murder. 'When can we go?' he asked.

'Mid week would be best. We do a Saturday changeover during the summer so once our guests have had breakfast and we've cleaned the rooms, weekdays are quiet. How about Thursday?'

That would suit him well. 'What time shall I pick you up?'

'I'm usually done by twelve. We could drop in on Mickey and then get some lunch somewhere.'

'Pull over,' said Elsa. 'You get a good view of Inverbank from here.'

Ian pulled into a layby and looked down into the valley below them. Lottie was jumping up and down wagging her tail excitedly, expecting a walk. The road they were on had twisted up into the hills from a small village a few miles back. Since leaving the village there had been no other houses, but now as Ian looked down into the valley and across a small river, he caught his first sight of Inverbank. It was a riot of colour. Even from this distance he could see that it was covered in flowers; hanging baskets, window boxes, planters. Every part of the house had something hanging from it or planted along-side it.

'I'm speechless,' he said.

'I told you he was quirky. Wait until you see inside.'

'How do we get there?' Ian asked.

'Keep going another couple of miles. There's a turn off to the right which takes us over a bridge. Then we double back to a private drive that goes to the house. There's a sign. You won't miss it.'

There was indeed a sign. And no one would miss it. It was a painted sign of a young man with long curly hair who stared out at the world through trailing fronds of foliage. The sign was framed in ornate gold and hung from what looked like a gibbet. Gold cursive lettering looped above the young man's head announced that they had arrived at Inverbank.

Ian drove another half mile along a white gravel drive and parked at the side of the house to be greeted by a man who could very well be the older brother of the one portrayed on the sign. He had the same dark curls but, unlike the man on the sign, who Ian took to be naked behind the foliage, this one was dressed. He was wearing a pair of very tight, very yellow trousers, a loose white shirt and a velvet waistcoat.

He greeted Elsa with open arms. 'Elsa, darling,' he said. 'It's too lovely to see you. What brings you all the way out here?'

'Mickey,' she said. 'I've brought someone to see you. This is Ian Skair.'

'Lovely to meet you,' said Mickey, shaking Ian's hand. 'And who is this little sweetie pie?' He bent down to stroke Lottie, who licked his hand and wagged her tail.

'This is Lottie,' said Ian, looking down at his dog, who sensing she had made a hit, held up her paw in greeting. This was a trick Nick had taught her but so far Lottie had failed to oblige. She was obviously waiting for the right audience.

Mickey took the proffered paw and bowed politely. 'Come in, come in,' he said, leading the way inside.

If the outside of the house had seemed flowery, it paled into insignificance compared to the inside. Mickey led them through an entrance hall. 'This is our honeysuckle hall,' he said, indicating pale yellow walls painted with trailing honeysuckle flowers.

Ian moved in for a closer look. 'Hand painted?' he asked, thinking that Mickey's legacy must have been larger than Tommie had led him to believe.

'All the décor is bespoke,' said Mickey. 'Created by Scotland's best.'

A chubby woman in workman's overalls appeared from a room Ian recognised as a dining room – a glance at the walls suggested it could be the daisy dining room.

'Ah, Flora, my love,' said Mickey. 'Be a sweetie and make us some coffee, would you? We'll take it in the orangery.'

He led them through another room, which Ian imagined might be the lily lounge, into the orangery. Orangeries, Ian was thankful to note, were pleasantly free of paintable walls. It was well supplied with oranges though. They were growing on small trees in tubs on every available surface.

'So,' said Mickey. 'To what do I owe the pleasure of this visit?'

'Ian's a detective,' said Elsa. 'He'd like to ask you some questions.'

'Ooh,' he said. 'Have I done something bad?'

Interesting, Ian thought. Exactly the question Tommie had asked. 'No, not at all,' he said. 'But I've been hired to look for Jamie McLeash. I'm told you used to know him.' Ian thought he detected a look of affection in Mickey's eyes.

'Of course,' he said. 'Jamie and I were at Stirling together.'

'And he stayed with you in London?'

'On and off for about four months, yes.'

'When did you last see him?'

'Mid-July six years ago.'

'That's very precise,' said Ian.

'Well, yes, of course. It was just before his boss was murdered. One remembers something like that.'

'Did you see him after the murder?'

'No, I didn't. I hadn't seen him for a day or two before it either.'

'Was that unusual?'

'Not really. We both worked anti-social hours. Jamie's immediate superior, the owner's son and a bit of a slave driver, often kept him working late. And sometimes Jamie stayed over at the hotel. He'd become friendly with the owner's younger son who lived abroad somewhere, but when he was in London he and Jamie spent a lot of time together.'

'So you weren't worried that he wasn't at home the day after the murder?'

'I knew nothing about it until the police came. Like I said, I assumed he had just stayed overnight at the hotel.'

'The police came to see you?'

'The next day. They said there had been an incident at the hotel and asked if I knew where Jamie was. I didn't know it was a murder until it was reported in the papers the next day and Jamie had disappeared.'

'Do you think Jamie was involved in the murder?'

'Jamie?' he laughed. 'Jamie couldn't have killed a mouse. He was one of the gentlest people I've ever met.'

This was something Ian kept being told. It was the one consistent thing he was hearing time and again from everyone who knew Jamie.

If this thing ever came to court, there would be plenty of character witnesses. 'And you've never heard from him again?'

'Not a word,' said Mickey. 'Until...'

Ian had a feeling he knew what was coming next. 'Until?'

'I was sent a postcard.'

'From Jamie?'

'I'm pretty certain it was from him, yes.'

'Do you still have it?'

'Somewhere, hang on a minute and I'll see if I can find it.'

'Told you it was quirky, didn't I?' said Elsa after Mickey had left them to finish their coffee.

'You weren't wrong. Are there bluebell bathrooms?'

'And japonica jacuzzi, I expect,' she giggled. 'But don't mock him. It's his first season and he's fully booked up to September. He had a piece about the hotel in one of the Sunday magazines a couple of weeks ago.'

'Must be hell for hay fever sufferers,' Ian muttered as Mickey returned and handed him the postcard – a picture of a flower market. 'Do you know where this is?' he asked.

'It's Columbia Road market, in London. Not far from Brick Lane.'

Ian turned it over and found the letter J printed on the back. Interestingly, it was postmarked Dundee and sent about three weeks ago. 'So apart from the J on the back, what makes you think Jamie sent it?'

'It's a place we used to visit together. I liked to fill the flat with flowers and Jamie just liked being there.'

'Do you have any idea why he might be getting in touch now, after six years?'

Mickey shook his head. 'And I don't know how he found me here either. I'd no plans to come back to Scotland six years ago.'

Ian wondered the same thing. He and Nick had searched fruitlessly for Mickey Rix, so how had Jamie managed to find him?

'Can I ask why you're looking for him?' Mickey asked. 'You're not working for the police, are you?'

'No, I'm not. A friend of his hired me after he too was sent postcards.'

'Good,' said Mickey. 'That's good. I wouldn't want to get him into any trouble. Do you know if the police are still looking for him?'

'The case was closed unsolved about three years ago. I'm assuming Jamie's no longer a person of interest.'

Mickey shook his head. 'He never should have been. Anyone who knew him... Oh my God, you didn't think he would be here, did you? I promise you he isn't. You can search the place if you like.'

It had crossed Ian's mind. A place miles from anywhere. A close friend... But it would be difficult to hide someone in a thriving hotel, wouldn't it? Too many strangers coming and going. 'No,' he said. 'But would you let me know if you see him?'

'You think he might turn up here?'

Did he think that? Probably not, but frankly it would be a relief if he turned up anywhere. *Just show yourself,* Ian thought. *Whatever it is you want, it's going to be much easier to help you if we know where you are.*

Ian thought Mickey now looked desperately sad and wondered what his feelings for Jamie had been. *Time to change the subject,* he thought. 'This is a very interesting place,' he said. 'All those hanging baskets and window boxes, do you grow the flowers yourself?'

'I'm starting to. I've grown some myself but not enough for a house this size. I've got a lovely supplier. A delightful man called Bryan Barr. He runs a one-man nursery up on the Angus coast and grows stuff to order specially for me to fit in with my colour schemes. Delivers it here ready to plant out. Flora's husband does that, well, he does most of the gardening.'

Elsa reached for Ian's arm. 'We should be going,' she said. 'It's well past lunchtime.'

'You've not had lunch?' said Mickey. 'Darlings, you should have said. I can get Flora to rustle up something for you.'

'It's fine,' said Elsa. 'You've all got quite enough to do without that. And I've got plans for me and Ian this afternoon.'

Plans? thought Ian, looking up in surprise.

Mickey winked at them. 'Far be it from me to interfere,' he said. 'But come again soon. Book in for dinner one night. Flora's got some good menus in the pipeline.

'We'll do that,' said Elsa, kissing him lightly on the cheek and heading to the car, Ian following in her wake wondering what exactly her plans involved.

20

Ian and Elsa held hands and watched from the aeroplane window as it drifted down through the clouds and landed neatly and silently in his garden. The pilot, Dora Meadows in full fantasy romance kit including pixie ears, turned and handed him a bundle of postcards. He reached out to take them from her and Lottie started barking. He opened his eyes with difficulty and groped for his phone. Half past two. Lottie was still barking and scratching at the door. 'What the hell, Lottie?' He tried ignoring her. She'd stop barking in a minute and he could get back to sleep. He turned over and pulled the duvet over his head. Lottie didn't stop barking. He pulled on a pair of jeans and a jumper, padded into the living room in the dark, eased open one of the shutters and peered out into the garden. Lottie stopped barking and peered out with him. A full moon cast silver shadows over the grass and flower beds. In the distance he could see the estuary sparkling. *The silvery Tay.* Exactly as described by William McGonagall in his poem. Usually it was muddy brown or, on a fine day, a watery shade of blue. Did McGonagall write his poetry by moonlight? He'd lived in Dundee, but Ian had no idea whether or not he had a sea view. Perhaps if he'd lived in Greyport, he'd have written better poetry.

Probably not, and there was something to be said for having been nominated the worst poet in the English language. He'd probably been overtaken by much worse poetry, since anyone and everyone could now post bad poetry all over the Internet. Some of it must be good poetry, he supposed, but it would take a persistent soul to trawl through cyberspace to find it. McGonagall probably felt the same kind of buzz as modern authors who were nominated for the Bad Sex Award. He wondered if Dora Meadows wrote bad sex scenes. He didn't think he'd trawl through her book to find out. He must remember to give the book to Felix, an interesting reminder of his old piano teacher.

Waiting by the window like this was a waste of time when he could be tucked up in bed. But then something caught his attention. Something was moving in the garden. He held Lottie by her collar and stared out of the window. Had he imagined it? No, there it was again. A shadowy figure in front of the hedge at the end of the garden, one hand on the gate. He grabbed an umbrella, not much of a weapon, but better than nothing, turned on the flashlight on his phone and opened the door, Lottie at his side. He shone the light at the figure who reached up and shielded his face from the glare. Ian could make out a hoodie, a face with a beard and some escaping strands of dark hair.

Lottie was growling softly, but then suddenly leapt forward, her tail wagging and ran towards the figure who bent down and patted her. 'Hi, Lottie,' he said in a soft voice.

Lottie had friends that Ian didn't know about? A friend of Stephanie's, perhaps? Not a comforting thought. Blamelessly innocent people didn't just drop in unannounced in the dead of night and Lottie had already been kidnapped once. He called her in a stern voice, and she trotted back to his side. The figure was still standing there. 'Kneel down and put your hands in the air,' Ian called, drawing on his police training and trying not to think about the disaster that had followed the last time he'd uttered those words. But the man gently lowered himself to the ground and held his arms in the air.

'I'm not armed,' he said quietly. 'I just want to talk to you.'

'Who are you?' Ian asked, noticing he had one fist clenched. 'Show me what you're holding.'

The man tossed a small object in his direction. Without taking his eyes off him, Ian bent down and picked it up. It was a small plastic model of a sheep. 'Jacob?' Ian asked.

'Good guess,' he said. 'You've worked out my clues.'

What was he going to do? They couldn't stay out here all night. For one thing neighbours would wake up and Jacob was close enough to the gate to escape. This could be Ian's only chance. 'Take your jacket off,' he said. 'And throw it over here.'

Jacob did as he was told, and Ian quickly checked the pockets, which were empty apart from some small change. Jacob was slight and skinny, shivering in his short-sleeved T-shirt and jeans. Nowhere to conceal any kind of weapon. 'Will you come inside?' Ian asked.

'If you leave your phone out here. You can put it under that flowerpot.' He nodded towards an upturned pot near the door.

Ian did as he was asked and led Jacob into the kitchen. The board in his office was covered with evidence he had collected, and he wasn't ready to share that yet. He pulled out a chair at the kitchen table, gestured for Jacob to sit down and then put the kettle on. 'Tea?' he asked. 'Or coffee?'

'Tea is fine.'

'Something to eat?'

Jacob shook his head.

He looked as if he needed to eat. 'Maybe later,' said Ian. 'When we've got to know each other a bit.'

'I need to leave before it gets light.'

'You're free to leave whenever you want, but you must be here for a reason.'

Jacob curled his hand around the mug Ian gave him and shivered.

'Put your jacket back on,' said Ian, handing it to him. 'I'm sorry to make you take it off, but...' He pulled up one leg of his jeans and showed Jacob the scar.

'I understand.'

This wasn't going to be easy. Ian had a short time and many, many questions. *Don't jump straight in with the murder.* 'How do you know Lottie?' he asked, smiling. A safe enough place to start.

'You don't recognise me, do you? Lottie knew me at once.'

'I'm sorry. We've met before?'

'In Edinburgh.'

That didn't really help. He'd spent a lot of time in Edinburgh. But not so much since he'd had Lottie. He must have looked puzzled.

'Outside a house in Morningside. You tipped out the contents of your bag and I helped you pick them up.' He reached into his pocket and pulled out Ian's card. 'I kept this.'

'You were the street cleaner?'

'I clean a lot of streets. It's a good way to people watch and not be noticed. To them I'm just there to clear up their litter. Not a real person.'

He was right. Ian hadn't taken any notice of him. Lottie had though.

'That wasn't the only time,' said Jacob.

It came to Ian in a flash. 'The Discovery pier and the book reading.' And, he remembered, possibly the man unloading plants at the garden centre.

'I took a chance with the book reading. Dora used to be my piano teacher and I wanted a bit of my old life, just for a moment or two. It was a big risk, but she didn't recognise me.'

It must be more than ten years since Jamie was at school. The quiet, fair-haired boy now had long, dyed black hair and a beard. It was safe to assume there was very little chance of being recognised by a woman who hadn't seen him in years. Possibly even his own mother wouldn't recognise him from a distance. 'So was wanting a bit of your old life why you sent the cards to Felix?'

A single nod.

'But how did you find out where Felix was?'

'It wasn't hard. He's famous.'

'But he's been out of things for months.'

Jacob drained his mug and put it down on the table. 'I spend a lot of my time in libraries. They're warm and free. I read all the newspapers and use the Internet. Felix's illness was covered by most of the arts pages, and it was easy to find the name of his agent.'

'And when he came to Edinburgh? Was that in the papers as well?'

Jacob nodded. 'A short announcement saying he was now recovering at the house of a friend and hoping to return to performing soon. Most of his friends are musicians and it's easy to find lists of them. They all want work, so they join online registers and upload their details. Rosalie Dacres was the only one who'd studied in Vienna at the same time as Felix and I remembered that Felix had talked about sharing a flat with her in London. And she advertises piano lessons, so it was easy to find the address.'

The guy was resourceful. He'd make a good detective. 'So that day you saw me throwing my stuff all over the road, was that the only time you've been there?'

'I can't get to the city very often. I'll go again when I can. I want to catch a glimpse of Felix and know he's okay.'

'He's recovering. They're reducing his medication and he's much better than he was. He's perked up a lot since we found you on Facebook. It was you we found, wasn't it?'

Jacob nodded. 'That was a brainwave of yours. I wasn't sure if anyone would work it out.'

'It was mostly my assistant. She's a bit of a techie whizz-kid.'

Jacob smiled. 'It was so nice to know that Felix wanted to reach out to me.'

Ian had no idea how Jacob had spent the last six years, but it must have been a lonely time for him. 'I can drive you to see him if you like?'

Jacob shook his head firmly. 'Too dangerous.'

'It's Felix who's paying me to find you. After you sent the cards.'

'I guessed that.'

'He'd love to see you. No one needs to know about it.'

'He lives in a house full of people and he might let something slip without meaning to.'

'He lives with Rosalie, who you already know is one of his

oldest friends, mine too. You can trust her not to tell anyone. And the only other person in the house is Nick, who's working as my assistant. She knows all about you and she won't say anything either.'

'If I was spotted, you'd all be in danger.'

'Danger from who?'

He looked down at his hands. 'Grosvenor,' he muttered.

That name again. At least he now knew Grosvenor was a person. 'Tell me about him,' he said gently.

'I can't,' said Jacob, gripping the edge of the table like a life raft. 'I don't know anything about him.'

Enough to know you're bloody terrified of him though. Jacob was clamming up. It was time to change tack. 'It was *you* who found *us,*' he said. 'Why do that if it's dangerous?'

Jacob stared into his empty mug. 'Because it's time.' He paused. 'I can't talk about it yet. I need to know I can trust you first. That you won't go to the police.'

Ian smiled. 'I've already been to the police.'

Jacob jumped up in alarm and started to head for the door. Ian held him back. 'It's okay,' he said. 'It was a very carefully orchestrated visit. They laughed in my face and told me not to bother them with it again. They said my evidence was too trivial.'

'What evidence?' Jacob edged back uneasily into his seat.

'Four sandwiches. All I told them was that I'd checked the coffee shop order. So now they think I'm some kind of blundering amateur. I promise that's all I told them. Not a mention of Facebook or postcards and definitely no names.'

Jacob looked up at him. He was almost smiling and for the first time Ian noticed the startling blue of his eyes. 'I have to clear my name,' he said. 'I didn't kill Leopold.'

'No one I've spoken to thinks you did. But you were there?'

'I was,' he hesitated. 'I was their insurance.'

'And after six years? Why reach out now?'

'Because something's changed.'

Ian had guessed as much. 'Can you tell me about it?'

'Not tonight. In a few days, maybe. I need to leave now.' He stood up and pulled his jacket around him.

'You'll come here again?'

'If I'm sure it's safe. Or maybe we'll meet somewhere else.'

'How will you know if it's safe?'

'Because I'll get a warning if it's not.'

He wasn't being much less cryptic than when he'd communicated through postcards. Ian got that he was scared but without knowing exactly why, there wasn't a lot he could do to help. He was going to have to let him set the pace. If Ian tried to rush things there was a danger that Jamie would sink even further into being Jacob and disappear again. Probably becoming even harder to find. He was going to have to let him leave. 'Can I give you anything? Money? Food?'

He shook his head. 'I'm well looked after.'

'Do you have far to go?' It was the middle of the night. Did he have a car?

'I can't tell you that.' He bent to fondle Lottie's head and then slipped out through the door and down the garden to the road. Ian retrieved his phone from under the flowerpot and listened for a car. But there was nothing. Only an eerie, moonlit silence.

He stood on the doorstep, wondering if he'd dreamt it all and if there was any chance he could return to his dream about holding hands with Elsa on an aeroplane instead. Then he went back inside. He picked up the two mugs to wash them and found a small plastic sheep on the table. He held it in his hand for a moment and then went into the office. He sat the sheep and his phone on his desk and turned to looked at his evidence board.

Insurance. That was the key. It was why Franz had made sure he was seen with Jamie both before and after the murder. But was that enough or was there more? Insurance of a much more sinister kind.

He'd used his sandwich theory to buy himself time, but at some stage, if he wanted to clear his name, Jamie would have to go to the police and admit who he really was. But not yet. If anyone had noticed his visit there had been nothing to identify him as Jamie

McLeash. Thinking about it, he hadn't really admitted it even to Ian. All he had said was that he hadn't murdered Leopold and that he wanted to clear his name. If he was asked, Ian was just seeing a client who wanted to keep his visit secret. Plenty of Ian's clients wanted that. There was no reason to report their visits to the police. And after all, hadn't he been told in no uncertain terms not to bother them with trivial evidence? The degree of triviality, Ian thought, a little guiltily, was something he would consider when he had more of it.

Ian went back to bed and slept uneasily until Lottie woke him at eight the next morning. His head felt woolly after the disturbed night he'd had, although Lottie seemed unfazed by it. They walked down to the quayside where Ian took some gulps of fresh sea air and started to feel better. A brisk walk home, some strong coffee and he'd be ready to plan his day, most of which involved lounging on his sofa with the Sunday papers. But first he wrote Nick a short account of the progress he'd made since her last visit almost a week ago. He didn't want to bother her with an email on a Sunday. None of what he had written was urgent. She'd probably skim it through before her next working day.

He'd underestimated her. She called him a few moments later.

'You're not supposed to work on Sundays,' he told her.

'Neither are you,' she laughed. 'But when you told me about Jamie, I couldn't wait.'

His fault really. He'd only told her Jamie had made contact. He might have guessed she'd want all the details right away. 'Yeah, he came to see me.'

'Really? When?'

'He turned up in the garden in the small hours of this morning.'

He heard her gasp of surprise. 'What did he say?'

'That he didn't kill Leopold and he wanted to clear his name.'

'How long did he stay?'

'Not long. I gave him a cup of tea and then he left. He was wary of me and very frightened. But he did say he'd come back once he was sure *they* weren't watching him.'

'Who are *they?*'

'No idea. But he said he was in danger from Grosvenor.'

'Grosvenor? That's interesting. So do we assume Grosvenor is a person not a place?'

'Seems so. And he told me he was their insurance.'

'Then you were right. It's not just Franz.'

'No, it's at least two people, one of whom must be the murderer. And they have some kind of hold over him.'

'He thinks they might be watching him? How will he know?'

'He said he'd get a warning.'

'That's really scary.'

'It is. The poor guy is terrified.'

'They won't come there, will they? You're not in danger yourself?'

'Nah,' he said, wishing he felt a bit more sure about that.

He distracted himself leafing through the Sunday newspapers that were piled up for the recycling bin. He rarely read them from cover to cover and usually put the magazine sections to one side, intending to catch up with them during the week. He wondered if he had the edition that had featured Inverbank. A couple of weeks ago Elsa had said. He flicked through some of the magazines before he found what he was looking for. He had waded through news about celebrities, unpractical cooking advice, hints on gardening and features about upmarket homes before spotting the headline '*Why battle with airport delays and long flights when you can staycation in glorious Scotland at this unique boutique hotel in the Highlands?*' Well, strictly Mickey's hotel was in the Trossacks not the Highlands. And he was irritated by this word *staycation*. He could probably forgive the portmanteau-ing of two perfectly serviceable words, although he'd never got his head around calling a holiday a vacation. What he objected to was its use as a verb. *I'm beginning to sound like my mother,* he realised with alarm. But

Mickey would have been delighted, he thought. No surprise that he was booked up for the whole summer season.

Apart from the headline it was a well written piece with some lovely photographs. Mickey's flower-strewn rooms were highly photogenic. Or the photographer was very skilful. Either way it was excellent publicity.

By Sunday evening, he was feeling more relaxed but was still wondering if it wasn't time to give up this case and hand it all over to the police. He'd sleep on it and see how he felt in the morning.

21

By the following morning he'd decided not to give up yet. It was an interesting case and he didn't want to disappoint Rosalie. And strangely, just as he was thinking this, she called him.

'Hi,' said Ian. 'Nice to hear from you.' He meant it. It was always good to hear from Rosalie.

'Ian,' she said, sounding subdued he thought. 'There's been a development. Véronique's arriving any minute.'

'Véronique? Felix's mother? It's only a week or two since she last visited.' Had Felix taken a turn for the worse? His first thoughts were for Rosalie and the strain this would be for her. She'd taken Felix into her home to recover. She also worked hard and her term would be starting soon. She would have students coming to the house for lessons and rehearsals to play for. She wouldn't have the time or the energy to cope with an invalid, however good a friend he'd been to her in the past. 'Is it Felix?' he asked. 'Is he okay?'

'Yes. Felix is fine. Almost back to his old irritating self. No, this is about Franz.'

Alarming. Franz, the older brother and possible conspirator in the murder of his father. Ian wondered, since the case had closed, if

Franz was still a person of interest. Was he about to ask Felix to shelter him? Or was he after Felix's money? Either of those would make Felix an accessory too, not to mention Rosalie. Should they report him to the police? And how would that affect Jamie? 'Franz is there?' he asked, trying not to sound too worried.

'No,' said Rosalie. 'He's dead.'

Dead! Ian's first thoughts were for Rosalie. How was she going to cope with two bereaved people? One of whom was already fragile. Then he wondered how it was going to affect the murder case. It was already a cold case. Did the death of a suspect make a difference to that? Would they just let it lie or would it all be raked over and the case reopened? 'I'll come right away,' he said.

'I didn't think I could ask you,' she said, sounding relieved. 'But thank you. I could really do with your support here right now.'

'Of course I'll come. I'm always there for you if you need me.' Luckily he had a light day. Nothing he couldn't put off. 'I'll be with you in an hour. Will you be okay until I get there?'

'It's sweet of you to worry about me,' she said. 'But I'm fine. Felix doesn't seem to have taken the news too badly. And Nick will be back from her singing lesson any minute. She's always good with Felix.'

'What time is Véronique arriving? Does she need a lift from the airport?'

'She's on a flight from Paris right now. She's not expecting to be met so don't worry. She can get a taxi. She'll probably be here around the same time as you.'

It was an easy drive to Edinburgh. Mid-morning and very little traffic. As he pulled into Rosalie's drive, he looked around to see if there was any sign of Jacob in his road-sweeping kit. Ian thought of him now as Jacob. He suspected this was a very different person from the Jamie of six years ago. One day, if they ever got to the bottom of this case and if a murderer was found, Jacob might be able to be Jamie again. Until then, as far as Ian was concerned, he was Jacob.

He put Lottie on her lead, got out of the car and looked up and down the road, but apart from an elderly dog walker and a woman with a pushchair, the pavement was deserted. Ian had no idea where Jacob lived and how easily he got around. He said he planned to be in Edinburgh again, but hadn't said when. For all Ian knew he could be planning to wait another six years. The man was a complete mystery. He'd now seen him four times; in Edinburgh, Dundee, at the garden centre and at his own house. He had no apparent means of getting from one place to another. All Ian really knew was that he spent a lot of time in libraries and might work as an occasional deliverer of plants.

As he got out of his car, a taxi pulled into the drive and Véronique climbed out amid wafts of perfume. She flapped her arms at the driver until he reluctantly left his seat and lifted a wheelie suitcase out for her. She stood muttering in French as she searched her bag for change to pay him, eventually digging out a leather wallet. She selected a twenty euro note and waved it at the cabbie. He rejected it with a barrage of unrepeatable curses. Ian hoped that the man's thick Glasgow accent meant that his language was incomprehensible to Véronique, although her mutterings were probably merely a French version of the Glasgow obscenities. Eventually she fished out a credit card and tapped it onto the machine. Ian heard the beep with relief and watched as the taxi drove away.

He picked up her bag and carried it to the front door. 'I'm so sorry for your loss,' he said.

She shrugged, not looking too bereft. 'I'd not seen him for many years and he may well be implicated in my husband's murder, so I find it difficult to feel any particular sorrow. I worry about Felix though. He's been through a difficult time, and he was just starting to recover.'

Rosalie came out and put her arms around Véronique. 'I'm so sorry,' she said, leading her inside. Ian and Lottie trailed in after them. Felix was sitting in the music room with Nick, but stood up and enveloped his mother in a hug.

Rosalie took charge. 'Nick, Ian,' she said. 'Come and help me with the coffee. We should leave these two alone for a while.'

She bustled them into the kitchen and put the kettle on.

'Do you know what happened?' Ian asked. He and Nick pulled out chairs and sat down at the table. Lottie jumped onto Nick's lap and Nick stroked her head.

Rosalie spooned coffee grounds into a cafetière, tapping her spoon on the counter while she waited for the kettle to boil. 'Véronique had a visit from someone from the Colombian embassy in Paris yesterday morning. He told her a small private jet had crashed in the mountains four months ago. Franz and two associates were killed.'

'Four months ago? And they only just contacted Véronique?'

The kettle boiled and Rosalie poured boiling water into the cafetière. 'They only recently found the wreckage,' she said, pressing the plunger. 'It was in a very remote area apparently. Colombia is a dangerous and disorganised place and Franz lived an isolated life in some mansion with a young woman called Aleena, a Colombian national. She reported him missing but the search took ages, and when they were found the bodies were only identified by what they were carrying with them.' She shuddered as she reached into a cupboard for coffee mugs. 'I'm not sure how Colombian law works but it looks as if everything was in Aleena's name. She organised a funeral and then found Véronique's address in Paris. The Colombian embassy was asked to break the news to her. At least they visited her in person. Can you imagine getting news like that over the phone? Véronqiue called me last night and asked me to break it to Felix.'

That couldn't have been easy. 'How did he take it?' Ian asked.

'He was very calm about it, wouldn't you say, Nick?'

Nick nodded. 'He was more concerned about Véronique,' she said. 'He called her right away. He was all set to book himself on a flight to Paris. But Véronique told him it would be better if she came here.'

'She was right,' said Rosalie. 'Felix is much better, but he's settled here and none of us think he's ready to travel anywhere yet.'

Rosalie found a tin of biscuits and arranged some on a plate. Lottie jumped off Nick's lap and looked hopefully up at them. 'Shall we join Véronique and Felix?' said Rosalie, asking Ian to carry the tray.

They found them looking through the contents of a small briefcase that Véronique had brought with her. 'His phone and wallet,' she explained. 'His girlfriend thought I might want to have them and they were sent over with the embassy mail.'

Nick picked up the phone. The battery was dead. 'It's the same as mine,' she said. 'I'll charge it, shall it?' She pulled a charger out of her bag and plugged it in. After a couple of seconds, the phone sprang to life with a picture of a large white house surrounded by palm trees, and several missed calls and messages. 'We'll not get any further than that,' said Nick. 'Unless anyone can guess his passcode.'

Felix picked up the wallet and opened it. There were a few business cards with Spanish-sounding names, some banknotes; pesos, dollars and euros, and an out-of-date credit card for a bank in Bogotá. Not much of a legacy, Ian thought.

Felix flicked through the business cards. He pulled out one and showed it to Ian. 'This one's for some guy in London,' he said, passing it to Véronique. 'Is that name familiar at all?'

'G. Fairchild,' she read. 'It's an address in Mayfair. I recognise the name of the street. It's not far from the hotel.' She turned the card over. 'There's a number on the back,' she said.

Ian took it from her. 'Six digits,' he said. 'It could be a door code or a password,' he said, handing it back to her.

'Do you suppose we should let him know about Franz?' Felix asked. 'He might have been a friend or a colleague.'

'I can write a letter,' said Véronique, sighing. 'There are probably other letters I should write.'

Felix patted her shoulder. 'Don't worry, Maman,' he said. 'We'll do it together.'

It was good to see Felix's concern for his mother. He had withdrawn so much into himself during his illness. Showing concern for others could well be one of the first signs of recovery, Ian thought.

'Could I see it again?' he asked. Véronique passed it to him, and he made a mental note of the name and address.

Rosalie suggested lunch in the garden and Ian was surprised how relaxed it was. Felix and Véronique were talking about buying a house in the South of France. 'I'm getting back into practice,' said Felix. 'It's great having the use of Rosalie's piano but she'll be teaching again in a few weeks and I'm going to need somewhere of my own.'

'You can stay as long as you like,' said Rosalie. 'We can work around my lessons. It's fantastic that you've started playing again.' She gave his arm a squeeze. 'It'll be like the old days when we shared a flat.'

'Felix has discussed it with his agent,' said Véronique. 'He's planning a comeback recital next spring but he needs to take things gently. We can't risk him burning out again. We thought we'd buy a nice little retreat for him. Somewhere to rest up between concerts. And I should like a house in a sunny climate. Montpellier, perhaps. You shall all come and visit us.'

'Me too?' asked Nick.

'Of course you too. You must bring your famous papa and we can have soirées.'

Ian could see it. A house by the sea with Bougainvillea in the garden and cicadas chirping at sunset. People in exquisite dresses sipping champagne, or perhaps Anna's papa could provide a few bottles of his best. A relaxed Felix playing Chopin and Piers singing Schubert while Rosalie played the piano for him. It all seemed very far from the violent death of half the family. So much trauma for the two of them. They deserved to daydream about the future. And what of Jacob? Could he become Jamie again and laze around with them in the sun, free of his past and his fear?

Should he tell Felix about his meeting with Jacob? Definitely, but not yet. Felix had had enough shocks for the moment. Jacob had told Ian a meeting would be dangerous and Ian had to trust him. He couldn't risk Felix reacting in a way that could put him at risk. It was better for him to concentrate on his mother for the moment.

Ian had work to do. It was a long shot and it was probably nothing, but before he did anything else he was going to find out all he could about G. Fairchild.

'I should get home,' he said. There didn't seem to be much he could do here to help. It would be better for all of them if he worked out more about the murder. Perhaps he would discover that both Franz and Jamie were innocent bystanders. It didn't seem likely, but it was probably better for Felix and his mother to know the truth, however bad.

'Don't rush off,' said Rosalie as he gathered up Lottie and headed towards his car.

'You've got a houseful,' he said, smiling at her. 'You don't need me hanging around and getting in the way.'

'You're not at all in the way. You've been a real support. I wasn't sure how to handle Felix and Véronique.'

'It's hard knowing what to say, isn't it?'

'They both seem to be coping, don't they?'

'They do, but it's good that they've got each other.' And she'd got no one right now with Toby on the other side of the world.

'I'm sorry I brought you all the way down here for nothing,' she said.

'It wasn't nothing. I'm always there if you need me. And I'm still working for Felix, remember.'

'You know, I'd forgotten about that with all that's been going on. How are you getting on with it?'

'I think we're making progress. But not a word to Felix yet. I'll give him time to let his brother's death sink in before I update him.'

Nick was fiddling with Franz's phone. 'Should I try and get into it?' she asked.

'It's impossible to hack an iPhone, isn't it?' said Ian.

'Pretty much, unless I can guess his passcode. But I get six tries. Felix can help.'

'And what happens when you've used up your six tries?'

'It just has to be wiped and set up like a new one.'

'Worth a try, I suppose.' It would be something to keep them busy.

Grieving must be that much harder without all the usual business of death – funerals, wills, possessions. 'But,' he added, 'check with Véronique first. She's the legal owner now. She needs to give her permission.' In fact, he wasn't sure what the legal position was with passwords. He assumed that, since Franz and Aleena weren't married, and Véronique was his next of kin, she could do what she liked with his phone and any information she discovered on it.

It had been a tiring day and it was a relief to be home. It hadn't been much of a day out for Lottie and she needed a walk. Just down to the village. He'd buy something for supper tonight and Lottie could have a run along the beach. He'd do a bit of work this evening to make up for his missed day, but what he needed right now was to clear his head.

As they walked, he thought things through. Had Franz's death changed everything or was Ian still pretty much where he had been yesterday? How was he going to clear Jacob's name if the only witness was dead? Suddenly, and much to Lottie's annoyance, he stopped dead in his tracks. Franz had died four months ago. Jacob's postcards had started to arrive just over three months ago. *Something had changed.* He and Nick had decided that, and Jacob had confirmed it. Was the death of Franz that change? Had Jacob been in contact with Franz until his death? And did that make him more or less guilty? And who or what was Grosvenor?

He returned to his desk only slightly refreshed, but at least Lottie was happy to curl up in her bed. She wouldn't need walking again today. Ian sat down and opened Google. He typed in *G. Fairchild* which brought up thousands of results. He added the Mayfair address which didn't help. All he discovered was that it hadn't been on the market for a long time, but that similar properties had fetched eye-watering amounts recently. He checked it on Google Street View and it looked pretty much like most buildings in Mayfair – upmarket with barred windows. Then he tried reverse phone number searches and all he could discover was that G. Fairchild's number hadn't been reported as a nuisance call. Neither did he appear on the electoral register for that address. In fact there were no residents listed there. Ian checked Street View again. It looked like a Georgian family home, but most of the houses in the area had been converted into offices and wouldn't have residents. He could check who owned it, but it was likely that it would be someone who rented out office space.

He sat back feeling frustrated. Should he call the number himself? He could make up an excuse, but it probably wouldn't tell him very much apart from whether G. Fairchild was male or female. Would that help? Probably not.

Then a thought struck him and he typed in *Grosvenor Fairchild*. And there it was. An exclusive gym in Chelsea. He navigated to the website. Exclusive wasn't the word. For a five-figure annual subscription and a personal recommendation from two existing members, one could have one's body honed to perfection by world beating masseurs and dieticians, and trained in a number of martial arts and self-defence techniques. The club logo was a hand holding aloft a knife. Further searches told him this was a Wing Chung knife. Wing Chung, he discovered, was a form of martial art which developed "the practitioner to make readily placed blocks and fast-moving blows to vital striking points down the centre of the body; neck, chest, belly and groin".

The knife itself, Ian thought, was not all that different from a fish filleting knife. A shiver ran down his spine and he felt suddenly nauseous.

22

I *should let Jacob know that Franz has died*, Ian thought. But how? He could hardly send a message that said, 'Franz Lansman died four months ago.' It sounded too abrupt. And he wasn't sure how secure Facebook messages were, that was more Nick's area of expertise, but should anyone read it, well, it might arouse suspicion. Better not to take any chances. He was getting used to Jacob's obscure coded way of sending information. Ian was beginning to understand how his mind worked. So with any luck it would work in reverse. He found a painting of the death of Franz Ferdinand. He had never heard of the artist and started one his explorations of Google's blind alleys as he clicked around finding out more. A book illustrator apparently, born in London. Would Jacob work out what Ian was trying to tell him? He spent hours in public libraries so there was a good chance that he would. If not, Ian would just have to hope that he made contact soon. He copied the picture into the message app and clicked send.

He was just wondering what to do next when Nick bounded in. 'You look very pleased with yourself,' said Ian, hoping she hadn't been blagging her way into online forums again.

'We managed to get into Franz's phone,' she said excitedly.

'We?'

'Felix, Véronique and me. We knew we had six chances, so we gave ourselves two guesses each. Felix went first and chose Franz and Leopold's dates of birth. I made up a number code using Aleena's name and tried the numbers on the back of the Fairchild business card. Véronique went last and tried her date of birth. Then she went all impatient and French, and flapped around with a lot of *oofs* and *merdes*. Then she typed in 123456 and we were in. I suppose security's less of an issue in remote parts of Colombia.'

'Wow, well done Véronique. And what did you find on the phone?'

'That's the most exciting bit. There were a lot of messages, mostly in Spanish. We typed them into Google Translate and they were boring stuff about car repairs and being late for dinner. There were some photos of a woman who I guess is Aleena and a house which is probably where he lived. Nothing very interesting but he'd downloaded the Onion app.'

'What's that?'

'It's an anonymous browser. No one can trace the websites you've visited. People use it to access the dark web.'

'Does that mean he was doing something criminal?'

'Not necessarily, but from what we've learnt about him it's quite likely.'

'It's not going to help us though, is it?'

She shrugged. 'We checked his contacts. They were mostly local, but guess what we did find?' She paused for dramatic effect, waved her arms around and took a deep breath.

'Grosvenor Fairchild,' he said.

She gaped at him. 'How did you know?'

'Did a bit of research of my own. He owns an expensive health club in Chelsea where they teach Wing Chung.'

'Wing what? Are you making it up?'

'No, I checked it out. It's kind of martial art that involves viciously sharp knives and a lot of stealth.'

'Interesting. And handy for bumping off inconvenient hotel owners. Was he involved with the hotel in some way? Shareholder or something?'

'I didn't get that far but it's an interesting idea. I might be able to check company records.'

Nick clicked on the phone. 'This is probably useful,' she said, scrolling down a screen. 'Franz sent him regular messages. First day of every month. Always the same, *Lambkin still in place*.'

'And did Grosvenor reply?'

'Yes, again always the same, *Item still secure*.'

'What about after Franz died? Anything from Grosvenor?'

'Yes. The first two are just question marks. The third says *Time for claim*. What do you think it all means?'

He didn't know but he felt uneasy. The word *claim* made him think of filling in insurance forms and Jacob's words were ringing in his head. *I was their insurance.*

'Do you know if Véronique wrote to him?'

'She sent a note saying she had found his business card in Franz's wallet and was sorry to have to tell him that he had died recently in a plane crash.'

'He won't have had time to reply yet,' said Ian. 'But I'd like to know if he responds.'

'I'll let Véronique know. She's staying in Edinburgh for a week or two. You look worried,' she said.

'I need to find Jacob,' he said. 'I think he could be in danger.'

'Do you have any idea where he is?'

Ian tried to think. If *he* was trying to hide and pass himself off as someone else, where would he go? City or country? Was it easier to hide while surrounded by people or out in the wilderness somewhere? He thought the city was more likely. Jacob was getting around. He'd turned up in Edinburgh, Glasgow and Dundee and it was easy enough to get from one to the other. On the other hand, Jacob had a kind of 'wild man of the forest' look about him. He'd stand out in a crowded city with his long black hair and straggly beard. Although perhaps not in the druggier areas and there were plenty of those in all three cities. But he'd also said he was looked after. Was someone sheltering him? If so, it would be easier somewhere off the beaten track away from prying neighbours. He rummaged in a drawer, pulled out a map and opened it out on his desk. He pulled up a chair for Nick and drew circles round the places where he had seen Jacob.

'What are we looking for?' Nick asked.

'Wish I knew. Somewhere remote but with easy access to the places I've circled.'

'Not possible,' she said.

He was inclined to agree. 'Perhaps we should concentrate on *how* he gets around. Perhaps whoever is looking after him travels around a lot and Jacob goes along for the ride.'

'Like a long-distance lorry driver?'

'Or just a regular delivery driver.' Ian wished he'd paid more attention to the plant delivery at the garden centre, but at the time he had been more concerned with the creep who was dating a girl at least half his age. He could check with the garden centre. They'd probably be able to give him a list of their suppliers. He wrote it on his to do list.

'That could account for Edinburgh,' said Nick, looking at the map. 'I suppose being in Dundee the same day as Dora Meadows could be coincidence. He noticed the name on a flyer or something and hopped on a delivery truck, but how could he have got to you in the middle of the night?'

'A lot of courier drivers work at night,' said Ian, wondering if he could find out if any of his neighbours had received a delivery in the small hours a few days ago. Or was it more likely to be one of the pubs or shops? Deliveries to private houses were, in his experience, usually made during the day. Although Grandad's veggie box arrived in the middle of the night to avoid Edinburgh traffic. His clipboard-bearing neighbour with the speedbump fixation might know. He seemed like the type to spy on comings and goings in the village. He added that to his list.

'Perhaps Jacob's working as a driver,' Nick suggested.

'I suppose that's possible, but he's living under the radar. With a false name he'd have no way of proving his right to work.' He sighed. They were getting nowhere. Just the prospect of trekking round garden centres and the risk of an even longer lecture about speed bumps made him feel tired. He folded the map up again. 'Let's hope he makes contact soon.'

'When he does,' Nick said, and Ian was gratified that she said *when,* not *if*. 'We should get him a burner phone. I could fix him up with lots of SIM cards so no one could trace him. But he'd be able to call you if he needed help.'

She watched way too many crime dramas. But then so did he, and actually it was not a bad idea. 'Let's do that,' he said. 'We'll go to Dundee now and get it all set up for when he does make contact.'

He'd just unlocked his car when his phone rang with a number he didn't recognise. It was Mickey Rix. 'You asked me to tell you if Jamie made contact,' he said.

'And he has?'

'No,' said Mickey. 'But someone was asking about him.'

'Who?'

'I've had a lot of enquiries since that piece in the newspaper. Most are telephone calls or emails, but yesterday I found this guy at the back of the hotel in one of the greenhouses. He said he was looking for somewhere to book for a weekend later in the year. And that was weird because most people come to reception and ask. They don't go poking around in sheds. I told him I was fully booked for months and asked if he wanted to leave his name in case we had a cancellation. He said not to bother. I didn't push it because I've already got a waiting list and I hadn't taken to the guy. Anyway, I didn't like the way he was creeping around and walked him back to his car. We got chatting and he said he knew Tommie.'

'Tommie?'

'Yeah, guy I used to live with.'

'Yes, of course.' Tommie who lived in the flat in Kensington where Jamie had slept on the sofa while he was at Lansman's.

'Then he asked if I'd seen Jamie McLeash recently and I remembered we'd talked about him when you and Elsa were here.'

'What did you tell him?'

'Just said I hadn't seen him for years.'

'Did you mention me, or Elsa?' Ian asked.

'Thought it better not to. If Jamie's in trouble I don't want to make it worse.'

'Quite right,' said Ian. 'What was he like, this bloke?'

'Big guy, and fit looking, bit of a smoothie I thought. He had a flash car, a white Audi with darkened windows. Do you know him?'

'I've an idea who it might have been,' said Ian, feeling a shiver run down his spine. 'Did he tell you his name?"

'No, and I didn't ask.'

'Well, thanks for letting me know. And call me again if you see him hanging around.'

'I'll do that,' said Mickey. 'And don't forget to bring Elsa for dinner sometime.'

'You're not too busy?'

'I'll always make room for Elsa,' he said. 'It's good to see her hooked up with a nice man.'

He hadn't thought that he had hooked up with Elsa. Was that the impression they gave? They just enjoyed each other's company. But he had more important things to think about. He felt very uneasy about a tall fit man snooping around. Was Mickey in any danger? Ian thought not. The hotel was well staffed. They probably had something in place for any troublemakers; rowdy guests, people demanding refunds or complaining about the food. No, Mickey was safe enough. But Jacob might be in danger.

He climbed into the car and sat gazing out of the window.

'Are we going to Dundee, or just sitting here for the rest of the day?' asked Nick.

'I think,' said Ian, his hand trembling as he started the engine. 'That we've just had our first sighting of Grosvenor Fairchild.'

'First?'

'Yes, and I think Jacob is in danger.' He opened Messenger and sent the only thing he could think of when he was in a hurry – a line of danger emojis, exclamation marks in yellow triangles.

'Should we go to the police?'

He shook his head. 'Wouldn't do any good. All we can tell them is that someone, a man whose name we can only guess, visited a hotel. There's no obvious danger and nothing to connect it to the murder. All we can do is make sure that Jacob is somewhere safe.'

It was an uneasy visit to Dundee. He let Nick make decisions about the phone while he held on to his own phone willing Jacob to reply to his message. The best thing they could do, he thought, was to get home as soon as possible. To the one place where Jacob knew he could find him.

The message came soon after they returned from Dundee. Ian was doing his best to answer emails while keeping his ears peeled for a message. Nick played with the very basic mobile phone they had bought.

Recognising with relief the distinctive ping of a Facebook message, Ian closed down his email and clicked it open. There were two pictures. One of the exterior of Dundee library, the other of a café. Ian wasn't a regular visitor to the library. He didn't know if it had a café, but a quick image search came up with the picture Jacob had used which was indeed the library café. He was beginning to think that Jacob actually enjoyed communicating by pictogram. Ian himself was beginning to enjoy it, or would have been if he didn't have the feeling that Grosvenor Fairchild was breathing down his neck. Well, it had been good enough for the ancient Egyptians and their hiero-glyphs. At the bottom of the message Jacob had typed *2.30 today*. He had picked up on the urgency of Ian's emojis. Ian sent him a thumbs up.

'How are you getting on?' he asked Nick. She had stopped fiddling with the new phone and was clicking through martial arts websites.

'I've saved your number to the phone and set it up with one of the

SIM cards,' she said. 'It's easy to change them. Do you suppose he's used to mobile phones?'

'No idea,' said Ian. 'He seems pretty computer literate, but he'd probably worry about anything that could be traced. He may not have used one recently.'

'They've not changed much in six years. He might find this one a bit clunky if he was used to a smartphone. The first SMS message was sent in the early nineties, but it involved a lot of fiddling around with number-pad keys. This one's only slightly better.'

She was a mine of information. Probably had a future in TV quiz shows.

'Give me your phone,' she said.

'Why?'

I'm going to set up a distinctive ringtone for all the SIM numbers. That way you'll know it's Jacob calling you. He tapped in his ID and passed it to her. She scrolled through his settings. 'What do you think of this one?' She pressed a key on his phone and his ears were assaulted by what sounded like a howling wolf. Lottie pricked up her ears and started barking.

'Horrible,' he said. 'But I'm not going to miss it, am I?'

'There are others, but that's the loudest.'

'Okay, go for it. And if he calls in the middle of the night when I'm asleep I've got backup from Lottie.' He looked at his watch. Nearly two o'clock. 'I've got to go back to Dundee,' he said, showing her the message.

'He's going to be in the library? How weird is that?'

'Not really. He feels at home in libraries. There's not much of a police presence. And he'll have both of us to protect him.'

'I'm coming then?' she asked.

Why not? She could explain how to use the phone and it might reassure Jacob to know that Ian wasn't the only one on his case. 'Sure,' he said, putting on his jacket. 'Not you though, Lottie.' To Lottie jackets usually meant walks. He scrunched the fur on her head. 'We'll go for a nice long walk when I get back.'

.   .   .

They found Jacob sitting at a table by a window with a cup of tea. He'd discarded his hoodie and brushed his hair back from his face. Ian looked around at the other café customers. None were sitting very close so they'd be able to talk without being overheard. The thought struck Ian that if he'd been asked to guess which of these people was a fugitive and suspected killer, Jacob would have been at the bottom of his list. He looked too gentle and frail, a deep sadness in his blue eyes. He looked up as they approached his table, caught sight of Nick and grabbed the edge of the table as if he was about to jump up and make a run for it.

'Nice to meet you again,' said Ian, hoping he sounded friendly and relaxed. 'This is Nick, my assistant.' Jacob stared at her warily. 'I told you about her. She's the daughter of a friend of mine and she's staying in Edinburgh with Rosalie and Felix.'

Jacob looked at her a little less warily. 'Does Felix know you're meeting me?'

Nick shook her head.

'We haven't told Felix we found you,' said Ian.

'Probably best not to,' said Jacob, wiping away a tear.

Nick reached out and took his hand. 'Once we're sure you are safe, he'll be the first to know.'

Jacob nodded and managed a weak smile.

'You got my message?' Ian asked. 'About Franz?'

'When did he die? And how?' Jacob asked.

'Four months ago. In a plane crash.'

Jacob nodded. 'That was when the emails stopped.'

'Emails?'

'Yes.'

'I think you need to tell us the whole story,' said Ian kindly. 'Tell us about Grosvenor.'

'I don't know anything about him. I hadn't met him before that night. I don't even know if Grosvenor was his real name.'

'His name's Grosvenor Fairchild. But tell us about that night.'

'I was going home, but Franz said I had to go to the meeting with him. It was in Leopold's office and Grosvenor was there. Something to do with finance, I was told. There was a strange atmosphere at the meeting.' He took a sip of his tea and stared out of the window for a moment. He shivered and then continued. 'Leopold was shouting at Franz, something about problems with one of the accounts. I think Grosvenor had put money into it and he and Franz had moved it all offshore. I don't know exactly. I had nothing to do with accounts. I stood up and said I shouldn't be there, and Franz shouted at me to sit down. Then he suddenly calmed down and suggested ordering coffee and sandwiches. He called from the phone in the office, which was odd. Usually only Leopold used that phone. Anyway, while we were waiting he started talking about the kitchen contracts. We were replacing a lot of the equipment, but that wasn't really boardroom level stuff and Leopold got quite bad-tempered about it. Anyway, Franz told me to go with him to pick up the coffees. I didn't know why. Not then. There was no reason for both of us to go. On our way downstairs he kept on muttering about how unreasonable his father was and then he said something like, "We're about to show him". He told me to go to the kitchen and get one of the knives. I thought he meant to show Leopold how old some of the kitchen stuff was and told him it would be better to take Leopold there and show him all of it. The knives were okay. A man came in to sharpen them every week. Franz yelled at me and told me I was just an intern and didn't know anything about how to run a kitchen.'

'Did he tell you which knife to get?'

'Yes. He told me to get the one on the end of the block. The one with the decorated handle that they used to gut the fish. That kind of made sense because the knife block was near to the door and that knife was right at the end. The lighting was a bit dim because of the renovation work. The kitchen lights were being replaced and there was just a small light over the door frame.'

'So you took the knife and you both went back to the office.'

'Yes. It all seemed quite friendly again and we sat and had our coffee. Grosvenor was wearing a pair of black leather gloves. I remember thinking it was odd to eat with gloves on.'

'And where was the knife then?'

'On the edge of the desk. But when he'd finished eating Grosvenor picked it up and started fooling around with it.'

'Fooling around?'

'Doing kind of martial arts stuff, waving it around over his head, until Leopold told him to stop it.'

'What did he do then?'

'He went and stood by the window. Leopold and Franz were going through a catalogue. Franz was getting really talkative about all this stuff. Like he was trying to hold Leopold's attention. And then...' Jacob put his head in his hands. He had turned pale and started shaking.

'It's okay,' said Nick. 'Take your time.'

Jacob looked up at them. 'Have you ever seen anyone being killed?' he whispered.

They both shook their heads.

'Then you're lucky. It never leaves you. There's hardly been a night since that I haven't woken up in a cold sweat, reliving it all. Mostly it's better if I don't go to sleep at all.'

'You need to try and tell us,' said Ian kindly. 'We can't help you unless we know the truth.'

'It was so ordinary and at the same time horrific. One minute he was standing by the window turning the knife over in his hands and the next he had stepped around behind Leopold and pushed it into the back of his neck.'

'Grosvenor?'

Jacob nodded. 'Leopold slumped down onto the desk. I just sat there watching the blood. In shock I suppose. There was a pool of blood on the desk. I stood up and tried to back away but suddenly felt dizzy. To steady myself I put my hand down on the desk and then nearly threw up because it was sticky. My fingers were covered in blood. Franz grabbed me and dragged me out of the office. I thought he was going for help, to call the police, but once we were outside, he pinned me up against the wall. He told me to run and said if I kept my head down, he wouldn't report me to the police. I couldn't believe what he was saying at first. And then it started to make sense. They'd planned it. My fingerprints were on the knife and on the desk and according to Franz I had a motive.'

Ian looked up suddenly. 'A motive?'

'I'd applied for a transfer to Vienna. Felix and I were going to get a flat together. But it was refused. I don't think Leopold was bothered. I think he was quite fond of me, but Franz was set against it. I threatened to leave and Franz told me they would see to it that I never worked in a hotel again.'

'Do you know why he was so against it?'

'I thought it was prejudice. But now I'm not sure. Perhaps he saw me as a rival. He made sure we were seen leaving together then he said he would email me on the first of every month and check up on me. As long as I replied he wouldn't report me to the police.'

'Did you keep the emails?' Nick asked.

'No, he told me to delete them as soon as I'd replied.'

'Do you always email from the library here?'

'Not always. I go to different libraries. It depends where we are.'

'What was the email address?' Nick asked. He scribbled it down on a paper napkin and handed it to her.

'An Onion email,' she said.

Ian looked at her blankly. 'You remember I said he had the Onion app on his phone?'

Ian nodded.

'Well, an Onion email is one that self-destructs once it's been deleted.'

'So it can't be traced,' said Ian. 'Clever.'

'We do have the text messages,' said Nick. 'But they don't mean very much.'

'They might alongside other evidence,' said Ian. 'Have you got the phone with you?'

Nick got it out of her bag and handed it to him.

Jacob stared at him open-mouthed. 'Text messages? You've got Franz's phone?'

Ian realised that there was a lot that Jacob didn't know. 'It was Véronique Lansman who told us that Franz had died. She was contacted by the Colombian embassy in Paris last week and flew over right away to be with Felix. They gave her Franz's wallet and phone. We found a business card for G. Fairchild in the wallet. That was just after your Grosvenor message. I put the two together and we found out a lot about him.' Ian turned the phone over in his hand a few times.

Nick got out her own phone and opened the web page for Grosvenor's health club with a photo of Grosvenor himself as part of the header. She turned the screen so that Jacob could see it. 'Is this him?' she asked.

Jacob nodded. 'That's him,' he muttered.

'You can thank Nick here for finding what was on the phone. I had assumed that iPhones were un-hackable, but she worked out the code.'

'It wasn't me,' said Nick modestly. 'It was just good luck. I suppose stuck out in Colombia he didn't really need a strong code.'

Ian typed in the numbers. Jacob should know about the texts. 'You need to read these,' he said, hoping it wasn't going to freak him out. He passed Jacob the phone. 'Do they mean anything to you?'

Jacob turned pale. 'Lambkin was the name he gave me. And I told you I was their insurance. This bit about the claim frightens me. But maybe Grosvenor doesn't know Franz is dead.'

'I'm afraid he does,' said Ian. 'Véronique wrote to him.'

'Then he'll come for me.'

'But why would he?' Nick asked. 'No one knows *he* was there.'

'He'd use me to clear his name. Jump in before I had a chance to say anything.'

The poor guy was stressed out. He'd been traumatised six years ago and living in fear ever since. Ian had sent him a lifeline with the news of Franz's death and now he'd sent him spiralling back down. Fear of Franz had been replaced by fear of Grosvenor. No wonder he was so thin. He was worn out by sleepless nights and the terror of what might happen next. 'Tell me about the last six years,' said Ian, hoping it would be a distraction. 'You said you were looked after.'

Jacob swallowed a gulp of his now-cold tea. 'After I left the hotel the only thing I could think of was getting back to Scotland. I thought I could go home and maybe my father would know what to do. I know we fell out, but he's a good man. He'd have helped if he could. But when I got to Kings Cross I only had enough cash for a ticket to Dundee, not Aberdeen. I didn't want to use my credit card because it could be traced. But while I was on the train, I realised what a stupid idea it was. I'd be arrested as soon as I showed my face and spend the rest of my life in prison. So I got out at Dundee and walked; out of the city and along the coast. I walked for hours and I'd no idea how far, or where I was. And then I collapsed. The next thing I knew I was tucked up in bed in a farmhouse with someone trying to feed me soup. It was the guy I've been close to ever since. He'd been in prison for a few years. I never asked why, but after he was released he'd had a bit of luck and inherited enough money to start a small business growing plants. He keeps a few sheep and uses the wool in his glasshouse. It means he can grow more exotic flowers. He offered me a cottage and paid me to keep an eye on the sheep. And I helped out with his bookkeeping and accounts.'

'And he drives you when you want to go somewhere?'

'More the other way around. I go with him sometimes to help with deliveries. He supplies customers all over Scotland and it's easy for him to drop me off at places where I can use the Internet. I started spending days in libraries where it's cheap to go online. I could answer Franz's emails, but I did a lot of other things as well; reading, keeping up with news, web surfing.'

'Sending postcards?'

He smiled. 'Yes. Franz sent his emails like clockwork once a month until four months ago and then they suddenly stopped. I sent a couple to him, but never had a reply. That's when I started to hope I could come back to life again. Maybe not completely as Jamie McLeash, but I could at least let my parents know I was still alive and I could contact Felix.'

'And then you contacted me,' said Ian, smiling.

'I picked up your card and that made me think that perhaps a detective could clear my name.' He paused and rubbed his eyes. 'But now... if I go back to being me, Grosvenor is going get me.'

'I don't get it,' said Nick. 'Grosvenor seems to have done all he can to hide the fact that he was there that night. But if he's going to drop you in it, he'll have to say he was there and was a witness. What's the point?'

'He might claim that Franz had told him who did it,' said Ian. 'Franz can't exactly deny it now.'

'But no one's going to take his word for it. He'd need evidence. Something the police didn't find at the time.'

'He's got evidence,' said Jacob.

They looked at him in surprise. 'What evidence?' Ian asked.

'That's what Franz was threatening me with. Not that he'd seen me do it, but that Grosvenor kept the knife.'

'Which had your fingerprints on it,' said Ian, beginning to understand why Jacob had kept quiet all these years.

'Will it still have his prints on it?' Nick asked. 'It's so long ago.'

'They last for ever,' said Ian. 'They planned this, didn't they? They will have thought about how to preserve the prints on the knife. My guess is that Grosvenor wrapped it very carefully, slipped it into his pocket or up his sleeve before climbing out of the window. He's going to arrange for it to miraculously come to light the moment he thinks Jacob's about to reveal the truth.'

'He'd have to know where Jacob is now.'

'He could be watching for him. At his parents' house perhaps, or Rosalie's. They knew about Jacob and Felix.' No wonder Jacob was scared. Franz was a witness and possible accessory. While he was alive, he could play Jacob and Grosvenor off against each other. Now it was only Grosvenor, Jacob's situation had become far more dangerous. And if he was Mickey's nosy visitor? 'That's what's worrying me,' said Ian. 'Jacob, I'm sorry, but we think Grosvenor might be in Scotland.'

Jacob turned pale. 'Where?'

Ian told him about Mickey's visitor, explaining his visit to London and how he had found Mickey.

'But you can't be sure it was him.'

Ian shrugged. 'No, I can't and I really hope it wasn't him, but we should be prepared.'

'What are we going to do?' Nick asked.

'Wait for Grosvenor to make a mistake and be ready for him when he does.' Ian hoped he sounded more confident than he felt. 'First,' he said, turning to Jacob. 'We've fixed you up with a phone. You can call me any time.'

Nick took the phone out of her bag and handed it to Jacob. 'It's only for emergency calls,' she said. 'You can't use it for email or the internet. But that means you can't be traced easily. I think only the police can trace calls through the GPS masts, but I'm not absolutely sure. There are probably people who've hacked into them. I've given you some spare SIM cards. Switch them if you've made a call and throw away the old one.'

Jacob took the phone and stared at it as if it was a bomb about to explode. Then he slowly put it in his pocket.

'We'll carry on using Messenger to keep in touch unless it's urgent,' said Ian. 'Now we're beginning to understand each other, it's the safest way.'

Jacob looked up at the clock on the wall. 'I need to go,' he said. 'My friend's picking me up.'

'Are you sure your friend's cottage is the safest place?' Ian asked. 'You could stay with me, or with Felix in Edinburgh.'

'I'd rather stay where I am. I don't feel safe with people around and I don't want to put anyone else in danger. From my cottage I can see and hear if anyone's coming.'

'Then I need to see where that is,' said Ian.

'No...' Jacob looked terrified.

'I'm not going to call at your house, or your friend's house. But I need to know exactly where it is in case, well, in case I need to be there in a hurry.' And where to send the police if they were needed. But he wasn't going to tell Jacob that. It might scare him into moving somewhere else. 'I'll go and take a look at it and if anyone sees me, I'll just be a dog walker enjoying the countryside.' He opened Google Maps and handed Jacob his phone. 'Just tap in your address.'

When Ian took the phone back from him, he looked at the screen. It was a long way from any kind of help. But Jacob felt secure there. He'd been safe there for six years and Ian could understand why he wanted to stay. He watched Jacob leave, pulling his hoodie on and slipping silently out of the library, down the steps and then into the crowds of shoppers.

23

Ian hadn't slept well. Too much pitching around in his head. He got up early and took Lottie out for a brisk walk. Then he went home, made a strong cup of coffee and sat down to make a list of things that were worrying him.

First on the list was the remoteness of Jacob's current hiding place. He opened up Google Earth and took a look at it. Postcodes in isolated areas were not always accurate but it wasn't hard to spot Jacob's cottage, simply because it was the only building for miles and a hundred yards or so from the rocky coastline. He followed a track which took him about two miles to the A92 Dundee to Montrose road. He zoomed out to find the nearest buildings and a mile to the north he discovered a farm with what he took to be glasshouses and polytunnels. But while Jacob's cottage was unnamed, the farm was called Barr Nurseries. *Barr*, he thought. Why did that sound familiar? Jacob hadn't given him any names, but Ian knew he'd heard that one recently.

A quick look at Google Maps told him it was a drive of forty minutes from Greyport. Too far in an emergency. If Grosvenor turned up on Jacob's doorstep there wouldn't be much anyone could do to help him.

His next worry was Grosvenor himself. How had he found Mickey Rix so quickly? It had taken Ian a morning of fruitless searching and the help of a friend. Then he remembered the newspaper article. Grosvenor could have visited Tommie just as Ian himself had done. Mickey's name might have come up and then he read about Mickey's hotel in the paper. Could he have been spying on Mickey for a day or two? Easy enough. There were plenty of places to pull off the road that he and Elsa had taken. It would be easy to conceal a car in the trees and watch the hotel through binoculars. Less easy to do that near Jacob's cottage, which was a relief. And in any case, there was nothing to connect Mickey's hotel to the cottage. They were eighty miles apart.

He looked out of the window. After a dull, drizzly start the day had now brightened up. He called Caroline. 'You up for another picnic?' he asked.

'Why not? Do you have anywhere in mind?'

'Just up the coast. There's a place I want to check out. It's great for dog walking and we can have a picnic on the beach.'

'Okay,' she said. 'It sounds fun. Shall I put a picnic together?'

'We can stop off in the village and get something,' he said. 'Do you mind if we go in your car?'

'Not at all. I can pick you up in about an hour.'

'Is your car okay?' Caroline asked as they loaded bags of food into her boot.

'It's fine,' he said. 'Just fancied a change.' In fact it was more than that. If Grosvenor had been spying on Inverbank, he could have seen Ian and Elsa arriving there and made a note of his registration number. It wasn't that difficult to track people through car registrations. Officially it was only the police who could do it, but he was sure there were other more covert ways. If Grosvenor had discovered that he was a PI he might be keeping an eye on him. It wouldn't matter much around Greyport and Dundee, but however small the risk, he couldn't take the chance of being followed to Jacob's cottage.

Then he suddenly remembered why the name *Barr* sounded familiar. 'Do you mind if we just pop into a garden centre on Perth Road?' he asked.

'Are you planning a makeover?'

'No, well, not right now. I'm interested in one of their suppliers.'

He hoped the garden centre didn't mind dogs. Caroline's car had a metal guard to keep them in the back but in a busy car park they'd bark at people and make nuisances of themselves. They put them on their leads and walked to the entrance. If they weren't allowed in Caroline could wait outside with them while he searched out what he was looking for. It would be a lot quicker if Caroline was with him though, because he wasn't good at garden centres. They were confusing places. It wouldn't be so bad if they stuck to garden stuff, but they sold everything. Or in his opinion, everything no one would want; scented candles, stuffed toys, tins of shortbread, packets of Edinburgh Rock, handmade soap, the list was endless.

They passed a sign that read *Well behaved dogs on leads are welcome* and wended their way through aisles of non-garden-related products until Ian spotted double glass doors that led outside to where there were actual plants. Miles of them. Plants as far as the eye could see.

'What are you looking for?' Caroline asked. She paused by trays of alpines. 'These would grow well in your garden, on the slope at the side of your path.'

He picked out a box. Might as well buy something while he was here. 'I need to find things that don't usually grow well in Scotland,' he said.

'Why?' she asked, looking puzzled. 'Shouldn't you be going for something that *does* grow well in Scotland? Why make your life harder than you need to?'

'It's not for me. I'm trying to find plants from a particular nursery. It's where we're going later.'

'Can't you buy direct from them when we get there?'

'I don't want to buy plants at all. It's the boxes I'm interested in.'

She looked around. 'Those look interesting,' she said, pointing to a sign that said *For exotic window boxes.* Unlike most of the plants that came in polystyrene trays, these were in wooden crates. Caroline was right. These were very interesting, and they looked like some he had seen in one of Mickey's window boxes. He pulled out one of the boxes and read the lettering on the side with mixed feelings – pleased that his theory was correct, but also scared that he had been right. Very scared. 'We should go,' he said. 'I need to make a call.'

Returning to the car, he took out his phone and tapped Mickey's number. 'Sorry to bother you,' Ian said when Mickey answered. 'This won't take a moment.'

'No problem,' said Mickey. 'What can I do for you?'

'You get your plants from Bryan Barr, don't you?'

'Some of them, yes.'

'Do they come in wooden crates with his name on the side?'

'Yes, we return the crates to him when we've planted them. It saves single-use plastic.'

'And this guy that was poking around, you said you found him in one of your greenhouses?'

'Yes, that's right.'

'Were any of those crates in there at the time?'

'They would have been. Bryan won't be back now until next spring. We've a stack of them in the greenhouse ready for him to collect on his next visit. There are about a dozen, I think.'

'You told me you and Jamie used to go to Columbia Road flower market. Did Jamie have a particular interest in flowers and plants?'

Mickey laughed. 'He was well known for it, always filling the flat with flowers. He used to buy them for the hotel too.'

That was it, Ian thought as he ended the call. A link in the chain. A horribly inevitable chain that had already brought Grosvenor to Scotland and to Mickey's hotel. How long was it going to take him to find Bryan Barr's nursery?

He turned to Caroline. 'I'm not sure you should come with me.'

'Why ever not?'

He talked her through the case. 'I'd be putting you in danger,' he said.

She grinned at him. 'Nothing new there then.'

She was right. Ian didn't often find himself in dangerous situations, and the last two he had been in, Caroline had been with him. But on those two occasions he hadn't known about the danger. This time he did. And there was no way he could risk Caroline coming into contact with a murderer.

She disagreed. 'First,' she said. 'You don't want this Grosvenor recognising your car. And if he spots it anywhere between here and Jacob's cottage, he'll follow you and it won't only be you who's in danger. And second, I'm good at defending myself and if it comes to it, two against one is way better than a hefty bloke against a man with a limp.'

'Thanks for that,' he said, glumly. It wasn't something he needed to be reminded about.

'And,' she said, 'what are the chances that he'll be there today?'

It would be a coincidence, he thought. And the best way to work out how to help Jacob was to know the lie of the land. The sooner he did that the better.

'Okay,' he said reluctantly as Caroline started the engine.

They drove in near silence for half an hour, Ian keeping an eye on Google Maps. With Caroline driving he was also able to keep a look out for white Audis. So far the road had been clear. Very little traffic at all. 'Next right,' he said, as they approached the turning to Jacob's cottage. They drove along a bumpy track for another mile and came to a gate. He could see Jacob's cottage in the distance. Pinned to the gate was a sign: *You are welcome to walk on my land but please keep dogs on a lead. There are sheep grazing for the next mile. Sheep worrying by dogs is a criminal offence. The penalty is a fine of £40,000 or up to a year in jail.*

To the right of the gate was another track leading to the beach. 'Drive down there,' Ian said. 'We'll park at the top of the cliff and give the dogs a run. Then we'll have our picnic and watch the cottage through my binoculars.'

Caroline found a place to park and she spread out a rug and unpacked the picnic. There was a rocky track down to the beach, but it was steep and would be a hard climb back up again. Right where they were would be fine. Ian wanted to watch the track to the cottage, but without looking as though he was watching it. Here they had a nice view of the sea on one side, fields on the other. The land immediately around them was lush and green. Near the cottage the ground became increasingly rocky. Beyond the cottage he could see large boulders partly obscured as the land dipped into a hollow before rising again near the cliff edge. If it was the same as where they were now, there would be a steep drop from the edge of the cliff onto a rocky shoreline.

The place was deserted and inhospitable. The only signs of life were a few sheep nibbling at grass between the rocks. Ian focussed his binoculars on the cottage and watched as Jacob emerged, looked furtively around and then tended a small flower garden. He pulled out some weeds and picked a handful of flowers, which he took inside with him and closed the door.

The sun went behind a cloud and Caroline shivered. 'Not the friendliest place, is it?' she said, packing up the picnic and calling to the dogs. 'Do you need to stay, or have you seen enough?'

They'd had the best of the day. It was clouding over and there was a brisk westerly wind. The sea, calm enough when they'd arrived, now seemed to be putting up a fight with the wind, tossing up angry breakers against the rocks. Ian shook his head. 'I've seen what I need to,' he said, wishing he'd persuaded Jacob to move in with him.

'You should go to the police,' said Caroline as they drove back towards Dundee.

She was right, but what would they do? No one had actually threatened Jacob. As far as Ian knew, Grosvenor had an unblemished record and was a model citizen, and there was no proof that he was even in the area. Ian was relying on his own gut feeling and a sense of foreboding. He'd turn back, he decided. Insist that Jacob return with him to the comparative safety of Greyport, where they could keep a lookout together and where an emergency call would bring the police in minutes. How much resistance could Jacob offer? A lot probably, but Ian was tougher, more experienced and he could be every bit as stubborn as Jacob.

But he had Caroline with him. He couldn't drag her all the way out there again, possibly involving her, at best in an unseemly argument, at worst, well... he didn't like to put that into words. They were in the outskirts of Dundee. It was a matter of minutes for her to drive him home to pick up his own car. He suggested this and watched as she opened her mouth to object. Then he heard his phone.

24

Ian jumped and pulled the phone from his pocket. It wasn't ringing, it was howling like a dog. The tone that Nick had set up so that he would know at once who was calling him. It meant only one thing. Jacob. And it wouldn't be a social call.

Caroline pulled the car over at the side of the road.

'What's up?' Ian asked, the phone feeling clammy in his hand.

'He's here.' Jacob's voice was barely more than a whisper. 'In the lane.'

Damn. If the sun had shone for a few more minutes, if the wind had held off a little longer, they might still have been there. He'd have seen the Audi bumping along the lane. He and Caroline had been halfway from the main road to the cottage. They could have blocked his way, headed him off and called the police.

'On my way,' he hissed into the phone. 'Lock your door.' Stupid thing to say, Ian thought. Who wouldn't lock the door with a murderer outside? 'And call the police.'

'No... no, I can't.'

Ian wasn't going to argue. There wasn't time. 'I'm on my way,' he said.

Caroline was already turning the car around. He'd call the police himself. It would take fifteen minutes to get back to the cottage if Caroline put her foot down, which she was showing every sign of doing. They were already hurtling out of Dundee at well above the speed limit. He hit the emergency number on his phone, realising as he did so that this was Kezia Wallace's patch and if he'd called her out on a false alarm she'd probably make sure he never worked again. That was a chance he'd have to take. Right now Jacob's life was more important. The emergency call centre was very efficient, talking him through the directions he was giving, thankfully still fresh in his head, and assuring him a unit would be there in fifteen minutes.

He glanced at Caroline, who was focussing on her driving with a determined expression, swerving in and out of traffic like a pro. 'Advanced driving course,' she muttered at him. Of course, he should have guessed. He was suddenly enormously relieved that she was with him. He'd spent too long worrying about her safety and what he might be letting her in for. He should focus more on what she did for him. She was feisty and cool-headed, and had come to the rescue more than once in the past.

She turned off the main road and a couple of miles further on she pulled up at the gate to the sheep field. Ian jumped out to open the gate, slamming it shut when she had driven through, slowing down for him to climb back into the passenger seat then bumping across scrubland, avoiding potholes and skidding around rocks. It was a desolate place of scrubby grass and boulders. A few sheep stared at them stupidly before panicking and leaping out of the way. Now they could see the cottage and the Audi parked outside. Caroline slowed down. Thankfully her car was quiet. With the wind and the sound of the waves, their approach wouldn't have been heard.

She pulled up behind the Audi and opened one of her windows. The dogs were restrained in the back and Caroline fed them each a dog chew. Good thinking, Ian thought. That would keep them occupied and stop them barking. The door of the cottage was open. They climbed out of the car and crept towards it.

The cottage was tiny. The door opened into a living room with a small kitchen beyond. Ahead of them was a staircase. Ian expected to hear angry voices, but as he peered in he could see it was empty. The room was bare, with only a wooden table, a couple of chairs and a small sofa. There was nowhere to hide.

There was a letter on the table. Ian scanned it quickly and felt a chill run down his spine. A confession. Typed on a computer and signed. Signed by Jamie McLeash, not Jacob MacDonald. But this was a bleak two-room cottage, no electricity and the nearest computer probably several miles away.

They edged quietly up the stairs and again found only an empty room.

'Look,' said Caroline, pointing through the window. From here they could see down the hollow at the back of the cottage and up towards the cliff edge. They watched as two figures emerged from behind the rocks. The smaller one staggering as he was goaded towards the cliff edge, the sun glinting off the blade of the knife which was held at his neck.

Suddenly Grosvenor's plan became clear. A confession followed by a jump off the cliff. The case would finally be closed. The murderer's confession in black and white. Grosvenor free to get on with his life.

'What do we do?' Caroline asked.

'I need you to wait here for the police. They won't be able to see what's happening from the front of the cottage. Tell them it's a hostage situation.'

'And you?'

Ian looked out of the window. 'I'm going out there,' he said.

Caroline nodded. She understood. If they waited until the police arrived it could be too late. But Ian might just be able to delay the inevitable.

He plotted a course, skirting around the rocks, staying out of sight until he was at the cliff's edge, staring down into the swirling sea, as black, foaming waves battered the rocks. Rocks that were sharp edged, razorlike, forty feet below. After a drop into the sea the body would be so battered with cuts and bruises that a single thrust of a knife would be undetectable.

Ian was now inches away from them behind a large rock and didn't dare move much closer. Not yet. His timing needed to be perfect. Too soon and there'd be no police backup. But if that didn't come in time? He couldn't think about that now. He looked back. He could see the cottage and police cars parked behind Caroline's car and the Audi. But the track between himself and the cottage was hidden by the dip in the ground and the rocks. Where the hell were they?

Then he watched with relief as three figures appeared slowly from the hollow and edged, as he had done, round the rocks until they were a few feet away.

Grosvenor hadn't seen them. His attention was fully occupied as he pushed Jacob to his knees, clutching at his coat collar with one hand, holding the knife to his neck with the other. He pushed Jacob down, forcing him to look at the jagged rocks below. 'All over in an instant,' he said to Jacob with a leer and shaking him menacingly by his coat collar. 'Better than spending the rest of your life in prison, isn't it?'

What could Ian do? Launch himself at Grosvenor, make a grab for the knife? He'd have Jacob over the edge instantly. Try to talk him out of it? Futile. Jacob had signed a confession. Grosvenor had the murder weapon with Jacob's fingerprints. Evidence that would condemn him. Jacob would be arrested and Grosvenor would claim to be the hero of the moment by tackling a known killer.

'Stop right there.' A voice Ian recognised and for once welcomed. Kezia Wallace had launched herself from behind one of the rocks and was hurtling towards the cliff, closely followed by two of her officers.

'Don't jump, Jamie,' yelled Grosvenor, turning to face her. Ian watched as, still clutching Jacob's collar, he slid his other hand behind his back and released his grip on the knife, letting it tumble down the cliff behind him. A slip of his foot and a flick of the wrist and Jacob would be over the edge, Grosvenor claiming that he had tried to save him.

Ian jumped from behind his rock and launched himself at them, delivering a kick to Grosvenor's shins while at the same time gathering Jacob in his arms and tumbling backwards with him into the safety of the grass. Their combined weight forced Grosvenor to release his hold on Jacob's jacket as Wallace leapt at Grosvenor, grabbed him from behind and wrenched his arms behind his back, snapping handcuffs onto his wrists.

'What?' shouted Grosvenor, struggling to free himself. 'I was trying to save him, you stupid interfering cow.'

Ian, who was now sitting up and no doubt still in shock, laughed. Hadn't he often thought of Wallace as an interfering cow?

Wallace scowled at him and turned back to Grosvenor. 'So what exactly did you intend using the knife for?' she asked. *Good question,* thought Ian.

'What knife?' Grosvenor asked, adopting an expression of injured innocence.

'The one you threw into the sea,' she said, gazing over the cliff edge. 'The one that unfortunately for you became lodged between those two rocks down there and which my officer will shortly retrieve.' The officer in question didn't look overly enthusiastic about the idea, but said nothing. 'You're under arrest,' she said, calling for the second officer to read him his rights. Then she knelt down beside Jacob, who was huddled into his jacket. All colour had drained from his face and he was trembling with fear. 'We'll get you to hospital,' she said with a tenderness that Ian would never have believed she was capable of. She nodded at Caroline, who had arrived from the cottage with a bottle of water and blankets.

'He's in shock,' said Caroline. She wrapped Jacob in a blanket and laid him gently down on the grass. Then she took off her jacket, rolled it up and placed it under his feet.

Kezia nodded approvingly as she took out her phone and called for an ambulance. 'Here in about ten minutes. You two okay to stay with him while we get chummy here back to our car?' Wallace patted Ian on the shoulder. 'Good job,' she said, smiling at him. A smile from Wallace? Probably the one and only.

. . .

The ambulance bumped across the grass towards them exactly ten minutes later. *Impressive,* Ian thought, considering how far they were from any kind of civilisation. But not a moment too soon. Jacob was pale and clammy, his pulse was racing and he seemed confused. Ian was thankful for Caroline's first aid skills but it was a relief to hand over to the experts. They slipped on an oxygen mask and gave him an injection. Then he was lifted onto a stretcher and carried to the ambulance. 'We've some checks to make and then we'll be heading to Ninewells in Dundee,' they told him.

A tinge of colour was returning to Jacob's cheeks and he stretched out his hand to Ian.

'We'll follow on,' said Ian. 'I'll be there, don't worry.'

'I'd better let the dogs out and give them a bit of a walk while you finish up here,' said Caroline.

Ian turned to go back into the cottage and found Kezia standing in the doorway. Her team had cordoned off the edge of the cliff with blue and white tape and were now doing the same to the cottage. 'You can't go in,' she said. 'This is a crime scene.'

One of the officers came out and handed her a plastic evidence bag. She took it from him and read the letter. 'You read this?' she asked, holding it up for Ian to see.

He nodded. 'It was on the table when we arrived.'

'What did you make of it?'

'A set-up,' said Ian.

'You could be right. We got here just in time. If it had gone to plan, we'd have found a signed confession and a body on the rocks. A nice tidy ending to a historic case. What I'd like to know is how *you* got involved.'

'And I'll tell you if you don't accuse me of wasting police time again.'

'Fair enough,' she said. 'You need to come in and make a statement as a witness. And I'll need your friend Jacob, or Jamie or whoever he is, to come and make one. I think you should advise him to bring a solicitor with him.'

'Are you going to arrest him?'

'He's got some questions to answer, but no, I don't think he's guilty of anything.'

'Even with a signed confession?'

'A good defence team would destroy that in seconds. First off, Jacob had no means of producing a letter here. Why would he go somewhere else, type a letter, get it printed and then come back here to jump off a cliff? He could just as easily have scribbled something on a scrap of paper with a pencil. And why now after six years? If he'd done it, he'd be congratulating himself on getting away with it. And that's even before some bloke tries to push him off a cliff in front of five witnesses. And yes, said bloke might try to claim he was trying to stop him jumping, but we all saw Jacob on his knees with a knife at his neck. If people are going to jump, they jump. They don't kneel down and roll themselves over the edge. That was going to be an execution. And I don't think Mr Grosvenor Fairchild was carrying out a bit of citizen justice to avenge his friend Leopold.'

Ian stared at her. 'You know who he is?'

'I've been keeping an eye on the case. After your fiasco with the sandwiches, I checked the records. I went a bit deeper than Duncan and discovered some interesting facts concerning the Lansmans and Grosvenor Fairchild. Of course, I have easier access to fraud squad records than you. Fairchild was already a person of interest before the murder and they were exploring a possible connection to Franz Lansman. But then his father was murdered, and Franz left the country. Without either of the Lansmans, the investigation was shelved.'

'Will the case be reopened now?'

'The financial case? Probably. There's a dossier on Grosvenor Fairchild and I'm guessing an arrest for assault and attempted murder will open up a number of avenues of enquiry. I'll be handling the assault case myself. Hopefully we can prosecute in Scotland and after that we'll hand him over to the Met.'

'And Lansman's murder? Jamie witnessed it. He can identify Grosvenor Fairchild as the killer.'

'That's just a case of one man's word against another's. There's no evidence. And for now, I'll be putting a police guard on McLeash's room at the hospital.'

'But you said you weren't going to arrest him.'

'I did say that, but our young friend does seem to have a habit of running off when he should be giving evidence and I can't be one hundred percent sure that Fairchild hasn't got some kind of backup plan.' She patted his shoulder. 'That's why I'm going to work my socks off on the assault case. I could do with your help.'

That was a surprise. 'How?' he asked.

'I assume you've a hefty folder of notes about McLeash and Lansman?'

He nodded.

'I can keep McLeash in Scotland and hold Fairchild for forty-eight hours while I build my case against him. After that I suspect the Met will want to reopen the murder case.'

'How can I help?' Ian asked.

'You'll be my route to McLeash. Find him legal representation and arrange for them to visit the hospital. Then be in my office at eight tomorrow morning.'

Caroline returned with the dogs and Kezia nodded to her. 'Nice to meet you again,' she said. 'And thanks for your help. You seem to have a knack of popping up just when you're needed.'

'Happy to help,' said Caroline. She turned to Ian. 'Are we ready to go?'

'I won't hold you up,' said Wallace. 'Are you going to Ninewells? They should have admitted McLeash by now. I'll call my officer and make sure you're on the list of approved visitors.'

She picked up her phone and arranged for Fairchild's car to be collected and forensically searched. Then she climbed into her own car and drove off.

And then Ian remembered the knife. Not the one Grosvenor had dropped over the edge of the cliff. The one that killed Leopold Lansman.

25

Working for Kezia Wallace. How did that happen? At eight the following morning, Ian nervously presented himself at the front desk of a police station in Montrose. He was shown immediately into Kezia's office and offered coffee and biscuits. Kezia herself appeared a few minutes later, armed with folders which she slapped down on the desk. Ian added his own folder.

'I hope my team are looking after you,' she said. Ian nodded. He doubted that they would dare to do anything else. Snap her fingers and they jumped. He wondered which side of that he would be on. As a specially contracted member of the team would he be expected to jump to order as well? Or would he be the finger-snapper?

'Right,' she said. 'We should get down to business.' She placed a piece of paper in front of him. 'Your contract,' she said, pointing to the bottom of the page. 'Sign here.'

He scanned through it. It seemed straightforward. Three days work and a generous fee. Local police funding must be in a better state than he remembered from his days in Leith.

'I can negotiate for longer if we need to,' she said. He picked up a pen and signed it. 'Fairchild will appear in court this afternoon on a charge of attempted murder. He'll be remanded. His solicitor is with him now. Smooth guy, flew up from London last night. But I don't think even the slimiest of solicitors will have much of a case. Grosvenor Fairchild was seen brandishing a knife on the edge of a cliff by three police officers and two independent witnesses.'

'What about the confession letter?'

'As I said, it's an obvious set-up.'

Ian thought *he* had been the one to say that, but he let it pass.

'But to make sure we've got it all covered,' she continued, 'earlier this morning I set up an investigation into printers. Did you know that printers have fingerprints?'

Ian didn't know that.

'And that Scottish libraries have an excellent system of records. Every print made in one of their libraries is traceable. So just in case Fairchild tries to use that as a defence I shall be ready for him. I don't expect there to be a record of a Jacob MacDonald or Jamie McLeash printing anything recently. And I've contacted the Met for a warrant to search the printers at Fairchild's home and business addresses. I confidently expect a match to this so-called confession from one of those.'

This morning? Did the woman ever sleep? Ian rather suspected *he* wouldn't be sleeping much over the next three days. Kezia's days, he imagined, were usually at least twenty-two hours long.

'We've pretty well wrapped up Fairchild. Now we need to talk about why I need *you*.'

Kezia glanced at his folder of notes. 'Looks like a thorough job,' she said. 'I'm sure you've got theories. Is there anything urgent in there that we need to sort out now?'

'The knife,' he said. 'The murder weapon was never found. You'll see I made notes about that. Jamie was made to fetch it from the kitchen, and it will have his fingerprints on it. I suspect Fairchild will make sure it's found somewhere incriminating.'

She tapped her fingers on the desk. 'Then *we* need to find it first. If it's among his possessions, we've nailed him. It's proof that he was there that night.'

'He might claim that Franz gave him the knife,' said Ian. 'We've only got Jamie's word for it that Fairchild was at the meeting.'

'Hmm,' she thought for a moment. 'What evidence do we have that Franz Lansman and Grosvenor Fairchild even knew each other?'

Ian flicked through his notes and found the transcript he had made of Franz's phone messages to and from Grosvenor Fairchild.

'Not enough,' said Wallace. 'We need the actual phone.'

'That's not a problem,' said Ian. 'It's in Edinburgh. I can get it couriered up here.'

'Good,' said Wallace. 'But it's not proof that they knew each other well enough to plan a murder together.'

'Might Fairchild try and pin it on Franz?'

She shook her head. 'No, that doesn't work. Not if McLeash's fingerprints are on the knife. That would let both of them off the hook.'

'And Franz was left-handed,' Ian added.

'Was he now? That didn't come up in the original police report.' She looked pleased with herself. One in the eye for the Met, Ian supposed. 'Right, I'll make finding the knife a priority.'

'So what do you want me to do?' Ian asked.

'Did you visit McLeash yesterday?'

'I did, but he was sedated. I'm going back this afternoon. I've got him a solicitor.' He'd had a stroke of luck with that. He'd called Rosalie and delivered the good news that Jamie had been found and was safe in hospital but needed a solicitor. A few years back, Rosalie had taught a girl who had gone on to win a prize for young pianists in London. Her father was head of a law firm in Edinburgh. Rosalie called him and he had arranged for one of his top criminal lawyers to represent Jamie. 'He's in Edinburgh and standing by to get up here the moment he's needed,' Ian told Kezia. 'He's already arranged for a psychiatric assessment.' Ian passed her a piece of paper. 'You need to add him to the authorised visitor list at the hospital.'

'Good,' she said. 'We'll make sure McLeash is ready for an interview the moment he's discharged from hospital. I'll slow that down as much as I can by insisting on medical and psychiatric reports of my own. He's obviously frail and we can play on that.'

'Why do you want to slow things down?'

'I believe as much as you do that McLeash is innocent. I'm bloody well going to nail Fairchild for the murder of Leopold Lansman and I need time to get the evidence together.'

So it wasn't so much her desire to see justice done and an innocent man exonerated, as a chance to further her career and go down in police history as the one who solved the murder. *Oh well, as long as it means Jamie can pick up the threads of his life again.*

26

The uniformed constable at the door yawned and checked his list. Ian had regrets about leaving the police, but sitting outside a hospital room wasn't a task he missed. They'd be working in shifts so he'd probably not see the same constable twice. If anything, the guy sitting on the plastic chair today looked even more bored than the one who had been there yesterday. He also looked about twelve. A sign of ageing, wasn't it, when policemen started looking young? Ian waved his ID badge at him. 'Okay,' said the young man, glancing up from the list. 'You can go in.'

Jamie was propped up in bed flanked by two enormous baskets of fruit. He had a drip in his arm and an oxygen mask covering his nose and mouth. Someone had shaved off his beard and trimmed his hair. He looked much younger, but tired and frail. Ian pulled up a chair and sat down next to him. 'Hi,' he said. 'How are you doing?'

Jamie pulled the mask down. 'Are they going to arrest me?' he asked.

'I don't think so, but they do want to talk to you.'

Jamie shrank back into the pillows. 'So why is *he* there?' he asked, nodding towards the constable at the door.

'Just a precaution,' said Ian, not elaborating. 'Nice fruit,' he said, wandering over to look at the baskets. Both had cards tucked into them; one from Felix, the other from Mickey. Ian had called them previous evening. 'They both want to see you,' Ian said. 'As soon as you're allowed visitors. Your parents as well.'

'My parents?'

'I called them last night.'

'I don't suppose they care if I'm dead or alive.'

'They do,' said Ian, sitting down by the side of the bed and helping himself to some grapes. 'They care very much.'

'You've seen them?' Jamie asked, looking shocked.

'I went to visit them a few weeks ago,' said Ian, remembering Andrea's sadness. 'They really regret what happened between you. Your mother particularly. She's kept all your photos and the card you sent. The least I could do was to tell them I'd found you.'

For someone who wanted to get his life back, Jamie looked distinctly unenthusiastic. Shouldn't he be looking forward to a reunion with his family? He was still in shock, Ian supposed. 'When you feel ready, of course,' Ian added. It wouldn't be until Kezia had interviewed him, but he didn't want to say too much about that right now.

'A woman came and asked a lot of questions,' said Jamie miserably.

'We fixed you up with a solicitor,' said Ian. 'He asked for a psychiatric report. The police will want one as well, so you can probably expect another visit and the same questions. That's good,' Ian added, noticing the expression of alarm on his face. 'A solicitor will help you. Make sure you answer the right questions and check they don't try to get you to say something you don't want to.'

'I can't.' His eyes were filling with tears.

No one in their right mind would think this guy was capable of hurting anyone. 'I'm not sure they'll give you any choice and...' He paused. 'It's the only way you can clear your name. Trying to run again will just make you look guilty. I'm working with Inspector Wallace and we're on your side. Kezia Wallace is not an easy person to get on side. Believe me, I've had run-ins with her a couple of times.'

'I've no money,' said Jamie.

'Jamie,' said Ian, reaching for his hand, 'or would you rather be called Jacob?'

'I've got to like Jacob,' he said. 'But I suppose I'm going to have to get used to Jamie again.'

'Okay, Jamie. Don't worry about money. Felix has found you the best legal team in Scotland.'

'I can't ask Felix to pay.'

'Why not? He was desperate to find you. He nearly killed himself because he couldn't bear the thought of life without you. And he's loaded – six-figure concert fees and huge royalties for recordings.'

'Yeah, and I'm just a pathetic loser.'

So that was it. Shame, and fear that the world had moved on without him.

'No, you were at the wrong place at the wrong time. And don't you think Felix deserves the chance to make up for some of the harm his family did to you?'

'I don't know…'

'Trust me,' said Ian, hoping he was being reassuring. 'All these people, your friends and your family, they want to help you.'

A woman in an overall arrived pushing a trolley with teacups and an enormous teapot. She looked at Jamie affectionately. 'Cup of tea, my love? And one for your friend?' Jamie shook his head. 'Now, we can't be having that.' She offered Ian a cup, which he accepted. 'He's not been eating,' she said. 'I've saved a chocolate biscuit for you.' She pulled a foil-wrapped biscuit from her pocket and Jamie accepted it warily as she placed a cup of tea on the locker next to the bed. As the woman clattered out of the room, Ian was pleased to see that she offered the constable at the door a cup of tea and a chocolate biscuit. Something to break the monotony. He would appreciate that.

'I need to let Bryan know where I am,' said Jamie. 'He'll be worrying about me.'

'I can go and see him,' said Ian. Bryan had taken Jamie in and looked after him when he most needed it. It was hardly his fault that he had inadvertently led Fairchild to him. 'Would you like to see him? I'm sure I could get him added to your visitor list.'

'No, he can't be seen mixing with a suspected criminal. He's been in trouble himself.'

'Yes, I remember. You said he'd been in prison, but surely that must have been years ago.'

'A criminal record's never really forgotten. Better that he doesn't risk it.'

Perhaps it was. He hoped Bryan wasn't about to be in trouble for harbouring a fugitive. 'Okay, I'll just go and talk to him. Tell him how things are.' He sipped his tea, noticing with relief that Jamie was doing the same. 'There's one thing you might be able to help us with,' he said. 'The knife. The one that has your prints on it. If we can link it to Fairchild, you'll be in the clear.'

'I don't know what happened to it.'

'The thing is,' said Ian, not wanting to alarm him. 'If, as you say it was some kind of insurance, then it must be somewhere that Franz knew about as well. Somewhere that either of them could produce it from if the other became a suspect.'

Jamie shook his head. 'I'm sorry,' he said. 'I just don't know.'

Ian patted his arm. 'Just let me know if you think of anything,' he said as he got up to leave.

27

Ian's phone rang at seven the next morning. It was Kezia. Of course it was, who else would call that early? On the other hand, he was due in her office soon. What could be so important that it couldn't wait an hour?

'No need to rush in,' she said. 'Fairchild was remanded yesterday afternoon and I've a meeting with the Procurator Fiscal to go through evidence.'

Was she giving him the day off when he was only two days into his contract?

'You can work from home,' she said, as if reading his thoughts. 'There's some good news. The confession matches a fault on one of the printers at Fairchild's health club. There's a tiny mark that the forensics guy could only see with a magnifying glass, but it's ninety-nine percent certain that it was printed from that printer, which should be enough for the Prosecution Service. The club also sent me member lists going back ten years. Franz Lansman was a member there for several years before the murder.'

'That's great, proof that they knew each other.'

'It's not proof. Fairchild will argue that there were hundreds of members and he couldn't be expected to know all of them. It's circumstantial but it will help.'

'What would you like me to do today?' Ian asked.

'I'm emailing you printouts of ANPR records of Fairchild's trips around Scotland. It confirms he was in the Callander area a few days before he attacked McLeash. He must have stayed the night somewhere. Try to build an itinerary and check possible hotels he might have stayed in. Phone and ask them to check their registers. Find out if they have room safes or lockers for valuables. Call in any likely places and I'll have one of my officers check it out. We need to find that knife as soon as possible.'

Sounded like a fun way to spend the day, but worth it, he supposed, if they found the knife. He spent the morning on it, eventually tracing Fairchild to a hotel at a motorway service station. Room safes, he was told, operated using a four-digit security number set by the occupant of the room. Any locked safes were opened by security staff after guests checked out. Fairchild had left his safe unlocked and had left nothing in his room.

Lottie started barking and hurled herself at the door just as the bell rang. It would be Franz's phone. Nick had arranged for its secure delivery along with the wallet. Ian signed for the package and carried it into the office. He needed to drop it off at the IT lab in Dundee and he could do that this afternoon. Then he remembered something. He checked the number of Fairchild's health club and called them, posing as a potential member concerned about the safety of his valuables during a gym session. He was assured that security at the club was second to none. On joining he would be provided with a state-of-the-art storage locker. He would set his own six-digit security number. This would be known only to himself and in the unlikely event of his resignation from the club the number would be reset. He thanked them for their help and said he would let them know should he decide to apply for membership. He declined the offer of a membership application pack and ended the call. He pulled on a pair of plastic gloves, gently prised the package open and carefully removed the wallet. He didn't want to contaminate the evidence, although any damage had probably happened when he and Nick explored its contents a few weeks ago. He pulled out the business card using tweezers, took a photo of the six-digit number on the back of the card and sent Kezia a text – probably not a good idea to interrupt a meeting with the Fiscal. He suggested exploring the customer safes at the health club. Then he drove to Dundee, delivered the package and took Lottie for a long walk.

When Ian arrived at Kezia's office at eight the following morning she was ecstatic. 'We've charged Fairchild with murder,' she said.

'You found the knife?'

'The health club was raided last night and the knife was found in a locker, opened using the code you sent.'

'Was it Franz's locker?'

'Better than that. The locker was registered by the club in the name of Franz Grosvenor.'

'Interesting,' said Ian.

'Very interesting,' she said. 'Particularly as there was no Franz Grosvenor listed as a club member at any time during the last ten years and that Fairchild's prints and DNA were found inside the locker.'

'And Jamie is in the clear?'

'He'll be needed as a witness, but yes, he's free to go. I gather the hospital are discharging him in a couple of days and he's going to his parents' home for outpatient treatment.'

'So do you need me any more?'

She gave him a withering look. 'You've still got a day of your contract left and there's a great deal of paperwork to do.'

'Of course,' he said, sitting down at the desk.

'But,' she said with a smile, 'we'll knock off early and go for a celebratory drink.'

A day of paperwork and an evening in a pub with Kezia Wallace.

Not what he would have chosen. But hey, his case was finished. Jamie could start his life again and Kezia could bask in the glory of having solved a murder case that had been beyond the Met. Things could be a lot worse.

28

I t was mid-January when the postcard arrived. Ian picked it up from the doormat and took it into the kitchen. He and Caroline plus the two dogs had just returned from Drumlychtoun where they had spent Hogmanay. Something had gone wrong with the heating system and the house felt cold. They wrapped their coats around them while Ian fiddled with the boiler and Caroline boiled a kettle. Lottie had dived under Ian's duvet and Angus sat shivering pathetically in the kitchen, huddled hopefully next to a stone-cold radiator.

As the radiators growled into action, they sat down at the kitchen table with cups of coffee and looked at the postcard.

'Winters must be very mild in the South of France,' said Caroline, sounding envious as she studied the photograph of Jamie, his hair expensively styled, light now and with streaks where the sun had bleached it. Wearing a pale-coloured linen suit with a navy blue open-necked shirt, he was sitting on a sea wall laughing at something he could see in the distance. He had put on a little weight and his cheeks were tinged with a light sunburn. He looked, Ian thought, very French. Véronique's influence, he was sure. She had found a house by the sea a few miles from Montpellier. Ian didn't know the area but it sounded like a fashionable, cultured place. The first thing Véronique did after she moved in was to build a studio for Felix in the garden and buy a Steinway grand piano. Felix had a recital planned in London in March. It would mark his return to performing, not, Véronique assured him, a return to his former life. She had had severe words with his agent and his performances would be rationed. He couldn't be allowed to burn out again. Felix planned a new, gentler repertoire. Three or four concerts a year would be plenty. His audiences were already clamouring for more but Véronique was adamant. And it meant his agent was able to double his fee. Felix himself was perfectly content to spend his mornings playing and his afternoons sitting in the sun.

Jamie had joined them in the autumn. No charges were made against him, although he would be required to testify against Grosvenor Fairchild when his cases came to trial. The solicitor they found had been excellent. He had visited Jamie in hospital and before allowing police interviews insisted on a psychological assessment which diagnosed PTSD. After that he stayed with Jamie throughout the long hours of statements and warding off any suggestion of press harassment. Once that was over, Jamie returned to his parents' home to recuperate. Ian and Lottie had driven to Aberdeen to visit them and they had gone for a long walk along the beach.

'Do you have any plans?' Ian had asked.

'I'm in therapy,' said Jamie. 'Someone my mother found in Aberdeen. She's very good, but I'm going to need her for a while.'

'That's good,' said Ian. 'No need to make big decisions right now.'

'I've got plans,' he said. 'And money. I hadn't touched my bank account for six years and it seems it's been growing.'

Ian smiled at him, expecting plans for a long holiday. But Jamie's answer surprised him. 'I'm going to buy the cottage from Bryan,' he said.

'Really? I'd have thought that was the last place you'd want to be.'

'One day out of six years? No, I'm not going to let that spoil it for me. It's been my haven. The one place I've ever really felt a peace.'

'So what are you planning to do there?'

'I'm going into business with my father. He's bored with retirement. He sold his business and is looking for something to invest in. 'I'll modernise the cottage, of course; put in electricity, a proper bathroom and heating. Then we're going to start a wildlife sanctuary. A place where kids can come and watch birds and go rock pooling. We've plans for a visitor centre and a safe stairway down to the beach. But first I'm going to France. I'll stay a few months and come back with Felix for his recital. The trial's due to start in May or June, but once that's over I'll be ready to start my life properly.' He threw a stick into the sea for Lottie and she plunged in to retrieve it, running back to them and shaking the water out of her fur. 'I shall get a dog,' he said, smiling at her.

'I can recommend that. Great company when you live alone.'

He smiled shyly at Ian. 'I don't know how to thank you for what you did.'

'There's no need to thank me. I was only too glad to help.'

'And your assistant? Is she still working for you?'

'Nick's back in New Zealand. She's training as a forensic hacker. She managed to persuade her father that she was never going to be a singer. But we're in touch. I'll pass on her thanks.'

'Will you and Lottie come and visit?'

'Of course we will.'

And now he had what he supposed would be the last postcard from Jamie. He'd buy a frame for it and hang it on the wall of the office.

'So what next?' Caroline asked.

'I've really no idea,' he said, smiling. He'd tidied up a few cases during the autumn and now his desk was cleared ready for a new one. There was no hurry. Something interesting would come along and in the meantime, he'd start looking for a new assistant.

Caroline was reading a news app on her phone. He should do the same. They'd cut themselves off during the festivities at Drumlychtoun but there was a world of events that they should probably catch up on.

'Just as well we don't live in China,' said Caroline.

'Why?' he asked idly. Living in China had never crossed his mind, nor was it likely to.

'There's some mystery disease. A place called Wuhan is in lock-down and making all its residents stay at home.'

'Tough,' he said, glad that Wuhan was a long, long way from Scotland.

ACKNOWLEDGMENTS

I would like to thank you so much for reading **Postcards from Jamie.** I do hope you enjoyed it.

If you have a few moments to spare a short review would be very much appreciated. Reviews really help me and will help other people who might consider reading my books.

I would also like to thank my editor, Sally Silvester-Wood at *Black Sheep Books*, my cover designer, Anthony O'Brien and all my fellow writers at *Quite Write* who have patiently listened to extracts and offered suggestions.

ABOUT THE AUTHOR

Hilary Pugh has that elusive story telling talent that draws you in and makes you feel you are in the room with her characters.
   Michelle Vernal

UK based author Hilary Pugh has spent her whole life reading and making up stories. She is currently writing a series of crime mysteries set in Scotland and featuring Private Investigator Ian Skair and his dog, Lottie.

Hilary has worked as a professional oboist and piano teacher and more recently as a creative writing tutor for the workers Educational Association.

She loves cats and makes excellent meringues.

ALSO BY HILARY PUGH

Bagatelle - The Accompanist free download included when you join my mailing list. Click the link below:

https://www.hilarypugh.com/romance-among-the-notes.html

Meet Ian Skair in:

Finding Lottie

Sign up for a free copy here:

https://www.hilarypugh.com/ian-skair-private-investigator.html

The Laird of Drumlychtoun

Ian Skair: Private Investigator 1

https://books2read.com/u/3yaeQp

Minuet and Trio - The Dancing Teacher

Buy the book

The River Street Family

Buy the book

Printed in Great Britain
by Amazon

42906277R00139